# FORBIDDEN MAGIC

## WITCH'S BITE SERIES BOOK FOUR

## STEPHANIE FOXE

STEEL FOX MEDIA LLC

*First edition, September 2017*
*Version 2.0, June 2019*
*ISBN 978-1-950310-07-4*

*This series may be complete, but the story never truly ends.*

*Thank you, dear reader, for joining me on this journey.*
*This one's for you.*

# CONTENTS

# PROLOGUE

The air is damp and cold despite the unyielding light that fills the cell. Condensation drips down the stone wall until it slips into a crack. Felix rolls up to a sitting position and scratches his unkempt beard. He hasn't had access to a razor in at least a week. He's not sure exactly how many days have passed though.

His granddaughter must be worried. Justine knows he'd never disappear like that, not willingly. And there aren't many people that could pose a threat to a witch like him.

Felix grits his teeth in anger. No matter how powerful he is, it seems he can never protect the people he cares about. The power he was born with is more of a liability than a benefit; no wonder so many of his kind are dead. He stares at his hand, wishing he could strip the magic away. If he hadn't been born with this curse, he would never have drawn Alexandra's eye.

Felix tilts his head back against the wall and closes his eyes. When he was young and stupid, Alexandra made him feel special and needed. He snorts. He was useful like all tools are. If he hadn't been so blind, perhaps he could have seen how she was using not just him, but their son as well.

Alexandra wanted one thing: power. She had traded in the colorful dresses that first caught his eye for severe black robes styled after the ancient witches she admired. Her favorite had been Aris, of course. A bloodthirsty woman who chased after power her entire, miserable existence.

Aris had led wars, massacres, and had beaten the entire magical world down until they submitted to her idea of unification. Felix sighs. The creation of the councils was good for witches and other paranormals in the end, but the cost it had required still seems too high.

These are thoughts he usually avoids, but sitting in a dark place with no sense of time has made the memories impossible to ignore. His son's wide eyes and pale face as he was killed haunt him. The sound he had made, half sob, half pleading, still rings in Felix's ears, even after half a decade. It was Alexandra's fault he had died, but she hadn't cared. She said he must have been weak.

Felix had taken his granddaughter and run that same night. He had fled to the one place Alexandra couldn't follow. He and Justine spent years flitting in and out of the shadows, hiding, training, scraping by. All it took was one mistake for a new monster to find him.

Footsteps echo down the hallway. Felix lifts his head and waits, cross-legged on the floor. The door swings open revealing a tall figure. The flickering light of the torches in the hallway cast shadows across the man's lean face.

"It's time," he says, tilting his head as he takes Felix's posture in. "Do you still intend to cooperate?"

"You haven't given me a choice," Felix rasps.

The man smiles. "It is easier to plan when the pawns have only one direction in which to move."

Felix snorts and pushes up off the floor. He pointlessly dusts off his grimy pants and follows the vampire out of the cell. Felix curls his fingers into a fist, his nails biting into his skin. If he didn't have Justine to think about he'd kill himself before he'd do this. It's wrong, like so many things he has done in his lifetime.

Then again, he's just a tool. He was always going to be used by someone, it's just bad luck this particular person got to him first.

F ive days earlier...

A cool breeze carries the smell of pine trees and the babbling of a small creek. I brush a stray hair away from my face and poke the grimy metal tooth of the bear trap with the end of my stick, flinching in anticipation of it snapping shut. Nothing happens.

Colin snorts behind me. "Are you going to set it off so we can move on, or are you scared of it?"

"I'm going to let you step in it next time," I mutter, knowing he can still hear me.

"I saw it, I wasn't going to step in it," he insists.

"Just keep telling yourself that," I say, looking back at him with a smirk.

He rolls his eyes and leans down to dig the map Agent Stocke gave us out of my backpack so he can mark the location of this trap on the grid.

I jab the stick sharply into the center of the trap. It leaps up, snapping the stick in half with a clank that hurts my ears. I flinch, just like I had for the previous three. Colin laughs but tries to turn it into a cough to cover it up.

"Go ahead and laugh it up, fur-ball," I say as I pick up the now safe trap and toss it as him.

"Fur-ball?" He asks as he catches it, still trying not to smile and drops it into his backpack. He gets to carry the heavy stuff since he is the werewolf. I might be just as strong as he is when I'm drawing on my vampire side, but I'm not going to waste all my energy on that. He was smug about it, and I let him stay that way to keep him in a good mood. Delicate male egos and all that.

"Yeah," I say, waving my hand at him. "Werewolf, fur-ball, same difference really."

"I thought JHAPI agents had sensitivity training and knew not to insult werewolves," Colin says, a smile still tugging at the corner of his mouth.

I pull on my backpack. "I'm just a consultant."

"Oh, so I didn't even get stuck with an agent, I'm stuck with a civilian." He looks up to the sky and shakes his head dramatically. "Goddess save me."

"You're lucky to have me," I say with a huff. "Now how much more do we have to cover?"

"It's only been three hours. We still have this entire area to cover," he says, pointing to the upper half of our section on the grid. There are four small x's designating where we found traps set by the NWR. They had protested Angeles National Park allowing the werewolves to run on federally owned lands for years. After the recent escalation of tension, the NWR decided to take matters into their own hands and set hundreds of traps throughout the woods.

The local packs had been trying to deal with it themselves, but after some human hikers wandered off the trails and ended up injured, one of them almost dying, they reluctantly agreed to accept JHAPI's help. That is why I'm stomping around in the woods with a werewolf trying to avoid stepping on a trap myself.

The NWR, being assholes, as usual, had laced some traps with silver making it difficult for the werewolves to touch. I get the thankless task of poking at everything first to make sure silver doesn't spew out of it and injure Colin. One of the first traps the pack had found did that. The wolf ended up with silver dust in his eyes and up his nose and he had almost suffocated.

Colin looks over the map one last time, then starts off again in the direction we had been heading before I saw the glint of metal under the pine needles and dirt the trap had been covered in. I had shoved Colin to the side just in time, despite his protestations afterward that he had seen it. Delicate male egos indeed.

My thighs protest the steady uphill trek. I adjust the straps on my backpack and keep scanning the ground despite the discomfort. I follow Colin around a tree and the ground changes from dirt and pine needles, to rock. I look up and freeze in my tracks. We're higher up than I realized, and the view is breathtaking. Tree-covered mountains stretch all the way to the horizon. Low clouds cast a haze in the distance, but the sky above us is almost cloudless.

I turn my face up to the sun, enjoying it in a way I haven't since I took the vampire magic from Javier. The hedgewitch magic inside of me sings with energy from being this close to nature. I grew up in cities, and never really left. Even living in the country I stayed inside when I wasn't in town. Maybe, when this is all over, I should get a cabin on the top of some mountain somewhere and become a hermit.

"It's a great view," Colin says, interrupting my reverie.

"Yeah," I say quietly. "I've never seen anything like this before."

"You never get used to it no matter how long you live here," he says. "I still stop and stare every time."

"Have you lived here your whole life?" I ask as we start walking again. I glance back at the view one last time before it's blocked by trees.

"Yep, born and raised in the pack," he says as jumps onto the top of a boulder that's over waist high to look around us. I lean against a tree and take a long drink of water. I'll take any break I can get.

"What do you do for a living?" I ask. Most witches work for the coven somehow. Contract work for magic goes through them, and so does your paycheck. They'll cover living expenses and give you some of it back, but it's meant to keep the witches dependent on the coven, so they don't give you much. I've always been curious if packs worked the same way.

"The pack owns a construction business. I'm a site superintendent." He hops down and starts walking again, correcting our direction slightly.

"Are all the employees pack members?" I ask.

"Nah," he says with a shrug. "The owner is, and quite a few of us are, but we hire humans and even werewolves from other packs. The business is too big to keep completely pack. It would have stunted the growth of it."

"That seems smart. I wish witches had the same thought process," I say, thinking back to all the opportunities my mother had been forced to pass on thanks to her coven.

"What coven are you with? Or is JHAPI your coven now?" He asks, glancing back at me.

"I'm not part of a coven. Haven't been since I was sixteen," I say, watching for Colin's reaction. He looks surprised but doesn't pry.

"How'd you end up working with JHAPI anyhow if you aren't an agent?" He asks instead.

"I'm working with the vampire council actually, and they insisted on having a representative on this team while they try to take down the NWR."

"They can do that?" He asks, his tone incredulous.

"Apparently." I hesitate, then decide if I'm wrong, JHAPI can deal with the mess. "I'm sure the werewolves could demand the same thing if they were interested. There is already a werewolf on the team though."

He snorts. "No self-respecting werewolf would leave their pack behind to join a government organization. Can't trust the government, and can't trust them."

I roll my eyes. "That's bullshit."

He comes to an abrupt stop and looks back at me, his jaw clenched tight. "And what the hell do you know about it? You're not a werewolf, you don't understand how a pack works."

I face him without flinching. If he wants to be all sensitive about it, that's his choice.

"JHAPI needs every type of paranormal to succeed. They need people that understand werewolves, witches, vampires. Hell, even goblins. Elise is an amazing agent and good person. What are you so worried about anyhow? That JHAPI is going to try to take something from you?"

"You should know exactly what we're worried about," he says, turning and walking away. "The council is the only authority we should have to answer to. The humans want to control us because they're afraid of us, just like the NWR. That's all

JHAPI is, another way for them to find an excuse to lock us up."

I snort, which earns me another glare.

"You should pay more attention then," I say lightly. "JHAPI has done more to fight the NWR than anyone else in the last hundred years. We're making progress. Having every human agent in the organization partnered with a paranormal keeps anyone from getting away with prejudice."

"Eventually the true goal of the organization is going to become apparent. It's only a matter of time —" Colin trails off, sniffing the air.

I pull on the vampire magic sharply, and all my senses swim into focus. Blood. Werewolf. A whimper.

Colin growls and lunges into a run. I sprint after him, my backpack bouncing around as I struggle to keep up with him. He flows through the trees and around the boulders while I struggle to keep traction on the dirt and slippery pine needles. I grit my teeth and speed up. I can't let him get away from me.

The smell of blood is getting stronger, and just ahead, through the trees, I catch a glimpse of fur. A wolf is hanging by one leg from a snare trap. Unease twists in my stomach. This isn't right.

I jump forward, tackling Colin. He growls in anger, and his elbow catches the side of my head as I ride him down to the ground. He flips underneath me, eyes glowing gold. He might still be in human form, but there is nothing but wolf looking back at me right now. He's operating entirely on instinct, but I can't let him go, not when I'm sure this is a trap.

## 2

I rear back and slap him across the face, trying to shock him into reason. He throws me off and lunges at me. I shift to the side with vampire speed and catch him in the stomach with a kick, then jump on his back and wrap my arm tightly around his throat, just like I remember Reilly doing to me in that gym.

I dig my arm in tight and squeeze. Colin struggles wildly, slamming me back against a tree. My shirt tears and my skin splits as I hit the stub of a broken branch, but I don't let go. I tighten my grip, and he sinks to his knees as his brain is deprived of oxygen and blood.

He drops forward onto his hands. I force him onto his stomach before finally loosening my hold on his neck.

"This is the second time I've saved you from walking into a trap, you asshole," I gasp.

He is shaking under me, his eyes still locked on the werewolf that is now struggling in the snare again. Blood is matted in their fur from where the snare has cut into their skin. There is also a sickening burning smell which tells me the snare is braided with silver. It's not enough to kill the wolf, but it has to hurt like a bitch.

"What—trap?" He gasps.

I unwind my arm from his neck and sit up slowly.

"I don't know, but that's one of your pack that went missing almost a week ago, right?" I ask.

"Yes," Colin growls, twisting his head to glare at me.

"Those injuries are less than a day old," I say pointing at the still wet blood on her leg. "She was hung up there recently, which means it was probably intentional. Which means it's a trap. The kind that makes a werewolf rush in without thinking."

Colin grinds his teeth together, but nods. I stand up and offer him my hand, which he takes. He looks at his pack member again and curls his hands into fists, still clearly struggling not to run to her.

"How did you keep up with me? And overpower me?" He asks. "I thought you were a witch."

It's been a secret for so long my first impulse is to lie and say I took a brew. I don't have to lie anymore though. The vampire council knows, and I'm sure the witch council has found out somehow. I want this pack to trust JHAPI, and he'll be able to hear a lie.

"I'm half witch, half vampire actually," I say cautiously. "This isn't really the time for an in-depth explanation, but I'm as strong and fast as a vampire. When I need to be at least."

"That's not possible," he says, his eyes wide.

I grin and let my fangs drop. Colin takes a step back in shock.

"Yet here I am," I say before retracting the small fangs. I'm still not used to them, they feel awkward and sharp in my mouth.

"This is insane," he says as he shakes his head and

turns back to the wolf. "We can't leave her hanging like that."

She is watching us, but every few seconds she goes back to twisting and clawing at the air. She can't seem to twist up high enough to bite the cable of the snare though.

"Of course not," I say, frowning. "We're going to get her down, but we have to figure out what the trap is first so we can avoid setting it off."

Colin squats down and scans the ground carefully. I walk in a wide circle around the wolf, scenting the air for other humans, but the smell is faint. They came and went last night or this morning.

"There's no trip wire," Colin shouts.

"There has to be something else then," I yell back.

I pull my cell phone out, it'd be great to have some backup, but of course, there is no signal out here. I shove it in my backpack which I take off and set on the ground. I don't want it restricting my movements.

I turn to walk back to him when I hear the sharp ping of metal tearing. The cable hasn't snapped, but about halfway down a few strands have broken. I furrow my brows. They could have easily used a cable strong enough to hold her up there indefinitely even if it did have silver in it.

I pick up a small rock and examine at the ground directly below her. The dirt looks a little fresher, and the pine needles are damp like they were stirred around.

I toss the rock. It hits the ground underneath the wolf dragging dirt and pine needles with it as it collapses the camouflage on the wide pit underneath her. Silver tipped spikes line the sides and jut up from the bottom ready to kill her if she falls. I grit my teeth.

"Don't throw any more rocks," Colin yells urgently.

"I wasn't planning on it," I shout back as I jog over to him. "What is it?"

He points at lumps of freshly disturbed dirt that are evenly spaced in a circle around the pit.

"I don't know what those are, but I don't think we want to find out," he says.

"They went to a lot of trouble here," I say, running my hands through my hair and taking a deep breath.

"Keri getting taken was a huge embarrassment for the pack politically," Colin says through gritted teeth. "If it looks like we just lost her in the woods, it'll be even worse."

"Well, for right now we just need to figure out how to get to her," I step back and scan the area, trying to decide how close we can get. "That cable isn't going to hold much longer, especially if she keeps moving. Can you talk to her? Try to calm her down?"

"I can try, but she's completely out of it. If she's been shifted this whole time, she won't be thinking anymore. The human side of us goes to sleep after a while," Colin says.

"Just try," I say. "I'm going to try to figure out how we can get to her without touching the ground."

Colin turns to Keri and walks as close as he dares. He kneels down and howls. The sound is soft, sad. She pauses in her wriggling and twists her head to stare at him. He starts talking then, a slow, but constant stream of chatter. He has her attention for a moment, but she growls and starts fighting the snare again.

Colin looks back at me.

"Just keep trying."

I jog over to my backpack and open the pocket I

stuffed my brews into. I brought two that can knock a human unconscious for over an hour. On a werewolf, it'll last maybe fifteen minutes. I pick the vial up and look back at Colin. He's still talking to her, but it's not working. Another two strands of the cable snap and curl up with a twang. She has to stop moving, or we're going to be out of time.

"Colin," I say, holding up the vial where he can see. "I can knock her out, but I'm not going to do it unless you agree."

Colin's lip curls up into a growl. He looks back at Keri who is still struggling wildly and rolls his shoulders.

"What is it exactly?" He demands.

"A knock-out brew. She'll just fall asleep for about fifteen or twenty minutes," I explain, holding the vial loosely between my fingers.

Colin looks unhappy, but he finally nods. I stand and throw the vial. It hits her side and breaks, the brew sinking into her fur and skin. She growls and snaps, then goes still.

"Now what?" He asks.

"I think I have an idea, but it involves trusting me some more," I say, crossing my arms.

He narrows his eyes at me. "Explain."

Colin's control is hanging on by a thread. One word answers, the growls, the tense line of his shoulders all betray the struggle. I know weres are protective of pack members, but this seems like more than that. It worries me.

"We can't walk up to her, and the cable will snap if we try to pull her up, so the only option left is to try a jump and grab," I say, tapping my fingers nervously against my arm. "And I have to be the one to jump because I can break the cable, but you probably can't since it is braided with silver."

"You may be fast, but there's no way you can jump that distance and land on the other side once you have her weight," Colin says, shaking his head.

"It's our only option," I say, dropping my arms. "I'm doing it."

I start toward Keri, but Colin grabs my arm. "You're going to get both of you killed."

"I'm not going to stand here and watch her fall into a pit of spikes and die. I'm not asking you to risk your life, I'm doing this. Let me," I say, yanking my arm out of his grasp.

"Fine. Prove me wrong then," he says.

I walk the perimeter until I find a gap in the trees on both sides. I'll have to be quick. I'll need to loop my right arm around her waist and reach overhead and break the cable with my left hand while somehow not losing any momentum. The landing is going to be a bitch.

I pull ruthlessly on the vampire magic. I've only got one shot at this. Now is not the time to ration my magic. Strength courses through my limbs and my fangs push out of my gums. I crouch down, my eyes locked on the cable and sprint forward. Step. Step. Leap.

For a half a second I'm flying through the air, then I hit the wolf. I wrap my right arm tightly around her, my fingers grasping at fur. We swing forward, and I yank on the cable with my left hand as I push white-hot electricity into the metal. It stretches and cuts into my hand before it finally snaps.

She's heavier than I expected and my eyes go wide as I realize we won't make it. Not by a long shot. Instead of flying, we're falling now. My feet hit the dirt, and I squeeze my eyes shut, expecting an explosion. Colin's racing heart pounds in my ears, but that's it. I tentatively open my eyes.

Maybe six inches in front of me is one of those potentially deadly lumps of dirt. I look down at my feet and breathe out a sigh of relief. By sheer dumb luck, I managed to land in a clear spot. The bad news is that I'm still at least six feet from safety holding an upside down, passed out werewolf. She's getting heavier by the second too.

Colin skids to a stop in the gap between trees in front of me and pants heavily, looking between me and the distance that separates her.

"Now what?" He shouts.

"Now we play catch," I shout back.

"You have got to be kidding me," he mutters.

I can hear it as clearly as if he had shouted it with how much magic is surging through me right now.

"Come on, I'm getting tired. Just be ready to catch her," I say as I attempt to adjust my grip without moving. I glance over my shoulder, and sure enough, there's another lump behind me that's even closer.

"Your plans haven't really worked out that well so far," he says, but he braces himself and holds his arms open.

I shift my left hand to her good leg and take a deep breath. I have to be fast, but it's too far to just toss her. If I can pivot without stepping on anything I think I can get enough momentum swinging her around me to throw her to Colin.

I wrap my right hand around her bad leg below the worst of the injury and nod at Colin to let him know I'm ready. I twist, swinging her around me in a wide arc. Her head gets perilously close to the ground.

I rotate back around to Colin and let her go, stumbling forward half a step before catching myself. She flies toward him, tongue flapping in the wind, and hits him in the chest. Colin topples backward and hits the ground with an armful of unconscious wolf.

My hands are shaking from the effort of maintaining the vampire magic for so long. I can't keep this up indefinitely. I pull harder on the sluggish magic and crouch down slightly. This is going to be a hard jump since I can't get a running start.

"Come on," Colin says, lifting Keri and moving out of the way.

I shake off the fear and leap. I get so close, but I'm more tired than I thought. I hit the dirt again three-quarters of the way there, my foot landing on one of those lumps this time. I hear a click and sprint forward. Screw jumping again.

Colin is running too, Keri clutched tightly to his chest. Everything feels slow as I run, even the rabbit-fast beating of my heart. I dive behind a boulder just as I hear something erupt from the ground. The explosion deafens my sensitive hearing. I curl into a ball as shrapnel flies overhead and hits the trees all around me.

The explosion set off another mine, and then another. I press back against the boulder and press my hands to my ears, letting go of the vampire magic in a rush.

After a few seconds of silence, I hesitantly lower my hands and look around. Thick silver balls are embedded in the trees all around me.

"Colin?" I shout, my voice sounding odd inside my head. My ears are still ringing. Dirt that was thrown up in the air is still on the wind making everything feel gritty. It smells like smoke and hot metal.

"Olivia, are you hurt?" Colin shouts back.

I struggle to my feet and glance down at my body just to make sure. "No, I'm not."

I spot Colin. He'd had the same idea, but he had found a bigger boulder thankfully. He's covered in dirt, and if he looks like that, I must be a mess too. I can feel the grit on my face, but I resist the urge to wipe it away since my hands are even dirtier.

"I told you there was no way you'd make that jump while holding her," he says smugly.

I roll my eyes. "You're welcome, fur-ball."

"She's hurt bad. I can still smell silver in her along with something else I've never smelled before," Colin says looking down at the still unconscious Keri.

I hurry over. The snare is twisted into the flesh of her leg. I dig into the wound, thankful she's still asleep, and free the cable. I drop it on the ground and run my hand over her flank, sending my healing magic flowing into her.

"I can heal her a bit, enough to make sure she survives the trip down the mountain," I say as I try to sort out all her injuries.

"You're a healer?" He asks, surprise overwriting the concern on his face for a moment.

I shrug. "A lousy one, but it'll be enough."

The silver is easiest to purge. I can feel the small particles dripping out of the wound on her leg. The snare had cut all the way through her skin and muscle, scraping and gouging the bone itself. I send the bulk of my healing magic there, encouraging the bone to heal and the muscle to begin stitching together from the inside out.

Werewolves heal extremely quickly, but injuries caused by silver can heal human slow. Giving it a jumpstart should encourage her own magic to kick in and take over. I can feel it trying, but something is interfering.

I spread my magic throughout her body and find it stuttering over a strange, foreign substance. It's

19

some kind of chemical, and it feels foul even to my magic. I let my magic eat at it, but it's slippery, and there's a lot of it. When my head starts to spin, I untangle my fingers from her fur and step back unsteadily.

"Sorry," I say breathlessly. "That's all I can do."

The unwelcome but familiar hunger makes my stomach twist. Colin isn't as powerful as Elise, but right now even his magic is tempting. I can almost smell it. I bite down on my tongue and take another couple of steps back.

"Are you okay?" Colin asks, his brows pinched tightly together in concern.

"I'll be fine. We need to get her to some kind of doctor as soon as possible," I say, shaking my head to clear it.

Colin nods then tilts his head back and howls. It sounds utterly inhuman, loud and clear and haunting. It echoes throughout the forest until he stops. His eyes are glowing lightly again, and the wolf peers out at me.

There is an answering howl. Colin grins.

"They'll be ready for us," he says, turning and starting down the mountain.

## 3

The view might be nice, but I refuse to step foot on a mountain ever again. My thighs are burning and shaking, and I'm not sure how much farther we have to go before we reach the bottom. Overusing my magic wore me out, and with no one to feed on, I'm running on empty.

I pause and lean against a tree for a second to catch my breath. I'm tempted to take my backpack off and leave it here, but the brews are too expensive to leave behind. Colin pauses about ten feet ahead of me and looks back.

"Do I need to carry you too?" He asks, amused.

"Shut up," I mutter, envious of Keri even if she does look ridiculous with her tongue hanging out of her mouth like that. Wolves are normally regal creatures, but I guess everything can look stupid in the right circumstances.

I shove off the tree and head down to where Colin is waiting. He starts walking again as soon as I step beside him.

"We're almost there, less than a quarter mile now," he says, answering the question I didn't want to ask.

I let out a sigh of relief. "Finally."

Keri twitches in his arms, a whiny growl escaping her lips. Her eyelids flutter halfway open and she huffs groggily.

"I'm surprised that didn't wear off sooner," I say with a sigh. "Do you think she'll try to hurt you when she wakes up?"

"Perhaps. The Alpha is close; I can smell him," Colin says with a shrug. "He will be able to calm her if needed."

"Ian Grzeski, right?" I ask. I read his name in the file when Stocke had been laying out the plan for this, but I hadn't seen him when we arrived. Stocke had simply introduced me to Colin, and we had headed up the mountain. There was a large area to cover and not much time. The full moon was in four days and the pack wanted to know they could run without risking life and limb.

"Yes," Colin nods. "He has been the Alpha since he was nineteen years old. The youngest Alpha in over two hundred years to maintain control of a pack for this long."

"He's also one of the most influential Alphas, isn't he?" I ask. He may not be on the council himself, but his aunt is, and they have a close relationship. The were-wolf council works a bit differently from the vampire council. The three werewolf council members each oversee a region of the country. If there is unrest, crime, or some kind of disaster in their region, it reflects badly on them. They are intended to mentor and help the Al-phas in their region though, not control them.

They have small packs of their own, but they are limited to only five pack members to prevent any council member from amassing too much power. The werewolves believe that centralization of power is a threat to freedom. Packs should thrive or fail on their own merits as long as they don't put other packs at risk through irresponsible decisions.

"Yes, our aunt is on the council. Ian is well-respected, as he should be," Colin says, pride apparent in his voice. There's something more though. I hesitate to call it fondness, but that's what it is. He isn't smugly proud of how powerful the pack is, he is proud that his Alpha has done well like a brother might be. I've never heard a witch talk about their coven like that, other than Corinne I suppose.

"Our aunt? Are you related to Ian?" I ask, surprised.

"He's my brother," Colin says with a nod.

A man with dark blond hair and thick beard tinged with red appears from seemingly out of nowhere ahead of us. He stalks toward us silently. He isn't that tall, or bulky, but his lean form is all muscle and all power. He glances at me, but his focus is on the twitching werewolf in Colin's arms.

"Why is she unconscious?" Ian asks in a deep voice as he comes to a stop in front of Colin. He brushes his hand over Keri's neck soothingly and her twitching slows.

"A knock-out brew," I explain. "She was struggling in a snare that was breaking and if she hadn't stopped, she would have fallen into a pit of stakes and died."

Ian's eyes flick toward me and his mouth turns down in irritation. He clearly wasn't asking me, but I'm not going to let him act like I don't exist. It was my decision to dose her anyhow.

"She wasn't able to hear me," Colin says. "There is a lot to explain. The trap we found her in was more elaborate than anything else we've found so far. You heard the explosions?"

Ian nods. "Even the humans heard. Agent Stocke has been very uneasy since then."

As if on cue my JHAPI-issue phone begins buzzing with missed calls and messages. I pull it out and turn it to silent. We're almost back, it can wait until then.

"I'll carry her," Ian says, gently lifting Keri from Colin's arms. Colin bows his head in acceptance and helps Ian move her into a better position.

"The NWR injected her with something," I say as we start walking again. "I did what I could to get it out, but there was too much for me fix completely. I don't know for sure, but I think it might be keeping her from shifting back."

Ian glances at me again, still suspicious.

"Olivia saved Keri's life, got the silver out of her leg, and started to heal the wound from the snare trap," Colin explains. He's trying to convince Ian to trust me.

"I'm sure Agent Carter is dedicated to doing her job," Ian says plainly.

The comment feels like an insult. This guy is determined to dislike me; though it might be more accurate to say he's determined to dislike JHAPI.

"Not an agent, just a consultant on loan from the vampire council," I correct. If he wants to be dismissive, he can at least get his details correct. Ian, of course, ignores me.

The steep, downward slope of the mountain begins to even out. The tall pine trees get farther apart and the shrubby bushes common in this part of California become more prevalent. The sunlight that I appreciated earlier is beating down on my back and threatening to put me to sleep.

Colin and Ian easily leap over a small, rocky creek with ankle deep water while I splash through it. My shoes will dry. Just ahead I can see the semicircle of JHAPI vehicles parked in front of the small cabin that is being used as the base of operations for this effort.

Agent Stocke is standing, arms crossed, in the center of it waiting for us. Her shoulders slump in relief when she spots me and Colin. She walks toward us, shoving her phone in the pocket of her pants.

"What the hell happened?" She asks as she falls into step beside Ian.

"The NWR set a different kind of trap," I say with a yawn. "They had Keri strung up in a snare over a pit of stakes and surrounded by land mines of some kind."

"Bouncing Betty's," Colin interjects, shaking his head in disbelief.

I wave my hand in acknowledgment. "I might have accidentally set a couple off, but luckily we avoided getting hit by the shrapnel. Cleaning up all those bits of silver is going to be a bitch though."

"Olivia stopped me from running into the trap," Colin says, ducking his head. "When I smelled Keri, and then the blood, I rushed in on instinct."

Ian gives Colin a disappointed look as he stops next to one of the vans.

"Open it," he demands. "I want to lay her inside rather than on the ground."

Colin nods and pulls the sliding door open. Ian sets Keri down carefully and Colin grabs a mostly empty backpack and gently places it under her head.

Ian run his hands over Keri, feeling for injuries he can't see, then inspects her leg thoroughly. The fur has all been rubbed off, and it's still matted with blood, but the pink-ish healing skin is visible. I did a good job on that at least.

Ian looks back at me. "You healed this?"

"I started too, but I ran out of juice," I say with a wan smile, wiggling my fingers.

"You said she was in a snare over a trap," Stocke says. "How exactly did you get her down?"

"Jump and grab," Colin says, trying to suppress a grin as he gestures for them to ask me.

"The snare line was breaking, and the NWR doesn't make mistakes like that. If the snare was intended to break, there had to be a reason. I tossed a rock underneath Keri and the camouflage covering the pit collapsed. Colin spotted the landmines. The only option was just to jump over the trap, grabbing her on the way." I cross my arms, ready for criticism. I'd dare any of them to come up with a better idea, especially in the limited time we had.

"She almost made it too," Colin adds.

I turn a glare on him. "She was heavy. And I made it far enough."

Stocke pinches the bridge of her nose between thumb and forefinger and takes a deep breath.

"It's a miracle you manage to stay alive," she mutters. "I've called the rest of the teams in, I don't want anyone out there with explosive devices we aren't prepared to disarm."

"So you've given up on helping us already?" Ian asks, his calm tone belying the tension in his shoulders.

Colin raises a brow at me as if to say, *See, I told you JHAPI couldn't be trusted.*

I smirk at him, they don't know JHAPI or Agent Stocke.

"Hardly," Stocke scoffs. "But I'm going to get agents qualified to handle disarming bombs. This is worse than we thought. I'll have people out here by tomorrow morning."

Stocke and Ian begin discussing logistics, but I

can't focus on their conversation. I walk around to the front of the van and plop down on the ground leaning my head back against the grill and letting my eyes slip shut.

"You alright?" Colin asks, nudging me with his foot.

I shake myself and blink at him. "Yeah, just tired. Using that much magic wears me out."

The rumble of a diesel engine draws my eyes to the rough, gravel road that leads to the trail we had just walked down. A jacked-up, red truck with tires way bigger than necessary bounces its way toward us.

"There's the doctor, finally," Colin says.

"Seriously?" I ask, staring at the flashy truck.

Colin shrugs. "Jimmy is a good doctor."

"Is he pack?" I ask.

"Yes, but he's a witch, and a healer. He married into the pack but declined the bite, for obvious reasons."

"Your pack has a legitimate healer on call? That's insane," I say, sticking my hand up toward Colin who takes the hint and pulls me up to my feet.

"He was definitely a welcome addition to the pack," Colin agrees.

The truck skids to a stop a few feet away and Jimmy drops down from the driver seat. He hurries around the front of the truck and heads straight for Keri.

"Ian," Jimmy says, greeting the Alpha as he approaches Keri. Jimmy kneels by the side of the van and buries his fingers in her fur.

I remember the last healer I met in person. He was dressed in a white suit like he thought he was some kind of angel. Most angels don't charge hundreds of thousands of dollars to save a life though.

27

The healer was insanely powerful. I had only been able to touch him for a second before my mother dragged me away with profuse apologies but his magic had felt endless. I hadn't stolen enough of it for him to feel the loss, but even the little bit I did manage to get has made my life easier.

My mother had been furious and had forbidden me from using the magic. I hadn't ever listened though. I've never been able to watch a person suffer without helping. Reilly was right about that being my weakness. I tuck my hands in my pants and watch Jimmy work.

Keri's body shudders slightly as his magic works its way through her. It smells clean, like rain and fresh cut grass. The wound on her leg fills in from the inside out, and the flesh flows closed in a wave. New fur sprouts out of her skin, growing until you can't tell she was ever hurt.

My eyes go wide. I always knew my healing magic was stunted, I just never realized the extent of it. This is wondrous.

Keri wakes up with a start, her lips curling back into a snarl. Ian immediately leans over her and grabs the back of her neck roughly. She goes limp and rolls onto her back, showing him her stomach. He stares at her for a moment, their eyes locked, then releases his hand and steps back. Keri watches Jimmy warily but doesn't make any other aggressive moves toward him.

"What in the hell was she injected with?" Jimmy asks, frowning.

"We don't know," Ian replies. He pauses, looking at me, then back at Jimmy. "Olivia said she thought it was keeping Keri from shifting back to her human form."

Jimmy nods. "It is, but it's not clear how. I've never felt anything like this before."

"Will you be able to fix it?" Ian asks, his brows pinched in concern.

"Of course, what do you think I am? A human doctor?" Jimmy scoffs. "It's just going to take time. I want to work on her at my clinic. I think I have few brews there that will help too."

"Whatever you need to do," Ian agrees.

Jimmy steps back and Ian scoops Keri up. The backseat of the truck has a stretcher they strap Keri onto. She noses at the straps, but Ian flicks her nose and she lays her head down with a huff.

"I'll update you in a couple of hours unless something terrible happens," Jimmy says, clapping a hand on Ian's shoulder.

Ian nods and Jimmy heads around the truck to climb up into the driver seat. The diesel engine roars to life and he takes off, driving faster than seems safe.

"Finally," Stocke says.

I turn to face the direction she is looking and see Ivy and the werewolf she was partnered with walking toward us. Not far behind them are Elise, Zachary, and another wolf in Ian's pack.

"Do you want to rinse off?" Colin asks, gesturing at my face and hands. We're both still smeared with dirt.

"Absolutely." I follow him to the small cabin behind us. It's a quaint structure with only one room and one bathroom. The floors are rough-hewn planks covered by a worn rug tossed down in the middle of the room. A threadbare couch is shoved against a wall out of the way and the center of the room is dominated by a folding table Stocke had brought in. Maps are set out in neatly organized piles along with a checklist of everyone involved in the search.

"Ladies first," Colin says, sweeping his hand toward the bathroom door with an exaggerated bow.

"Oh, so now you have manners?" I ask, raising my brow at him as I take him up on his offer.

"I'm a gentleman," he says, leaning against the door jamb and crossing his arms.

The hot water tap does nothing when I turn it on but the cold water tap sputters out icy water. I scrub at my hands with my fingernails to get the worst of the grime off then coat my hands with soap and rub them together vigorously. Once they're clean enough to be passable, I start on my face.

"Ian will come around, I think," Colin says quietly.

I squint back at him, water dripping into my eyes. "He seems pretty determined to prove we're not trustworthy."

"He's the first Alpha that has ever willingly worked with JHAPI. He has to be cautious," Colin insists.

I shrug and splash more water on my face. Colin hands me a towel and I dry off, having to chase rivulets of water that are dripping down my neck.

"Cautious is fine, I get that. I just hope that Ian is being honest with us," I toss the towel back at Colin. "We had to leave behind at least five werewolves we know were captured by the NWR in Las Vegas without even attempting to find them because the packs wouldn't admit some of their people had been taken."

"My brother wouldn't do that," Colin says, his jaw clenched tight.

"Let's hope not," I say before brushing past him and leaving the bathroom. Colin lets me go without a word.

I step back out into the sunshine and glare up at it.

"I thought those explosions had to be your doing," Elise says. Her belt buckle is a black, hissing cat today. This one seems like a statement piece. The pack was more uncomfortable with Elise being here than any of the other agents. After talking to Colin I understand a little better why, but it's still bullshit.

"Yeah, I seem to have that kind of luck," I say tentatively. She hadn't spoken to me more than was absolutely necessary since 1 left for the Summit. I'm surprised she's approaching me now.

Elise smiles and snorts. "I've never met anyone with worse."

"How did you and your little group do?" I ask.

"Found a few traps, nothing exciting though," she says with a shrug. "Glad to see you're alright though. Zachary was about ready to race across the mountain."

Colin steps out of the doorway behind me and I move out of his way. He pauses, looking at Elise, then purses his lips and sticks his hand out.

"Colin Grzeski," he says, introducing himself.

"Agent Elise Hawking," Elise replies, glancing at me with a slight air of disbelief. The pack had treated her like a leper as soon as we had arrived. The werewolf assigned to her team had looked like he was being punished somehow.

Colin stands stiffly, the two of them eyeing each other, both waiting to see what the other might do or say.

"Olivia has a reckless streak," Colin says finally.

"You have no idea," Elise agrees, raising one brow.

"You're not allowed to bond over my character flaws," I mutter, picking at some dirt still under one of my nails.

Colin grins and starts to say something else, but a shout from Ian interrupts.

"Sorry, gotta run. See you around," he says, deliberately looking at both of us. He jogs away toward Ian who is watching me with an unreadable expression.

"That was interesting," Elise says quietly, turning to stand next to me.

"Felt like progress," I say, nudging her shoulder.

"Yeah, it did," she agrees with a smile and something in my chest loosens. Maybe we can be something like friends again.

## 4

I park in the underground garage of the hotel. This is a nicer place than the last one we stayed at. Reilly even sprung for a suite with separate bedrooms, which was a relief. I guess he's less worried about keeping an eye on me now that we're more like allies and less jailer and prisoner.

I let my head fall back against the headrest. I'm tired, still grimy from where I couldn't wash the dirt away, and the hunger is making me feel weak. My personal phone buzzes in the seat next to me. I stare at it grumpily. I've been getting messages and calls at least three times a day since I turned it back on. I unbuckle my seatbelt and grab the phone, my finger hovering over the unlock button.

With a huff, I unlock the phone and open the messages. There are a few from Lydia, but most are from Patrick. It looks like he's been texting me every day since about a week after I left. There is a gap right after the incident at the Summit, but only a few days.

November 9 09:34 pm: Are you okay? Were you hurt?

November 9 09:42 pm: Olivia, please just let me know you're okay...

November 12 02:06 am: I'm just going to keep trying.

November 12 03:12 am: I'm sorry.

November 13 08:23 pm: Mr. Muffins peed on Emilio's pillow. He was furious. Muffins is smug.

Tears prick at my eyes, and I press my hand to my mouth. I miss that stupid cat so much. If I can't be there to harass Emilio, I'm glad she's still giving him hell.

I take a deep breath and text back a quick reply praising Mr. Muffins and letting Patrick know I'm fine. Most of the anger toward the clan, and especially Patrick, has faded. Things with Reilly, on the other hand, are getting increasingly more awkward.

My phone buzzes again, and Patrick's excited reply flashes across the screen. I climb out of the car and head toward the elevators that take me to the main floor of the hotel. I keep my responses to Patrick short. Part of me wants everything to go back to normal, but normal went out the window a long time ago. I'll stop ignoring him, but I don't think I can go back to the easy friendship we had. At least not yet.

I'm sharing a suite with Reilly, but I haven't actually been to the room. We checked in early this morning before sunrise, and I had left right away to meet with the team.

A spacious elevator carries me up to the twelfth

floor. I step out, and a small placard on the wall points me in the direction of room 1289. The room is near the end of the hall. I unlock the door and slip inside, shutting it softly behind me. The sun hasn't set yet, but it's habit to stay quiet when I know someone is asleep. Even if that person is *dead* asleep.

I tiptoe through the open sitting area. Recessed lighting is cycling from blue to purple to red and back again giving the whole room a strange vibe. Two couches face each other in the center of the room underneath a chandelier. The bright pieces of glass twinkle in the shifting light.

On the other side of the couches are two thick double doors. One is open, revealing a glimpse of the bathroom and a large jacuzzi set up on a marble pedestal. That looks like my next stop after I grab a change of clothes. I still feel gritty from where dirt and debris made it down my shirt.

To my left is a closed door, and to my right, I can see into a bedroom. Reilly's bare foot is sticking out of the covers. I guess the other room is mine.

I open the door to my room and flip on the lights. My bags are all piled on the king-sized bed, but it's what lines the wall to my left that catches my eye.

There is a long, wooden table and on it, neatly organized, is my wet dream come to life. There are four cauldrons; one in pewter, copper, iron, and the crystal one I bought in Vegas. A gas stove with two large burners takes up one end of the table, the chrome gleaming invitingly. On the opposite end is a shelf stacked with ingredients. Herbs. Little vials of shimmering liquids. A set of sharp knives.

I walk forward, mesmerized, and open the drawers at the bottom of the shelf. They are filled with crystals of varying sizes. Many of them I had never been able to afford before. There is one drawer with four sections, each containing pure gold in different forms. Powdered, rough nuggets, cubes, and slivers.

I pick up a bundle of lavender and inhale deeply. It's potent and as fresh as dried herbs can be. The ingredients are all vibrant and eager to be used.

I had complained most of the way from Cesare's clanhouse in Portland to Los Angeles about how I needed to be able to brew. I had spent at least an hour expounding on all the things I wish I had, and the best ingredients, and the best tools. Apparently, Reilly had been listening and not ignoring me like I thought.

I check the time. It's almost sunset. I walk back to the sitting area and pause a few steps away from the door to Reilly's room. His toes twitch and his breathing changes, growing deeper and faster.

My fingers itch with a need to brew. Since I have all of this, I want to try something new. Reilly sits up abruptly, his eyes going straight to me. The sun sets completely; the vampire magic inside of me stirs, happy that it's gone.

"You're filthy," Reilly says as he steps out bed, unconcerned that he's only wearing those stupid silky boxers he favors.

I avert my eyes from his bare chest. Just because we're roommates doesn't mean he gets to wander around half naked in front of me. He could give a girl ideas. Very bad ideas.

"There was an incident with a small explosion," I say, shrugging.

He's standing in front of me in a flash. I take a half step back, but he catches me by my shoulders and searches me for injuries.

"I'm fine," I say, shoving at him. "And put on some clothes. This isn't a nudist colony."

"That's too bad," he says with a grin, glancing down at my body.

I roll my eyes. "Not gonna happen."

"So you keep saying." He turns away and heads back into his room. I had forgotten about the raised, white scars that crisscross his back. I've never seen a vampire with scars before, hell, I had no idea they even *could* scar.

I plop down on one of the white couches, dirt from my clothes rubbing into the fabric.

"What exactly happened?" He asks from the other room.

"The NWR set out one of the missing pack members a bait. I had to navigate some land mines to rescue her," I explain, for the third time. "Just read the report tomorrow, I don't feel like rehashing it right now."

Reilly walks out of his bedroom buttoning his shirt. He's wearing his usual black slacks, but he still hasn't put on shoes.

"We were told the only thing in those woods were bear traps," Reilly comments.

"Yeah, Stocke wasn't pleased. She's calling in a bomb squad or something, and she isn't going to let the team back out there."

Reilly nods. "Good."

I tap my fingers against my thigh and gnaw on my lip for a second. "Thanks for the brewing equipment."

He finishes the last button and looks up. "Of course. You need more brews than JHAPI will issue you. Make what you need and then some. I think we're going to need everything you can brew to deal with Cesare and whatever this Bound God turns out to be."

"Sure thing, I'll just skip sleeping for the next couple of weeks," I sigh. That's Reilly, always practical. I can't complain though, he gave me everything I asked for. I do want to brew everything I can. Despite my shiny new magic, there's something about having a brew in my pocket that makes me feel ten times safer.

"Speaking of, I have arranged a meeting in a few days with someone who should be able to get us the information we need. You have to come," Reilly continues.

"Then Zachary is coming," I say. If he gets to hand out orders, I do too.

"We need to keep this small. The more people that know, the higher the risk of Cesare finding out," Reilly says, adjusting the cuff of his sleeve.

"We can trust Zachary. He's been secretly investigating the coven on his own already. You don't get to cut him out. You have your clan mates, and I have my friends."

Reilly's nostrils flare in frustration.

"I liked you better when you were scared of me," he mutters.

"I was never scared of you," I say, narrowing my eyes at him.

"Lie," Reilly says smugly, his cheeks dimpling as he smiles.

I roll my eyes and stand up. It takes more effort than it should. "I'm going to—"

"You're exhausted," he interrupts. "You need to feed."

"If you'd let me finish a sentence," I say sarcastically, "I was going to tell you that I'm going to brew something to help with that. I need to do it now while I'm hungry so I can test it."

He frowns. "I've never heard of anything that could curb a vampire's appetite."

"Well, I'm not a vampire," I say walking around the opposite end of the couch toward my room.

"You're half vampire," Reilly insists, following me.

I stop and turn to face him. "Look, I'm good at this. I may not get it right the first time, but I'm going to figure it out. I've been doing this since I was five years old and there has yet to be anything I haven't been able to brew."

"It's still a risk," Reilly says, his mouth pulling down into a frown. "If you're hungry, you can feed. You shouldn't risk hurting yourself just because you don't like that you need blood and magic."

"I'm trying to make myself stronger," I insist. "If I'm in the middle of a fight, and I get exhausted like this, I can't stop and feed. I need something that can help when feeding isn't an option."

"I don't believe that's what this is about," Reilly says, crossing his arms.

"Believe what you want," I say, turning away and walking up to the worktable.

"I'm staying in case this goes horribly wrong," Reilly says from behind me.

I wave my hand at him dismissively. I don't care what he does as long as he stays out of my way. I examine the cauldrons I have to choose from. The cauldron is the base of the brew. I run my fingers over the iron cauldron and frown. That one isn't quite right. The pewter, however, warms under my hand.

I move the cauldron to the gas stove and turn on the burner, then hesitate, and turn it back off. Not until later, I think. The heat should come in at the end once the magic has already had its way with the ingredients.

A hesitant thrum of magic grows in my chest as I pick out the ingredients. My hands aren't as sure as they usually are when I'm doing this. I pick up two crystals and stare at them, neither is perfect, but perhaps the garnet will work. Bat wings are one of those ingredients I hardly use, but I lay it out with a smile. A creature of the night feels right.

Some of the hesitancy fades as I begin preparing each ingredient. The cinnamon bark grinds into a coarse powder. I sneeze, and it billows up like a cloud.

"Are you sure you know what you're doing?" Reilly asks.

"Shush," I say, shooting him a glare. "Don't interrupt." I turn back to the workstation and carefully slice, chop, and crush each ingredient. I add a few more things as they come to mind, but when I'm ready to brew, it still feels incomplete. I frown and fill the cauldron with cold water; it'll come to me.

Deep-red magic sparks out of my chest and flutters around the cauldron. I grab the cinnamon and sprinkle it into the water. The sparks chase it down, and the water glows red and warm even though I still haven't lit the fire. Steam curls off the surface and I hurry to add the bat wings. The brew darkens and begins to churn.

I twirl my finger over the surface and the bubbling liquid beings to spin. More magic pours in; my fingers shake slightly. I curl them into a fist to hide it. I've brewed tired before; it isn't going to stop me. Gritting my teeth, I let my magic flow.

The crystal goes in whole, followed by a handful of gold. Something rich to complement the color. I turn away from the cauldron and dig through the drawers until I find a bar of dark chocolate. I break off a piece and hold it over the cauldron. It melts in my fingers and drips into the brew.

The red sparks dance in, over, and around the cauldron. A warm glow emanates from the cauldron as well, growing in steady beats that match my heart. I stir the brew gently. The brew clings to the rod as I lift it out, then plops back down in the cauldron.

I still need…oh. Of course. I grab the knife I chopped with and prick my finger. Sparks gather around the wound and carry the blood straight into the brew.

"That is odd," Reilly says quietly.

I ignore him but smile to myself. It is odd, but also strangely cute. My magic is straining to give me what I want. It can feel the need, but it still isn't sure how to do it. Whatever this does, it won't be perfect. I can only hope it helps.

The lighter on the gas stove clicks twice, then a flame erupts from the burner. I crank it up to high and watch the brew intently. The red grows darker and darker until it's closer to purple. I stir it quickly; the thumping beat of the magic grows faster. My heart races right along with it.

My heart pounds painfully like it might explode, once, twice; then magic vanishes into the brew with a loud clap. The flame goes out.

I lean against the workbench trying to catch my breath. The brew smells like blood. I'm not sure if that's a good sign or not. I grab a small vial and dip it in the brew making sure I don't touch it.

"Be careful," Reilly warns.

"I've got you here to rescue me." I grin and toast him with the vial.

Taking one last deep breath, I throw it back like a shot. The thick liquid coats my tongue and burns its way down my throat. Too much cinnamon. I grimace and resist the urge to spit it out.

A sharp cramp tears through my stomach. I double over and wrap my arms around my middle, the empty vial bouncing on the carpet and rolling under the table.

"I think I'm going to be sick," I gasp out. I turn and run for the bathroom, my legs shaking under me. Halfway to the toilet, I collapse on the cold bathroom floor.

I curl into a ball, pressing my hands to my stomach. The brew backfired. I'm not nauseous, I'm hungry. I've never been this hungry. Fangs punch out of my gums and dig into my bottom lip as I blink back angry tears. I've never failed at a brew this badly before. This shouldn't have happened. It shouldn't be possible.

Reilly kneels next to me, but his face is blurry. I blink and realize he's shouting at me.

"Olivia," he repeats, giving me a hard shake. "What do I do?"

I jerk upright and sink my teeth into his neck. Blood. Magic. Power. I need it. He goes still as I crawl into his lap and push my hands into his hair to make sure he can't get away.

I moan around the blood pouring down my throat and pull on his magic greedily. I've been so hungry. I don't know why I haven't been doing this every day. I should take all of it.

"Olivia, that's enough," Reilly whispers. He smooths back the hair draped over my face.

I growl and dig my teeth into the meat of his neck. He hisses and tries to jerk away, but I'm wrapped tightly around him. Reilly stands with a muttered curse, slipping his arms under my thighs to support me. He's walking, but I don't care, not while I can still feed.

Icy cold water pours over my head, and I jerk back in shock, my teeth tearing loose. Reilly pushes me against the wall of the shower and shoves his arm into my throat. Sense trickles back into my brain. I untwist my fingers from his hair, spluttering at the cold water still pouring over my face.

"Shit," I gasp hoarsely.

Reilly's eyes flash with anger, and he grinds his teeth together. He looks truly dangerous like this.

"You are not testing that on yourself again," he growls.

"No kidding," I say. "That shouldn't have happened. I don't understand."

He slowly releases his hold on me, watching warily to see if I attack again. I close my eyes and slide out of the spray of water. He stands in front of me in his soaking wet suit, feet still bare.

"I'm sorry I attacked you," I say, feeling like an asshole.

He shrugs, unconcerned. "What went wrong?"

"I don't know," I say, shaking my head. "I've never fucked up a brew that bad before. I didn't think it was possible."

"No one is infallible," Reilly says. "You're not doing this again."

He turns and walks out of the shower, leaving wet footprints on the bathroom floor.

I smack my hand against the tap and turn the water off, then sink to the floor as I wipe my hand across my mouth. It comes away streaked with Reilly's blood.

I let my head fall back and shut my eyes. I don't like giving up, but I can't be stupid either. I can't risk losing control like that again. My only choice right now is to feed.

---

I can't sleep. All I can think about is the taste of Reil-

ly's blood. It hasn't ever been like that before. I en-
joyed sitting in his lap a little too much. I roll over
with a groan and crawl out of bed. It's time for another bath. Maybe the hot water will relax me
enough that I'll actually be able to sleep. I have
training tomorrow afternoon, and I can't afford to be
up all night.

Reilly's door is closed. I tip-toe to the bathroom
and shut the door behind me as quietly as I can. Hot
water pours out of the tap as soon as I turn it on,
steam curling into the air. I drop my clothes in a pile
and climb into the huge bathtub. It really is big
enough for at least six people.

The hotel has supplied bubble bath in several
scents. I grab the vanilla and lavender and dump
some in. Too much judging by the volume of bubbles
it's already creating.

I shrug and slip down into the rising water. The
crackle of bubbles popping and the rush of the hot
water is soothing. I lean my head back against the
edge of the tub and stretch my legs out in front
of me.

The door opens, and I freeze as my senses jump
into high alert on instinct. Reilly's warm scent flows
over me. I turn my head slowly. He prowls toward
me. His shirt is hanging open over his slacks and his
abs ripple as he walks.

"Wh-what are you doing?" I ask, stuttering over
my words. My mouth is suddenly parched.

"Something I should have done a long time ago,"
he says as he comes to a stop right next to the
bathtub.

I stare at him with wide eyes as he kneels down
next to me and traces his finger down the side of my
neck, then further down until his hand disappears
into the bubbles. My breath catches.

"You want this," he says, sure of himself.

"No, I don't," I say weakly.

He leans in closer. "Lie."

My heart pounds in my chest as the last of my self-control vanishes.

"I hate you a little," I say breathlessly as I push him back. He goes unwillingly, pulling his hand out of the water as he moves back to his feet.

I stand up slowly, letting water and bubbles slide down my body. Reilly watches with heavy-lidded eyes, then wraps his hand around the back of my neck and pulls me into a kiss. It's everything I had dared hope it would be.

He pulls away from my mouth and kisses down the side of my neck, lips and teeth grazing my skin. He reaches up and twists his fingers in my hair, holding me as tightly as he can like he's afraid I might run away. My lips part as his breath sends goose-bumps down my back.

He presses the tips of his fangs against my skin. His tongue darts out, tasting my pulse before he bites down hard on my neck. I moan and dig my nails into his back. He pulls me out of the tub, and I wrap my legs around his waist. He holds me tightly, and carries me out of the bathroom with long, purposeful strides. His lips and teeth never leaving my neck.

We walk into his bedroom and he pulls away, his tongue catching a drip of blood clinging to his lower lip. He throws me down on his bed. I bounce once on the soft mattress and watch with hungry eyes as he strips out of his shirt, then slowly pulls off his belt.

I want him to touch me everywhere. I've been holding this back for too long. Hell, it's just plain been too long. I have needs, and Reilly with his dimples and muscles is going to fill every one of them.

He drops the belt on the floor and unbuttons his

pants. He shoves them down and I see his hard, thick—

I shoot up straight, panting and sweaty. My arms flail out into the dark room searching for warm skin, but I'm alone. Fuck. Stupid, shitty, unnecessary dreams. I drop my head into my heads and groan in frustration. Sexual frustration. I'm torn between relief and the overwhelming desire for that to be real.

Then again, it would be a disaster if it was. I don't trust Reilly, certainly not enough for that to be more than a fling. The fact that I'm attracted to Reilly at all is a mark against him. My track record with men is unlucky, to say the least.

I throw the covers back and swing my legs over the side of the bed. I need a cold shower. I slip out of my room silently and head toward the bathroom. The door to Reilly's room is standing wide open unlike in the dream. I pause in the center of the sitting area and watch the slow rise of his chest.

The last time I barged in on him sleeping, he was laying in the bed on top of the covers in ridiculous silky boxers. My cheeks heat at the memory. I turn and walk resolutely into the bathroom, dumping my clothes in the middle of the floor.

Cold water hisses out of the shower head and I step underneath it, gritting my teeth against the shock of the change in temperature. I brace my hands against the shower wall and shove my head under the flow, trying to think of anything to distract myself.

Brews. That's what I need. More knock-out brews. Healing brews. Literally anything. If I can't sleep, I can be productive. Hedgewitch magic was the first I ever stole, and I know I can always come back to it when I need it. It's reliable. Unlike men.

## 5

It's just past one pm when I turn down the long driveway that leads to JHAPI headquarters. In the distance is a sprawling ten-story building, one of several structures on the hundred acre property. Hu had told me they had buildings meant for training with magic that were built with special materials that were impervious to some of the more destructive elements, like fire and electricity. I'm eager to test that out.

I stop at the white line that is drawn a few feet in front of a tall wedge barrier with yellow and black reflective stripes painted across the front of the steel, just in case you missed it. They are serious about preventing anyone from driving in here without permission.

A man in uniform with a badge pinned to his chest and a gun belt around his waist steps out of the guardhouse and approaches my car. I roll down my window and hold out the paperwork Stocke had given me yesterday.

"I'll need to see your license too," the guard says as he takes the paperwork and scans through it.

I dig my license out of my wallet and hand that

over as well. He looks between the license and the paperwork, then nods and hands it all back to me.

"Park on the ground level in the parking garage, then go straight inside to get your security badge."

"Will do," I say with a smile.

He nods and waves me forward. The barrier sinks down into the pavement until all that's visible is a patch of concrete slightly lighter than the rest. I drive forward.

The driveway continues for a quarter of a mile before you reach the parking lot, and the garage is on the back side of that. I drive around in circles before I finally find an empty spot. I park with a sigh of relief and text Hu that I'm here.

I grab the duffel bag that has my spare clothes out of the backseat. The only other people walking through the parking garage are wearing the standard black suit of JHAPI agents. I look down at my purple tank top and black leggings and shrug. Hopefully, they'll let me in the door.

A covered walkway extends from the parking garage to the entrance I think I'm supposed to be using. I follow behind the other agents, taking in the scenery as I walk. A huge concrete dome is just visible past the far corner of the main building. A group of six people jog along a paved trail that circles the entire back half of the property.

Stocke had mentioned that the second half of the training process to become a JHAPI agent was conducted here at the headquarters. They weeded out the weak and untrustworthy on the other side of the country, then shipped them here to finish.

I push open the glass door etched with the JHAPI logo and step into the cold, but bright building. It's bustling with activity. Chatter and the quick footsteps of people walking with purpose echoes off the tile floor. A glass elevator zips upward, disappearing into the tall ceiling of the atrium about five floors up. Every other floor is lined with a balcony. The entire space is brightly lit from the glass front of the building which starts out wide at the bottom and narrows to a point at the top.

Access to the elevators and the doors that lead farther into the building are blocked by metal detectors and guards. Every person that passes scans their badge and waits for the guard to wave them through. The lines are moving efficiently with no more than two or three people waiting at a time.

I stop gawking and head toward the information desk. Hu said he'd meet me here, but I'll need to get the security badge before we can go anywhere. There's no line, so I approach the closest person behind the desk and set my paperwork on the counter.

"Hey," I say, getting their attention, "I need to get a security badge."

They glance at my outfit, but take the offered paperwork and start checking it against something on their computer.

"ID please."

I hand that over as well and lean against the counter, taking in the room again. Hu waves at me from behind one of the barriers and slips out the exit behind another agent. I wave back with a smile. Hu, despite being scary as fuck when he needs to be, always seems to be in a good mood.

"Here is your security badge," the woman at the desk says, drawing back my attention. "It is valid for two months, and you'll need to swipe it at every checkpoint. It will work for every area you have access to. If it doesn't work, assume you aren't cleared to access whatever is behind that door."

"Thanks," I say, accepting the rectangular badge.

The picture is from my driver's license, which is a huge improvement over the last picture I was forced to wear around. I pull the lanyard over my head and pick up my duffel.

"We need to head back out the direction you came in," Hu says, arriving in front of me. Thankfully, he's already dressed in gym clothes as well, so I don't feel quite as out of place anymore.

"Lead the way," I say, adjusting the duffel bag on my shoulder.

We head back outside and follow the sidewalk that wraps around the building. As we pass the corner, the rest of the facility becomes visible. There isn't just one concrete dome; there are at least six that I can see.

"What are those things?" I ask.

"The training facilities JHAPI built for the paranormal agents. They're concrete, so you can't set it on fire or melt it with electricity," Hu explains. "Each one is divided up into sections on the inside. I reserved two for us so that we have more room to move around."

"Why aren't they enclosed?" There are high arched openings every few feet.

"For air witches mostly, but also to keep things cool when the fire witches get started. It keeps the air fresh inside too," Hu says as we pause to let a group of joggers pass over the sidewalk in front of us. The jogging trail winds throughout everything back here.

"I've never seen anything like this," I say, a little awed by the extent of the facility.

"In that direction," Hu points to the left past the domes, "they have obstacle courses meant to wear out vampires and werewolves. They made sure there was something for every type of paranormal when they built all of this."

"I can see why funding is such a big deal to them," I say. All of this must have cost millions upon millions to build.

"Have you been practicing the basics we went over the last time we trained?" Hu asks.

"Yes, every spare moment," I say, lifting my hand with a grin. The electric magic crackles into a twitchy sphere in the palm of my hand. It took days to get to the point I could contain it at all, but after that, shaping it became surprisingly simple. The magic wanted to be controlled. I had simply needed to find the focus it required.

"That's great!" Hu says, stopping to examine it.

"That's not even the best part." I flick my wrist and twirl the magic around my hand in a slow figure eight, grinning in satisfaction as Hu's eyes widen.

"We're going to get to work on more than I planned today," Hu says, straightening back up. "I'm glad I asked Elise to come help."

"Oh, she's going to be here?" I ask, surprised.

"Yes, she'll be joining us a little late, but I wanted you to be able to work on dealing with multiple attackers."

"Sounds good," I say flexing my fingers. "I'm excited to get to really use the electric magic. It behaves so differently from the rest."

"Elemental magic can be temperamental like that," Hu agrees. "Each kind has its unique issues."

"I thought that since I've used elemental type magic for so long that it would be easier to control," I say with a sigh.

"I've never met anyone with more than one type of magic before, of course, but I think you could provide some fascinating insights into magical theory. It's too bad you don't have magic of each type. There are so many experiments I'd like to run," Hu says, a wistful look in his eyes.

"That would be a lot of magic to steal," I say, raising my brow at him.

"Oh, I don't mean literally every possible magic. I just meant one of each of the four types. Physical, mental, elemental, and the odd one: space-time." Hu glances at me, slightly embarrassed. "I studied magical theory in college."

"Space and time?" I ask raising a brow. "No witch can time travel."

"No, but some do have the talent of foretelling, or my least favorite, psychometry," he says with a shudder. "It's so creepy. And, of course, that's just a loose set of categories. Impervs clearly use physical magic, however, hedgewitches, who technically use earth elemental magic, create brews that cause both physical and mental changes. My Professor insisted they fell into all three categories because of that."

I come to a stop, taking in all this information. "I have so many questions."

Hu laughs. "Sorry, I love magical theory, so I get kind of carried away when I talk about it."

"Foretelling can show the future, and psychometry can show the past, but neither of those affect space," I say gesturing around us.

Hu grins and leans in eagerly. "There is an old branch of magic that some people believe completely died out after the Great War led by Aris and Izul. They were called shadow walkers."

"Shadow walkers?" I interrupt with a laugh. "That sounds dramatic."

"That's the basic translation," Hu says, waving away my gibe. "It comes from the Latin phrase *nocte viator*, which literally translates to *night traveler*, but over the years it became shadow walker."

"What can they do, exactly?" I ask.

"That is the interesting part," Hu says, his eyes bright. "There are different theories. One claims they can travel from shadow to shadow, basically invisible. Another says that there is a realm that mirrors this one that the shadow walkers created, and can return to at will. A place where it is always night and magic doesn't work."

"So, basically, a witch's version of a scary fairy tale," I say, biting down on a smile. Hu is passionate about this, I don't want it to seem like I'm laughing at him. I'm just laughing at these theories.

"There is historical evidence they existed. For some reason, during the Great War, they started being killed off. With rarer magics, especially back then, it wouldn't have been that hard to completely stamp out an entire magical talent from the world."

"I wonder how many we've lost," I comment as we start walking again.

"Probably dozens. There was a branch of physical magic that involved manipulation of gravity that was ended sometime in the early fifteenth century. Some argue there used to be witches that could manipulate ice as an element as well."

We pass one of the domes. It seems even bigger when you're standing right next to it. A flash of light startles me, and a wave of heat blows past us. A fire witch and an air witch are dancing around each other, flinging magic back and forth with friendly taunts.

Hu keeps walking. I drag myself after him, but I wish I could stay and watch. I've never seen magic used like that outside of a fight where I could appreciate it.

We walk into the second dome, marked by a sign as Training Area B. The concrete floor is divided into four equal sections. Hu reserved the two sections on the left giving us almost a football field worth of space to work with. We drop our things on a concrete bench.

Hu strips off his shirt, folds it and lays it on top of his bag. He stretches and the thick muscles of his shoulders and back ripple under the bright tattoo.

"Alright," Hu says, rubbing his hands together. "Now that you can control your magic the key is thinking about how you should direct it. My fire can be used to strike and to protect."

He holds his arms out and the fire flares around him like it had at the airport outside of Vegas. It flows around his chest, ready to lash out with barely contained energy. His hair moves as if he's caught in a breeze as the air around him shifts from the heat.

"If you were to hit me with any sort of offensive magic, even one of your brews, the fire around my chest would try to consume it," Hu explains. "It won't be perfect, but everything I can do to give myself an edge is beneficial."

I flex my fingers, thinking. "Back at Javier's clan-house when the coven attacked the electric magic spread out like a net when it came up against the other witch's magic."

Hu nods. "That's good. How long did it hold up?"

"Not long," I say, remembering the recoil as my magic collapsed, and I was thrown back onto the floor. "It was two against one. I was up against an air witch using wind to feed the magic of a fire witch."

"Mistake number one," Hu says. "Never let them work together like that. You don't want to be stuck between them, but you want to keep them from supporting each other as well."

"Easier said than done," I say with a shrug.

"We aren't here for easy," he says, crouching

slightly. "Dodge or block what I'm about to throw at you. Your choice."

"What—"

Hu lifts his hand and a stream of fire spirals toward me. My eyes go wide and I pull on the vampire magic, leaping to my left just in time to feel the fire shriek past me. Sweat beads up on the back of my neck from the intense heat. I skid to a stop a few feet to Hu's left.

He doesn't give me a chance to think, just twists toward me and casts his magic again. I flee, feeling like I've forgotten every bit of magic I practiced over the last few weeks. Before Hu can cast again, I use the vampire magic to move as quickly as I can toward his back, then come to an abrupt stop and lift my hand. Electricity rushes out of my raised palm and spreads out into a crackling net between us.

He's faster than I thought was possible for a witch and his magic crashes into mine in a shower of sparks. The collision rattles me and I grab my wrist with my opposite hand to keep my arm steady. Fire pushes against the bright, white electricity, each of us pushing more and more magic as it becomes a contest of sheer power.

I grit my teeth against the effort and try to think. It's becoming increasingly obvious I'm going to lose this battle. Hu takes a step forward and my eyes go wide as I'm physically pushed back, my feet sliding across the rough concrete.

I twist my arm and snap my hand closed. The net of electricity crashes around the fire, bright white drowning out the red-hot flames. The crush of magic on magic explodes and Hu and I are flung apart. I twist mid-air, using my vampire magic to land on my feet and sprint forward, throwing a quick bolt of lightning that forces him to stay on the defensive.

55

A growl makes the hair on the back of my neck prickle, but it's too late. Huge paws hit my shoulders and I'm crushed down onto the concrete, just barely catching myself with my forearms to prevent my face from taking the brunt of the fall.

I lay underneath Elise, who teasingly nips my ear, and try to catch my breath.

"Fucking cheaters," I pant.

Hu is laughing so hard he can barely breathe.

Elise steps off of me and sits back on her haunches, tongue lolling out of her mouth as she does her best impersonation of a friendly dog who didn't just tackle someone in the middle of winning a sparring session.

I sit up with a groan and glare at them both. Smug assholes.

Hu walks over, still grinning. "You did great, Olivia. However, make sure you counter-attack faster next time. And don't waste as long pushing back in a contest of strength."

Elise huffs in agreement, her tail thumping against the ground as is to emphasize his point.

"You really go for realism in training," I say as I struggle to my feet. My forearms are scraped from the impact, but I have a feeling I'm only going to end up with more scrapes and bruises before we're done.

"No other way to do it," Hu says.

"And here I thought you were the nice one on the team," I say with a grin. I'd still be lost without Hu's help, and honestly, I find this kind of training exhilarating. "I guess the other lesson is to pay attention to my surroundings and threats that may show up after the fight has started?"

Hu nods and lifts his hands for a high five which I deliver with a resounding smack. "There's hope for you yet."

Two hours later I'm laying on the concrete with a burn across my scraped forearm, a bite mark on my ass, and a grumpy, singed werewolf ripping my tennis shoe apart.

"You literally bit me on the ass, Elise," I shout across the open space. "I have a right to defend myself."

She looks up from the shoe and turns her tail toward me as if to rub the damage in my face. Hu is laying a few feet away, just as exhausted as I am, but somehow still able to laugh hysterically.

"I don't have another pair of shoes with me you vindictive puppy," I mutter.

Elise rips the sole of the shoe completely off and looks at me smugly.

"Oh my gosh, I'll heal it, alright?"

She snorts and begins her shift back to human. The electric burn begins to heal as she shifts, but an oozing pink slash that stretches from her lower back to her left thigh remains once she's back on two feet.

"That hurt worse than silver," she announces as she strides toward me, naked and unconcerned.

"I got burned and bitten, stop whining," I say as I stand up.

She reaches me and holds her arm out haughtily. I roll my eyes and grab it, sending my healing magic coursing through her. With her already accelerated healing, it's almost effortless to heal the burn. I tug her forward so I can examine the skin. The mark is completely gone, and her ass is back to its usual, spectacularly muscled self.

"Good as new," I say, dropping her arm.

She twists around to inspect it and nods in

approval.

"We've got that meeting in a couple of hours," Hu says as he walks past us. "I don't know about you two, but I want a shower and dinner beforehand."

"Absolutely," Elise agrees. She looks back at me. "Come on, I'll show you where the showers are."

All my injuries ache, but I'll wait to heal them until I'm in the shower. I need to take a few brews and healing myself is easier with fewer distractions. I grab my duffel bag, and Elise pulls on a bathrobe laying on top of her backpack.

"JHAPI frowns on its agents walking around naked in all areas not designated for training," Elise says, answering my unasked question. "I forgot once and almost got suspended."

"I'm sure you made somebody's day though," I say with a laugh.

"Why do you think I didn't get suspended?" She says with a wink.

The showers are attached to a traditional gym. We walk past the humans and paranormals lifting weights and running on treadmills. Most are wearing PT uniforms with their names on the back.

"Agents in training?" I ask.

Elise nods. "Most actual agents don't have time to work out, so you won't see many of them in here at once."

The women's bathroom is empty as we head back to the shower area. I dig a healing brew out of the duffel bag and drink it. It warms me from the inside out. The aches vanish, and the scrapes fade to pink. A nudge from my healing magic and the burn is fixed as well.

"So, you made it out of the den of the vampires alive," Elise says as she brushes past me.

"Barely," I agree with a laugh. I toss my bag down

on a bench and start stripping out of my workout clothes.

Elise faces me, hands on hips. "What the hell is actually going on with Reilly? And don't lie to me."

I freeze with my shirt in my hand. I had hoped to avoid this conversation, but Elise was bound to get me alone eventually.

"It's...complicated," I say.

"I will bite you on the ass again if you don't give me a straight answer," Elise growls.

"Okay, okay," I say, lifting my hands in surrender. Everything has changed. If Elise had cornered me like this a few weeks ago, I would have thrown Reilly under the bus and hoped for the best. "Until the Summit I didn't trust Reilly at all. He drug me out of Texas and threatened to kill the clan I had worked for if I ran."

Elise's face shifts from determined to furious. "I'll arrest him right now."

"He was bluffing," I say, sitting down on the bench heavily. "I thought I was the pawn in his political games, but it turns out Reilly is just as much a pawn as I am. His sire is the one pulling all the strings on all this."

"I still might arrest him," Elise says, crossing her arms. "What does his sire want with either of you?"

"You know all that stuff Zachary has been investigating? The crazy coven?"

Elise nods.

"Cesare is a traditionalist. He wants vampires to enslave humans, and to do that, he has to take out anyone that could stop him. Cesare believes that the god they have trapped somewhere is real, and he wants to release it so that it can destroy the other paranormals races; witches, werewolves, goblins." I shake my head. "For some reason, he thinks I can kill

59

it once it has weakened the other races enough. He forced Reilly to find me and start preparing me."

"No offense, but I don't see you killing a god any-time soon," Elise says with a raised brow.

"I don't either," I say with a shrug, looking down at my hands. "I can steal magic, but the more I steal, the more I need. It takes time to learn how to control it, and I don't know how much time I have."

"So, what's the plan?" Elise asks.

"The plan?" I ask.

"For stopping Cesare," Elise says, crossing her arms. "You're not just going to let him get away with it. I know you better than that."

"No, of course not," I say, looking up sharply. "We're going to stop him. We just have to figure out if this god is even real and where it is."

Elise stares at me for a moment, her lips pursed as she considers something.

"I'm not convinced on this whole god thing, but you clearly need help," she says as she turns away and steps into one of the shower stalls. She turns on the water and steps under the spray. "If Zachary is in-volved in all this, then so am I."

"You don't have to help with this," I say.

"Oh, I know," she says, sticking her now wet head out of the stall. "And you're welcome."

I huff out a laugh and finish undressing. I am grateful, but this task still feels too big. Sometimes I wish I could just walk away from all the crap with Cesare and focus on finding the coven that killed my mother. My mother thought I was a part of all this though, and I can't walk away from something she asked me to stop.

I stand up and step into the shower stall next to Elise. The water sprays down over my head I let it drown out the worry, just for a moment.

## 6

E lise is glaring at Reilly. And not in a subtle way. It's a full-on, about-to-start-a-fight kind of glare, and I'm stuck in between them. I kick her shin under the table, but she doesn't waver. I should have lied to her.

"And then Elise tore up her shoe," Hu says, finishing up his dramatic re-telling of my training session with tears of laughter streaming down his face.

Reilly is laughing as well. His shoulders are relaxed, and he looks completely free of worry. He glances at me, his dimples deepening as he smiles. I want to lick his face.

I shift in my seat and turn away from Reilly. That dream has damaged my mind. It was easy to ignore the attraction when he was still threatening me.

"Glad to hear you're learning," Reilly says. His eyes flick toward Elise, but he continues to ignore the glaring.

I shrug. "Hu is a good teacher."

Hu smiles at me. "I was worried you might end up hating me. Some people don't take well to being pushed like that."

"I could never hate you," I say waving my hand at him dismissively. "You're too nice."

"You've never tried to wake him up in the morning then," says Aaron Cook, his partner, as he walks into the room. Zachary follows closely behind him. Elise finally turns toward the table and drops the evil look. "He turns into the grumpiest person you'll ever meet."

"Not everyone wants to wake up and go for a run at five am," Hu grumbles as Cook sits down next to him.

Ivy and Corinne arrive next, and it's a relief to see that Corinne looks healthy again. The color is back in her cheeks, and she has a healthy tan.

"How much longer are you stuck on desk duty?" Cook asks as she takes the seat next to him.

"Ugh," Corinne groans. "I have a doctor's appointment tomorrow afternoon, and they should clear me then. I'm *better*."

"Only because I have been keeping you from trying to use your magic again too soon," Ivy says punching Corinne's shoulder lightly.

I can't even imagine how hard it would be to go so long without using any magic at all. They would have had to sedate me.

"Desk duty is terrible," Corinne says, sighing. "I have a new appreciation for Staci's patience. I don't know how she manages to stay sane doing all the paperwork."

"She's a nerd. She likes it," Cook says with a snort.

Corinne and Hu smack him at the same time. Cook flinches, and I bite down on a laugh. He hasn't been as combative toward me; I don't want to start anything today.

"Don't be an ass," Corinne says. "She's a good agent."

Cook holds up his hands in surrender. "Never said she wasn't. We'd be lost without her."

I relax back in my chair as the rest of the team trickles in. Despite the explosions, everyone seems to be in good spirits after working with Ian's pack to clean up those traps. Having Corinne back is even better. She is the glue that holds the team together with her ability to befriend anyone.

Agent Stocke and Staci walk in last, along with the analyst that briefed us on the issues in Los Angeles when we first arrived. Agent Tomlinson is a thin man with wire-framed glasses and a sharp intelligence. He sets the folders he is holding down on the table and clears his throat. The conversations die down, and everyone turns their attention to him.

"Per Agent Stocke's request, agents equipped to handle explosives were dispatched to the Grzeski pack lands yesterday. They found two more areas with hidden explosive devices and will continue their search tomorrow," Tomlinson says, starting the meeting. "The werewolf council reached out yesterday with their appreciation, which is unprecedented to put it lightly."

"They actually used the word thank you?" Elise asks leaning forward.

"They did indeed," Tomlinson says with a small smile. "They also requested that your team meet with Ian Grzeski tomorrow afternoon to establish an ongoing relationship with JHAPI to eliminate the NWR in this area."

Elise sits back in her chair, shocked.

"Can we bring the entire team?" Stocke asks.

Tomlinson nods.

"The only stipulation was that Olivia Carter attends the meeting," he says, looking straight at me. "You made quite the impression."

Ivy stares at me, her brows knit together like she's not sure how to feel about me receiving praise for helping JHAPI.

"Who knew Olivia would end up a diplomat," Zachary says, amused. He gets a few laughs; I send him a good-natured glare and shrink back into my seat.

"Ian Grzeski has very close ties to the werewolf council. Whatever happens tomorrow, will set a precedent for how other packs deal with JHAPI across the country," Tomlinson continues. "The JHAPI Director will be personally following up with the team on this and has given Agent Stocke the authority to negotiate on behalf of the organization to cement cooperation with the werewolves."

Tomlinson sits down, and Stocke stands from her seat at the head of the table.

"I have more good news," Stocke says, looking proudly at the team. "During the attack on the Summit, and subsequent raids, several NWR members were captured. One of them has been identified as the third highest ranking member of the NWR, Evan Peterson."

That name is familiar. I remember Martinez and arguing with the other man about someone called Peterson while I was chained up in the van.

"Peterson is being transferred to a higher security facility here in Los Angeles. We will be given access to interrogate him tomorrow evening," Stocke says.

"What are the odds he makes it here without a repeat of what happened with Martinez?" I ask, still bitter that he managed to escape.

"That was a disaster," Ivy says.

I'm surprised she's willing to agree with me, out loud no less. Corinne winks at me from across the table.

Stocke purses her lips and gives me a withering glance. "We learn from our mistakes. He is being brought in by plane, and they have tripled security."

"Do we have permission to test the new truth potion?" Staci asks eagerly.

My stomach twists. Surely they wouldn't interrogate the prisoners like that.

"Tomlinson?" Stocke asks.

He taps his pen against his notepad. "There has to be a recorded test proving it will cause no harm to the person that takes it. Truth potions have a very bad reputation."

Staci sits back in her chair and nods, resigned. She had to have expected that response though. I'm all for using half-tested brews on people, but the truth potion is dangerous.

"I can hear if Peterson speaks a lie," Reilly offers. "As can Agent Hawking."

"I'd like you in the room then," Agent Stocke nods. She looks over at Elise. "There is another NWR member that I'd like you to interrogate. Zachary, you'll be her second."

Zachary nods in acknowledgment.

"Alright, I'll see you all tomorrow at one pm," Stocke says, wrapping up the meeting.

Everyone stands, and I trail out behind the group. Reilly pauses at the doorway and waits for me to catch up.

"What exactly did you tell Elise?" Reilly asks as he falls into step beside me.

"The truth. She wanted to arrest you," I say, smirking.

"Arrest me? I should be given a medal for putting up with you," Reilly snorts.

"Putting up with me?" I say, raising a brow. "I'm pretty sure you're the one that's difficult to handle."

"Someone definitely needed to handle you," Reilly says with a grin.

I roll my eyes.

"Are you hungry?" Reilly asks.

I curl my hand into a fist and take a deep breath before responding. "Yes. I tried to not overdo it in training, but I couldn't hold back. Hu would have roasted me."

"I'll feed you when we get back to the hotel," Reilly says, not taunting me for once.

"I know I need to feed, but I can't keep weakening you like this," I say, guilt twisting in my gut.

"We'll figure something out," Reilly says with a shrug.

I keep my mouth shut, but I don't want Reilly to turn up with some random vampire. I have to try to brew something to help again. I'll be more careful this time. My hedgewitch magic hasn't failed me yet. I always find a way. Eventually.

## 7

"That is not just Ian's pack," Elise comments as Zachary parks the car in a paved area on the side of Ian's sprawling house.

"Who else is it?" Ivy asks, trying to peer around her head from the backseat. Corinne and I are crammed in the back of Zachary's sedan with her. It's just big enough for three adults to sit, but not comfortably.

"No idea," Elise says. We pile out of the car just as Agent Stocke parks.

There are at least twenty werewolves milling around outside Ian's house. I recognize Colin and a few other familiar faces from the day we spent trying to clear traps from the forest. However, there are four distinct groups. They must be different packs with the way they are watching each other with almost as much wariness as they are watching us.

Ian steps out of the crowd and waits as we cross the lawn.

"Agent Stocke," he says in greeting, shaking her hand. "Thank you for agreeing to meet with us on such short notice."

Stocke nods. "It's our pleasure. I am surprised to

see so many packs here today. We were only expecting to get the honor of speaking with yours."

"I invited the other Alphas in Los Angeles to join us since whatever we decide also affects them," Ian explains.

"Well, we're certainly glad they're here. Do you mind introducing me before we get started?" Stocke asks.

"Of course, please come with me," Ian says.

Two men and one woman approach our group. I hear an odd noise and glance back at the house. A little face peers out of the blinds, but disappears in a flash when they realize they've been spotted.

"Agent Stocke, this is Alpha Pollard, Alpha Renner, and Alpha Costa," Ian says pointing to each of them in turn. Alpha Costa, the woman, is the only one that steps forward to shake Stocke's hand. The two men nod impassively.

"I am not convinced this meeting is a good idea," Costa says. "In the past, the government has tended to shoot first and ask questions later, especially when a wolf has lost control. However, your agent saved the life of one of Grzeski's pack without causing her harm, and at great personal risk. If nothing else, I am willing to hear you out."

Alpha Renner scoffs quietly behind her. Apparently, my great personal risk doesn't mean much to him.

"I'd like you and Olivia to join us inside," Ian says to Agent Stocke. "The rest of your team can wait with my pack."

I glance at Agent Stocke, but she takes Ian's demands in stride and nods to the rest of the team. They head towards the rest of the werewolves to wait. Elise looks back at me, and I can tell she's frustrated. I'm still not sure why they want to talk to me specifically, and it's making me nervous.

I follow the small group into the house. The tile floors are spotless, and the walls are decorated with pictures of pack members and a few paintings of men and women that must have been the previous alphas.

Ian leads us to an open study with a window that looks out into the backyard. The walls are lined with built-in bookshelves. There is a round table with eight chairs near the middle of the room. We all sit down, but with only six of us, the werewolves manage to leave a chair on either side of Stocke and me, segregating us from the group. I guess this is going to be us against them.

"Thank-you again for meeting with us," Stocke says, leaning back in her chair with one hand comfortably on the table. "The werewolf council expressed interest in a more formal relationship between JHAPI and the werewolves. Of course, they don't have the power to mandate that for your packs. Are any of you interested in our help?"

With that, Stocke takes control of the meeting. Instead of the two of us being interrogated by them, it feels like they're the ones being interviewed.

"Is that what you're actually offering?" Renner sneers. "Help?"

"Yes," Stocke replies, tilting her head. "JHAPI was created to protect, first and foremost. They knew the best way to do that was with an organization that was not just human. We leave human crime to the FBI, and we focus on threats to the paranormal community."

"Sounds like an excuse to police us even more," Renner mutters.

"Note that I said threats to the paranormal community, not threats from them," Stocke says raising a brow. "My team was the first created specifically to eliminate the NWR. Recently, JHAPI has created two more teams like ours so that we can respond to more threats, more quickly. Having the support of the werewolves across the country would only help us in achieving that goal."

"Are you trying to recruit more werewolves to your agency?" Ian asks. He's the only one that doesn't seem angry or suspicious today, which is a big change from the first time I met him.

"Yes, along with other paranormals," Stocke says. "However, the first priority is just gaining the support of the packs."

"It seems like you care more about what the vampire council has to say," Pollard says, speaking up for the first time. He is older than the others, his hair and beard both dark gray. "They have dumped millions into your organization, and you have one of their own on your team."

"We don't know what she is," Renner says, turning his steely eyes to me. "Only what she told Ian's beta, which could have been a lie."

The table is silent a moment while they all stare at me. I hold their gazes steadily, all the nerves gone.

"Well? You aren't going to answer?" Renner snaps.

"I haven't been asked a question," I say, leaning forward to rest my elbows on the table.

Ian smirks and asks the question for Renner. "Are you a vampire or a witch?"

"Both, apparently," I say. The table is still as they all listen carefully to my heartbeat. "My mother was a witch, and my father a vampire."

Renner sniffs unhappily and leans back in his seat. "I don't like it."

"My name is Olivia, not It," I say sarcastically.

The gets a laugh out of Costa and a smile out of

Ian. Only Pollard stares at me impassively. He must not have a sense of humor.

"You've never cared about the were's input," Renner argues. "JHAPI is happy to let the witches and vampires keep pulling the strings."

"Ever since the organization was founded, we have done everything possible to gain the input of the werewolf council," Stocke says, looking directly at Renner in challenge. "It has been the choice of the werewolves to rebut every offer of cooperation. This is just another example of that. We are fighting the same enemy you are, and we are doing it better, yet you still don't want to work with us."

Renner's hands curl into fists on the table.

"What are you implying?" He demands.

"I'm not implying anything," Stocke says. "I'm stating a fact. The werewolves have let their paranoia and suspicion hold them back. You could be the driving force behind JHAPI, but instead, you're left in the dark while the rest of the country forges on without you."

Renner growls, the sound reverberating around the room. I glance at Stocke, shocked at how plainly she's speaking. It's like she's trying to piss them off.

"Did you come here just to insult us?" Pollard asks, putting both hands on the table like he's ready to stand up and walk out. Costa, however, is watching the exchange with a thoughtful expression.

"No," Stocke says. "I came here to be honest. I'm not going to dance around the issues to save your pride. Has anything I have said been less than truthful? Has it been in any way wrong?"

"You're making us out to be paranoid conspiracy theorists," Pollard says unhappily.

"Is she wrong though?" Costa asks, looking around her. "It's in our nature to mistrust anyone outside of our pack. I don't agree that this has held us back nearly as much as she implies; caution is not a fault. However, it might be time for us to consider what they have to offer."

"Perhaps the decision will be easier to make when we know what JHAPI wants from us, and what they are willing to do for us," Ian says. He doesn't seem bothered by Stocke's comments. Or perhaps he just has a very good poker face.

"We want your honesty and cooperation when agents need to communicate with a pack. We need you to report when your pack members go missing, and we would like to be able to speak with pack members that might be witnesses," Stocke says. "We would also like to be involved in more joint operations like the one to clean up Angeles National Forest."

"I am willing to consider this," Costa says, leaning forward. "However, I have some questions."

"I'll answer anything you care to ask," Stocke says.

The meeting drags on for another half hour. Stocke rises every challenge the alphas throw at her. Ian asks a few pointed questions, but I get the impression he's trying to help us more than hinder us. Renner never stops being angry and paranoid, but even if we only win over two of them, it's still progress.

My stomach is rumbling by the time we all head back outside. The other alphas make a beeline for their packs, but Ian hangs back with us for a moment.

"I would like to invite you and your team to have dinner with my pack on the night of the full moon," Ian says. "It's a good time for them to get to know you as people. That will go farther toward changing minds than any of these meetings."

"We'll be there," Stocke says. "Reilly Walsh, the other representative will be with us as well. I trust that won't be an issue?"

Ian shakes his head. "We have no issues with the vampires so long as they have no issues with us."

## 8

I open the door to the hotel room, then pause. There's someone in here, and it's not Reilly. I grab a knock-out brew from my pocket and pull on the vampire magic. Smells and sounds rush to my senses. This particular scent is familiar and particularly unwelcome.

I slip inside. Bodyguards are standing on either side of the doorway to my room with their hands folded in front of them. Their eyes are focused on the brew I'm holding, but they don't make a move to take it away.

Cesare is standing in front of the workspace Reilly had set up for me holding the vial of my most recent failure. He sniffs it, then grimaces and sets it back down.

"I assume that was ineffective?" He asks without looking at me. He flips through my notes and picks up a small vial of my blood. I curl my hand into a fist to resist the urge to snatch it away from him.

"Yes," I say as evenly as I can. "Didn't hurt or help."

Cesare looks at me and sets the vial down. He stalks forward, his eyes cataloging my outfit and the brew clasped in my right hand.

"Reilly tells me your training is going well," Cesare says. "You are finally getting control over the elemental magic you stole."

"Yes," I repeat. I know, logically, that Reilly is still keeping up the pretense of reporting back to Cesare, but it makes my gut twist with a feeling of betrayal. I don't want Cesare to know anything about me.

"Let's sit," Cesare says, waving at the couches.

I follow him reluctantly and sit on the couch across from him. One of the bodyguards takes a position by the front door while the other stands behind me. My skin prickles with unease. I can't see him, and I doubt I could move fast enough to avoid a strike. The move feels calculated. Cesare wants me to feel unsafe.

"How is Javier Moreno?" Cesare asks.

"I don't know. We haven't spoken since I left Texas," I say.

"Perhaps I can arrange a visit," Cesare says. "You should stay in touch with your friends. After all, they do mean a lot to you."

"I'm sure Javier is busy, but I'll call him soon," I say, curling my hands into a fist on my legs. I don't want Cesare doing anything with Javier, not even arranging a visit.

"How often do you feed from Reilly?" Cesare asks.

"Not often," I say.

"Still," Cesare says, tapping one long finger against his chin. "Find someone else. If you can't, I'll have someone sent to you. I don't like the idea of you weakening him if you were to take too much. Reilly is useful to me."

"I'll find someone," I say, trying not to sound too desperate. My pulse is picking up despite my best efforts to stay calm. I am angry and worried, and I don't know how to hide it if he can hear my heart beating.

Cesare flicks his finger toward the vampire standing behind me. I flinch when a hand appears next to my face.

"Feed now," Cesare says. "I'd like to see it, and it's best if you stay well fed."

"I fed last night," I say, making no move to take the hand.

"And you're going to feed again," Cesare says, his voice slipping into irritation. "Don't be petulant about it."

I grit my teeth and take the vampire's hand. My fangs push out of my gums painfully slow. I hesitate before biting down, but I don't have a choice. I don't want to find out what Cesare would do if I refused.

I sink my fangs into the meat of the vampire's wrist and pull lightly. He is powerful, but nothing like Reilly. I feed as slowly, taking the smallest amounts of blood and magic possible. The vampire's hand twitches slightly, and I take that as an excuse to pull away.

"You took so little," Cesare comments.

"I took enough," I say, and I did. The hunger is always there, but I fed from Reilly just last night.

Cesare flicks his finger at the bodyguard who removes his hand and joins the other vampire at the door to the room.

"I suspect you don't view Reilly as a true threat, not any longer," Cesare says, leaning forward and looking me in the eye. "Don't for a second make that mistake with me. Like any other tool, you are replaceable."

His voice is velvety smooth, but his words cut like a knife. I stare at him for a few breaths, then nod.

"Don't worry, I won't forget," I say sharply.

He grins, his fangs glistening in his mouth.

"I'll see you again soon, Olivia." He stands and then is gone along with his bodyguards. The door slams shut behind them.

I stay perched on the couch, staring forward. If he wanted to scare me, he succeeded, but I doubt it had the desired effect. I dig my nails into my palm. I'm going to make sure Cesare doesn't succeed, even if I have to find a way to kill him myself.

The door opens again, and I stand up, electric magic at my fingertips and all my senses rushing to high alert. Reilly pauses in the entryway, taking in my stance and the lingering scent of Cesare at the same time. His jaw clenches tightly, and he looks around as if he's expecting to see Cesare still in the room.

"He's gone," I say, forcing my hands to relax.

Reilly looks me over. "What did he do?"

"Threatened me, mostly," I say, plopping back down on the couch. "He doesn't want me feeding from you anymore, and I guess he knows I'm not scared of you. He made some not-so-veiled threats against Javier intended to keep me in line."

"I smell blood," Reilly says, walking toward me slowly.

I wipe my hand across my mouth, but it's clean. Reilly pinches his brows together, and I sigh heavily.

"He insisted I feed while he was here. He really doesn't want me feeding from you," I explain.

Reilly growls and kicks the other couch in a violent outburst that has me jerking back onto my feet. The couch cracks in half and smashes against the wall with a loud smash.

"What the fuck?" I shout. Reilly faces the now dented hotel room wall, his shoulders heaving.

"He's never checked up on me unannounced like

this before," Reilly says, his voice rough with anger. "He suspects something."

"Did you really think you would be able to do any of this without him getting at least a little suspicious?" I ask, incredulous. "He has no reason to trust me, and you said yourself that he knows you're attracted to me...or whatever."

I look down at my feet, uncomfortable. We hadn't talked about that since his apology. I don't trust Reilly enough to let anything happen, and he had gone back to his meaningless flirtations.

Reilly sighs and drags his fingers through his hair.

"This was a message meant for me," he says tiredly. "Threatening you was secondary."

"Why do you think that?" I ask. There's something he's not telling me.

"He came when I wasn't here, something he wouldn't have known unless he was watching my movements," Reilly says, finally turning to face me. "Cesare doesn't do anything by accident. Every word, every action, is deliberate."

"So, he didn't want to see you?" I ask, confused.

"No," Reilly says shaking his head. "He wanted to remind me that he could get to you at any time, and there's nothing I can do to stop him. It's a lesson I learned a long time ago but had apparently forgotten."

"I don't understand. Does he really mistrust you that much? Wouldn't he make you bring me back to the clanhouse if he did?" I ask.

"No, I wouldn't be useful to him there. If it got to that point, he would just kill me and be done with it," Reilly seethes. "Cesare finds whatever weakness you have that he can leverage, and he makes sure you never forget that he knows what it is."

"I thought you didn't have any weaknesses," I say, half-joking, but Reilly's face darkens.

"Only monsters without a conscience can claim that," he grinds out.

"Cesare can threaten all he wants," I say squaring my shoulders. "He's not going to try to kill me until after this Bound God is dead, and we're going to stop him before that happens."

Reilly looks at me, old grief showing in his eyes as he laughs humorlessly. "You sound just like her."

"Like who?" I ask, confused.

"It doesn't matter," he says, turning away again. "We're going to get the answers we need tomorrow night."

Reilly walks into his room and shuts the door, leaving me with a broken couch and more questions than answers.

## 9

The sun is still up, but I'm already awake. I've been laying in the oversized bathtub long enough for the water to get cold and my fingers and toes to go all pruny. My phone buzzes loudly on the tile. I grab it, dripping water all over the floor and the screen.

For once, it's good news. Corinne was just cleared for active duty. I text back congratulations and accept the offer to meet her and Ivy for dinner before the interrogations later tonight. I dry off and get dressed quickly. They want to meet me there in about twenty minutes.

Since the restaurant is close by, I decide to walk rather than take the time to go down to the parking garage and then get the car out. The streets are crowded with pedestrians. Everyone must have had a similar thought since the weather is perfect. Sunny and seventy degrees even though it's early December.

Bob's Burger Barn looks like the kind of place a guy would have taken a girl he was going steady with back in the fifties. The booths are shiny red vinyl, not a crack in sight. The waitresses are all wearing full skirts and white blouses with collars. A perky redhead greets me with a smile, and since I don't see Ivy or Corinne yet, I let her lead me to a booth near the window.

She lays out three menus, and I sit back to people watch while I wait. It's mostly families here. They might know about vampires and werewolves, but none of them understand the turmoil that's going on so close them. They've never heard of the Bound God. They don't get almost blown up on a regular basis. A little girl with brown hair is pouting because her mother won't buy her a milkshake. If only that was the worst of my problems. Being an adult sucks.

The door tinkles and Ivy walks in alone. I wave to get her attention even though I wish Corinne had arrived first. I doubt Ivy really wants to sit and chat with me.

"Corinne is running a few minutes late," Ivy says in lieu of a greeting as she sits down across from me. She takes one of the menus and flips through it.

I shift in my seat, but the vinyl squeaks and causes Ivy to glance at me.

"I hate vinyl," Ivy says, looking down at her side of the booth accusingly. "It's uncomfortable and always feels sticky."

"Yeah, it's pretty terrible," I agree. We lapse into silence again. Neither of us is good at small talk

Ivy smacks her menu down on the table, and I jerk in surprise. She looks at me and folds her hands together.

"I think Corinne did this on purpose," Ivy says. "She wants me to apologize."

"For what?" I ask, drawing my brows together.

"For shooting you," Ivy says with a huff. "I still think it was justified, but she keeps going on about my trust issues and how my perception of you as an outsider made me behave irrationally toward you."

"That sounds like Corinne," I say, biting back a smile.

"You risked your life to fix your mistake," Ivy says after a pause, "and I can respect that."

"Uh, thanks," I say, grabbing a roll of silverware to have something to fidget with. I don't like receiving compliments or apologies, a mix of the two is almost unbearable.

"I still don't like that your personal need for revenge or whatever else might affect the team again," Ivy says. She looks up at me, face serious. "We all have our shit, but you can't let it put anyone in danger."

"I didn't ask for Martinez to become obsessed with me," I reply. "And I'll never put the team in harm's way. I'd leave before I would do that."

Ivy nods and looks back down at her menu. "I guess all they serve here is burgers. Even their salad has a burger on it."

"They serve milkshakes too," I say with a smile. Thank heavens that talk is over.

Corinne appears at the edge of the booth, smiling a little smugly, and Ivy scoots over to give her more room. She winks at me as she sits down.

"I can't believe I'm finally cleared," Corinne says. "It's been an eternity."

"We're all glad to have you back," Ivy agrees with a rare smile.

It's terrifying to think how close Corrine came to dying. Death seems so far off until it touches you. I push the morbid thoughts aside and grab one of the menus. There is food to be eaten.

---

Maximum security is no joke. The prison is a

fortress. I feel a little violated from all the pat downs by the time we get inside the place.

Armed guards pace the long halls, always in groups of two or more. The walls and floor are all the same shade of dreary gray. There are no windows; there are cameras though, every five feet at least. There is not a single spot in this entire place that is not being monitored twenty-four seven by someone.

The interrogation rooms are high tech as well. They have the traditional one-way mirror, but there are also large screens set above it that show different angles of the room. Another screen shows a thermal scan of the room. I guess we'll literally be able to watch Peterson sweat.

Cook and Hu are in a neighboring room watching Elise and Zachary's interrogation. Reilly and Stocke are still in the viewing area with Staci, Corinne, Ivy and me.

I take a seat next to Staci and observe Peterson. He's unassuming. Not tall, but not really short either. His hair is brown and average length. He isn't ugly or handsome. He is someone you simply wouldn't ever look twice at. Until you see his eyes.

Peterson is staring straight ahead, his gaze is filled with hate. He doesn't know who is on the other side of the glass, but that doesn't seem to matter.

Stocke is staring back at Peterson, tapping the thick file she is holding against her arm.

"He's going to react badly to your presence I think," Stocke says.

"Good," Reilly says with a toothy grin. There's no way to mistake him for human even without the fangs showing.

"We do need to get some information out of him," Stocke says, exasperated.

"Angry means talkative," Reilly says. "He won't be thinking straight after he realizes what I am."

"How long has he been waiting?" Stocke asks the guard standing in the doorway behind us.

"Forty-five minutes, ma'am," he replies.

"Alright, he's stewed long enough. Let's do this," Stocke says.

She and Reilly put on the tiny earpieces that will let us speak to them if needed and leave the room. A minute later, the door to the interrogation room opens and they walk inside. Peterson pretends to ignore them, but he can't hide the subtle twitch of his hands.

Stocke walks around to the front of the table and looks at Peterson. Reilly stays behind him. Peterson tries to look over his shoulder, but his arms are shackled to the chair and he can't turn far enough to see who it is.

"That's going to unnerve him," Ivy comments with a grin.

"Evan Peterson," Stocke says, her voice is clear through the speaker overhead. She opens the file and reads it with pursed lips.

Peterson looks up at her, stoic.

"Charges of terrorism, hate crimes, murder, attempted murder, property damage, vandalism. The list goes on and on," she says, dropping the open file on the table with a thunk. "You're not exactly an upstanding citizen."

His mouth twists into an expression of disgust and he snorts.

"Oh, you disagree?" Stocke asks. "You think you're a good guy?"

Peterson grinds his teeth together, the muscles in his jaw clenching and unclenching.

Reilly steps closer, his shoes making a clear sound

against the concrete floor. Peterson's hands curl into fists and the muscles in his neck stand out with the effort of not trying to look behind himself again. The thermal camera shows Peterson's face getting warmer and warmer.

"They have to be careful not to make him too angry," Corinne says, concerned.

"I don't see how they're going to get anything out of him other than how much he hates paranormals," I say, leaning back in my chair.

Stocke leans forward and braces both of her hands on the table. "What are you, Peterson? Come on, I know you have something to say."

"I am a warrior of the light," he snaps, baring his teeth. "I don't sell my women to vampires like cattle. I fight the war no one else is willing to fight."

"That's a start," Stocke straightens, raising both brows and nodding slightly. "Do you mind answering a few questions?"

Peterson scoffs and shakes his head.

"I'll take that as an enthusiastic yes," she says as she walks around to the side of the table. She leans her hip against it and crosses her arms. "Did you know Martinez was a witch?"

"I suspected," Peterson spits out, enraged once again. "No one believed me, but I was right. We should have known with the way he always slithered back from even the most dangerous missions still alive while good men were left behind."

Reilly nods, confirming for Stocke that Peterson told the truth.

"It's a little ironic that your best man was one of us," Reilly says, speaking for the first time. "I guess humans really are the weaker species."

Peterson stiffens, his face going red.

"Get that thing out of here," he demands. "Or are you planning on feeding me to it?"

Stocke laughs. "Man, I wish. However, legally, that's not allowed."

"They take and kill humans every day. And what do you do? You arrest *me* and not them," Peterson says stretching forward as far as he can go.

"Let's play a game," Stocke says, pulling out the chair across from Peterson and sitting down.

"What?" Peterson growls out.

"I'm going to guess where important people or stockpiles in your organization are, and you are going to tell me if I'm right or wrong," Stocke explains.

Peterson scoffs and leans back. "I'm not going to tell you anything."

"You won't be able to stop yourself," Reilly whispers directly into Peterson's ear. "You can't keep me out of your mind."

Peterson jerks away, yanking against the restraints that hold him in the chair with a shout.

"Get the fuck away from me parasite!" He rages.

Reilly laughs and walks around the table to stand next to Stocke.

Stocke picks up the thick folder and flips through it before settling on a page. "Here's a good place to start. I'm going to guess the location of your stockpile of silver. Think about it real hard for me."

Peterson grunts and jerks at the restraints again, unable to tear his eyes off of Reilly.

"The stockpile is in Raleigh, North Carolina," Stocke says definitively. The slightest movement of Reilly's head indicates a negative.

"It's in Indianapolis," Stocke tries again.

Reilly tilts his head. Not quite right, but Peterson

is getting nervous. The thermal camera shows his face heating even more.

Stocke lowers the folder and looks him in the eye. "Chicago."

Reilly smiles. "That's it."

Peterson growls and spits at Reilly. "Get out of my head abomination! Get out!"

Stocke adjusts the folder and settles in to list off the other places they want to confirm. Peterson continues his struggle.

"He really thinks Reilly can read his mind," I say in surprise and amusement.

"They're using his own worst fears against him," Ivy says, nodding in approval. "It's a brilliant tactic. Stocke is good at getting into people's heads like that."

"Zachary's father was like that too," I comment.

"You knew his father?" Ivy asks, her brows pinching together.

I shift in my seat. I hadn't realized that wasn't common knowledge. "Yeah, I was kind of half adopted by his family way back when. I hadn't seen Zachary in years before he showed up in Texas though."

"Oh," Corinne says, realization forming on her face. "That's why Cook has always been so rude to you."

Ivy laughs. "That makes so much more sense."

I cross my arms and intensely regret speaking up.

"Zachary recovered from the heartbreak just fine," I mutter. "Did he tell everyone about that?"

Corinne pats me on the shoulder. "He sure did," she says pityingly.

I turn my attention back to Peterson, who is getting angrier as the interrogation goes on. Each time Reilly can detect the way his heart speeds up as

Stocke guesses a location correctly, he becomes more convinced Reilly is somehow reading his mind.

The other team crowds into the viewing room as Stocke and Reilly are wrapping up.

"What the hell did they do to this guy?" Cook asks as he watches Peterson let loose a stream of curses at Reilly.

Ivy launches into an explanation. I move to the back of the room, ready to be out of this place. It was satisfying to see Peterson break like that, but all the information they got just reminds me how much more there is, and always will be, for JHAPI to do. It's exhausting.

"That was genius," Corinne exclaims as Reilly and Stocke walk back in the room.

"We'll see," Stocke says, shaking her head. "Everything we got in there could be highly inaccurate."

"You got him angry enough to be honest," Ivy says. "He was scared. You got something right at least."

A guard comes to return Peterson to his room. He tries to fight the guards, but his movements are too restricted to be effective.

The team files out of the room and I trail behind. Reilly waits for me.

"Are we still going to talk to your mysterious contact tonight?" I ask.

Reilly nods. "Yes, Zachary said he would meet us in the hotel parking garage around eleven pm."

"Where are we going, exactly?" I ask.

"My contact owns a bar downtown," Reilly says, looking me up and down critically. "Wear something nice."

"Only if you promise me tequila," I say.

Reilly shakes his head with a sigh. "I promise," he says, resigned.

## 10

Reilly parks the car in a dimly lit parking lot overshadowed by an ornate building. I'm not sure if it's gothic, or just gaudy. Flowering vines grow up the stone walls of the castle-like structure. A giant, neon sign spells out FANGERS, flashing brightly with red light.

"What the hell is this place?" I ask as I step out of the car and adjust my tight dress.

"An eye-sore," Zachary mutters.

"The most popular nightclub in Los Angeles," Reilly says, ignoring Zachary, and nodding toward the line that wraps around the building. "It caters to vampires, so of course, the humans want in too."

"Are we even going to get in?" I ask, incredulous. I've never seen that many people lined up for a night-club before. And, if I'm honest, judging by the out-side, I don't really get it.

"We're on the list," Reilly says, adjusting his cuffs. "Did you really think I'd bring you two here just to stand in line?"

I snort. "You like showing up places unannounced."

Reilly leads us to the front of the line. A few

people give us the stink-eye, but most of them are staring at us eagerly. They must be assuming we're all vampires.

"Reilly Walsh," Reilly tells the bouncer in a bored tone. The hulking man looks over his list and nods once. Another employee behind him lifts the rope and lets us past.

The red carpet leads into a dark tunnel. The stone around us is cold and damp. We're walking up a fairly steep incline. Zachary stumbles behind me and reaches out to steady himself on my back.

"Sorry," he says quietly. "It's ridiculously dark in here."

"They're going overboard on the creepy vampire vibes," I say, pulling him up to walk beside me. I keep a hand on his arm to make sure he doesn't walk into a wall. Until Zachary had tripped, I hadn't realized that I was relying on the vampire magic to see.

The tunnel turns sharply left and right several times before we finally reach a section that is lit. Red light shines from tinted bulbs hanging from the ceiling. The thump of music echoes toward us. The beat is loud enough to feel in my gut.

The tunnel ends abruptly at a short staircase. Another bouncer sits in front of the heavy, wooden door, but he doesn't request ID or anything else; he opens the door without comment.

Music pounds out of the central area of the nightclub. We walk inside, and I look around in awe, it's a spectacle. While the outside was gaudy and kitschy, the inside is whatever everyone always hopes a nightclub will be.

Hot guys and hot women are grinding underneath the flashing lights. Dancers hang from the ceiling in cages and from long silk scarves performing elegant acrobatics. The bartenders are flashy, spinning the bottles as they pour. A DJ stands on a platform raised above the rest of the room with flashing lights dancing behind him.

"What now?" I lean over and shout at Reilly.

He grabs my arm and leads Zachary and me toward a staircase I hadn't noticed in the back of the room. It leads down.

The heavy pounding of the music fades into the background as we descend to the lower level. The flashing lights give way to flickering firelight simulated by wide screens built into the walls. There is no dancing down here, but there are couches and private nooks where couples, and small groups, are flirting and feeding. The entire atmosphere is more intimate and dark.

"Do you want a drink?" Reilly asks.

I nod. "Absolutely."

We weave our way over to the bar. Reilly and Zachary both get leered at on the way over. I have to tug Zachary along when a particularly busty woman with big, blue eyes winks at him.

"You're no fun," Zachary complains.

"She would eat you for breakfast," I say, laughing at him.

"I'd let her," Zachary says wistfully.

Reilly orders me a shot of tequila at the bar then wanders off into the crowd. I lean back against the bar to wait for my drink. The mix of people down here is fascinating. It's mostly vampires and humans, but a few are definitely werewolves. A witch here and there, but not many of those.

"You don't find places like this in Dallas, Texas," Zachary comments.

"No kidding," I agree, shaking my head.

A vampire leans into a necker next to me, knocking my elbow. I glare at them and turn back to the bar. The woman looks a little peaky to me already. I narrow my eyes. I doubt she should be fed on anymore.

The necker's eyes glaze over and a light sheen of sweat forms on her brow. I frown and pick up the shot the bartender sets in front of me, but I'm too distracted to drink it. That vampire has to stop feeding from her soon, or she's going to end up passed out in the parking lot from blood loss.

Her cheeks lose their color, and her lips follow. I smack my drink down on the bar. The vampire isn't paying any attention to me though, his eyes are shut as he slurps down the necker's blood.

I reach out of flick him on the nose. Electricity leaps from my finger and leaves a bright red mark all the way up his forehead.

"You've gotta leave some blood for her, asshole," I snap as I yank the necker toward me. She collapses onto my chest, her head flopping around. She can't even stand.

The vampire hisses, his fangs still bloody, and swings at me. I duck under the fast but clumsy attack and shove the necker at Zachary who catches her and pulls her back into the crowd. With her out of the way, I face the now furious vampire.

"Who the fuck do you think you are?" He demands.

I grab the shot and toss it back, then slam the glass down on the table. "The lady about to kick your ass."

He growls and lunges, but he doesn't have Reilly's speed or finesse. Hell, he couldn't even keep up with Hu. I step to the side and kick him in the balls as hard as I can.

The fight has drawn attention now. Two vampires appear behind the guy I just kicked. One of them helps him up while the other takes a step toward me.

"Enough," Reilly says from behind me. He looks at the three vampires and gives a short bow. "Apologies for the—"

"You are not apologizing for shit," I interrupt as I shoot a glare at Reilly.

Reilly grinds his teeth together and grabs my arm roughly, attempting to drag me away from the group, but I jerk out of his grasp.

"We are not here for this," Reilly hisses quietly.

"I think you should let him apologize, you dumb bitch," one of the vampires shouts at us.

"I think you should kiss my ass," I shout back, stepping in front of Reilly.

A crowd has formed around us, leaving only the space between me and the vampires empty. The one I kicked struggles to his feet, his face crimson with anger and embarrassment.

"I think the lady is right," a smooth voice says, cutting through the chatter. The entire bar goes silent. A vampire with long, blond hair and a face that you can't help but stare at walks up to the edge of the circle, the crowd flowing around him like they're afraid to touch him.

The three vampires step back, each bowing their head slightly.

"She attacked me, completely unprovoked," the first one explains.

"You were about to embarrass yourself, Gerard," the blond vampire purrs. "And me. Do you know how long it has been since someone drained a necker in my bar?"

Gerard shrinks back, shaking his head.

In a flash of movement I can't follow the blond vampire is standing over Gerard. He wrenches back

95

Gerard's head with a handful of hair and bends down close to his face.

"Literally fucking never," the blond vampire growls. He yanks Gerard forward, sending him sprawling across the floor of the bar. "Get out, your clan is no longer welcome here."

The crowd parts again as the disgraced vampires scurry away, and the blond vampire turns to me with a smile that sends a chill down my spine.

"Olivia Carter, you make quite the entrance," he says with a grin. He approaches, eyes flicking to Reilly for a moment before he stops in front of me and grabs both of my hands. "My name is Adrian, I'm sure you were dying to know."

"I was getting curious," I admit, taken aback by the hand holding and the fact that he knows who I am.

"Olivia," Zachary says urgently. "Shouldn't she be waking up by now?"

I pull my hands away from Adrian and hurry over to the necker Zachary is still holding. Her neck is still bleeding sluggishly, and her breathing is unsteady.

"Shit," I say, pressing my hands to her neck. I don't have any of my blood replenishing brews with me. I came prepared for a fight, not this. I push healing magic into her, trying to restore the damage to her neck at least.

Adrian appears at my shoulder holding a small vial.

"This might be useful," he says as he tips it into her mouth. The brew rushes through her body, warming it as it restores her blood.

"I've never seen a bar keep that on hand before," I comment as lower my hands. The necker is beginning to stir, but she's going to have a hell of a headache.

Adrian smiles and tosses the empty vial over his shoulder. A man in a black suit deftly catches it and slips it into his pocket.

"People dying gets messy," Adrian turns to his bodyguard. "Get her back home."

Zachary hands the groggy woman off and adjusts his blazer.

"And who might you be?" Adrian asks, leaning toward Zachary. I can't be sure, but it looks like he's smelling him.

"Zachary Brunson," Zachary says, extending his hand.

Adrian takes it and kisses his knuckles before turning and pulling Zachary's arm into his. Adrian slips his arm into mine as well and begins leading us toward the VIP section we had been barred from earlier. I glance back at Reilly who is watching us with a frown on his face.

"Come along, Reilly," Adrian says in a sing-song voice. "I haven't forgotten about you."

Reilly rolls his eyes but follows.

---

Adrian leads us past the thick, red velvet curtains that hide the VIP section from view. The music is quieter back here, but the beat of the bass is more intense. The flashing lights are replaced with a dim red glow that doesn't quite reach the dark corners of the room.

There are couches scattered around the space and narrow walls that turn the room into a maze. A woman is suspended from the ceiling by a set of aerial silks. She undulates and rolls upward, her long legs moving with effortless precision.

At the very back of the room, on a raised pedestal, sits what can only be described as a throne. It's made of plush black velvet and twisted iron that extends several feet high. Adrian releases our arms and moves ahead of us at vampire speed, his long hair trailing behind him. He turns and sits down on his throne, crossing his legs and leaning back to take in the three of us.

His bodyguards move a couch in front of the throne and motion for us to sit. Zachary and Reilly each take an end, leaving me to sit in the center. I cross my legs uncomfortably and stare up at Adrian.

"Now, I think I already know what you want," Adrian begins, "but I do love hearing people ask for my help. So, indulge me," he says, spreading his hands wide in invitation.

We had already agreed to start with the most important question. Reilly shifts and leans forward slightly.

"What is the prophecy of the Day of Breaking?" Reilly asks.

"Ah, a history lesson. Let's see this one was prophesied by Allaghar the Prolific," Adrian sighs, his lips pulling down into a frown. He clears this throat, then begins to recite.


"Bound will be unbound
    God will fight God
    Filled with the blood of the weak
    The Key must be found
    Lest Chaos consume
    And magic be lost
    The Key must return to ash
    What was born of it


"It's a bit long winded if you ask me, but it gets the

point across," he says with a shrug. "The old goblin languages don't really translate well."

"The prophecy is from a goblin?" I ask. Maybelle had scoffed at Gerard's premonitions, but I always wondered how he knew so much.

"Of course, all the great prophets have been goblins," Adrian says, waving my question away. He twirls a lock of hair around his finger and his eyes stray to one of the dancing girls. I have a feeling we can't afford to lose his attention.

"What is the key to the prophecy?" I ask.

Adrian turns his focus back to me. "That's the question everyone has been asking for two millennia. I'm sure I'll figure it out eventually."

"Is the Bound God even real?" Zachary asks, doubt evident in his voice.

"Many powerful people certainly think so," Adrian says, tilting his head to the side. "Do you doubt the prophecy, Zachary?"

"Yes," Zachary says, crossing his arms. "It's been two millennia like you said. He hasn't made an appearance in all that time."

I glance at Zachary. He has been unconvinced that this god exists since the beginning, but the prophecy makes my skin itch. There has to be something to it. Cesare is evil and power hungry, but I don't think he is gullible.

"Hmm," Adrian taps his finger against his lips. "I suppose we can't all be believers."

"How do you kill the Bound God?" Reilly asks.

Adrian sits up, eyes bright with interest. "Now we're on the right track. However, what might you need to know before you kill someone?"

Reilly sighs, grinding his teeth together in annoyance before he responds. "Where is the Bound God?"

"Bingo!" Adrian exclaims, pointing at Reilly. "Though, the answer to that is interesting."

He leans forward and snaps his fingers at a shot girl walking through the section with a tray of drinks. She hurries over.

"Bring me a drink," he says before looking at us. "Would you like anything?"

We all shake our heads, and I wonder what exactly he is going to be drinking. Reilly always turned his nose up at human foods. I really hope it's not a goblet of blood.

"Now," Adrian says as the girl hurries away. "Location is an interesting thing if you think about it. For example, if someone is dead, their rotting corpse sits in a grave. But," he smacks his hand down on the armrest, "that's hardly where *they* are."

"Are you saying the Bound God is dead?" Reilly asks, his brows pinching together.

"No, of course not," Adrian says dismissively. "I'm saying there are places outside of the physical realm. Places I can't point out on a map. The legends claim this alleged god is trapped in just such a place, and the Praesidio coven guards the entrance to this realm."

I stiffen at the mention of the coven. We hadn't been able to find out their name before.

"The Praesidio coven," Zachary says. "Where are they?"

"They stay close to the source of power," Adrian says, eyes flicking from Zachary to me, "since they control the witch council."

"Who is the coven leader?" I demand, leaning forward and bracing my hands on my knees. I want to run up onto the pedestal and shake the answers out of Adrian, but I have a feeling he could kick my ass if I tried.

"A witch named Alexandra Hunt," Adrian says.

The shot girl interrupts my next question, and I have to suppress a groan. It's a goblet of blood. I press my lips together in disgust. It smells inviting, which only makes my stomach turn more. There's just something about drinking it out of a glass that makes me want to gag.

"Now, I'm sure you're going to want to walk out of here and Find her," Adrian says, emphasizing the word find. "But you should know that's a very bad idea."

"Why?" I ask, curling my fingers into my palms. He's going to have to give a damn good reason to dissuade me from doing just that.

"The NWR is an organization of humans, yet your fellow agent was hurt trying to Find one of them." Adrian lifts the goblet to his mouth and takes a long drink, his eyes closing in bliss. He swallows, then continues. "Alexandra is old, crafty, and meaner than Jason Martinez. Do you really think she would leave herself vulnerable?"

I sit back and close my eyes for a moment as the memory of Corinne's face when the curse attacked her flashes through my mind.

Zachary shakes his head, frustrated. "How do you know anything about that?"

"I know everything," Adrian says, taking another sip. "Almost."

"Who is blocking my investigation?" Zachary challenges. "Since you know so much about JHAPI."

"Who isn't, would be quicker to answer," Adrian says with a laugh.

Reilly smirks, but Zachary is unamused.

"Oh, come now," Adrian says, seeing Zachary's irritation. "It should be obvious at this point. The witch council is protecting their own. Cesare Sangiovanni seeks to hide his scheming. The human politicians just want their organization to succeed. Your one-man battle against the system is futile."

Zachary crosses his arms, but Adrian is right, it should have been obvious. We're not here because we're trying to go through the proper channels though. We're here to get answers no one else has.

*Find the book. Find the magic.*

My mother's words echo in my mind.

"My mother stole a spell book from a powerful coven years ago, and created me," I say, searching Adrian's face for recognition. He nods, encouraging me to continue.

"Cesare has it now. What's in it?" I ask.

"I suppose only Cesare and your mother know that," Adrian says, raising his brow. "I can tell you that it is very old. It was written by Izul himself."

Reilly looks up sharply. "Is Izul the one that trapped this god?"

Adrian swirls the remnants of blood in his goblet. "Another answer that is most likely hidden in Cesare's lair."

"Does the coven know what Cesare is planning?" I ask.

Adrian downs the rest of the blood and sets the goblet on the arm. He stands and walks down the two short steps coming to a stop in front of me. I look up into Adrian's blue-gray eyes.

"Yes, but that's not the question burning in the back of your mind though, is it, Miss Carter?" He asks, his voice low as though the question is only meant for me.

I have been struggling with the brew I need to free myself from this dependency on other people's magic for days. It's starting to seem impossible. Adrian may not be a hedgewitch, but he did to claim to know everything. Almost.

"Has anyone ever cured a vampire?" I ask.

Adrian's eyes go wide.

"Oh, now that I didn't expect," he says. "Cured is an interesting choice of words."

"It almost a curse," I say. "The price you pay for speed, strength, and a long life is very high. I imagine someone has regretted the trade-off."

"Still, you're hinting at something you aren't asking outright," Adrian insists, crossing his arms.

I huff and tap my fingers against my thigh. "If I don't feed, I get weak. I've been trying to brew something that will satisfy the hunger, or at least diminish it."

Adrian gives me a pitying smile.

"Darling, that is simply the price you pay for your heritage. Vampires hunger. You can't take all that power and expect that to be the end of it." He reaches down and takes my hands, holding them between his own. "The more you have taken, the hungrier you've gotten?"

I grit my teeth and nod.

"It will always be that way. Accept it, and you can control it. I can smell the hunger on you right now, and it smells like weakness." He releases my hand. "I want to speak to Olivia privately."

"Why?" Reilly demands, his voice bordering on a growl.

Adrian turns cold eyes on him, his face shifting from playful to deadly in the space of a breath. "I'll ask whatever price I want, Reilly Walsh. I answered your questions without demanding payment in advance."

The two bodyguards appear on either side of the couch, and Reilly stands stiffly. Zachary hesitates, looking at me for confirmation. I nod. Adrian is eccentric, but I don't feel threatened.

Reilly and Zachary follow the guards toward the exit, but Reilly pauses near the curtain and looks back at me before speaking directly to Adrian. "Hurt her, and I'll kill you."

"You could try," Adrian says with a wide grin that looks anything but friendly.

I stand and make a shooing motion at Reilly. His dramatic offers of vengeance are kind of appreciated, but I don't think antagonizing Adrian is going to make whatever he wants from me better. Reilly gives me a stony look but finally leaves.

Adrian faces me and the music around us fades. I glance around and realize the room is empty. Even the dancers are gone. I'm not sure when they left.

"You are unique," Adrian says, stepping in close to me. "And it makes me curious."

"What do you want?" I ask hesitantly.

"I want to know what it feels like when you feed from someone," he says, his eyes straying to my lips. "And I want to know what you taste like."

My mouth goes dry. The only vampire I've ever willingly let feed from me was Reilly, and those were different circumstances. He was also dead sleep at the time.

"That's it?" I ask warily.

"Yes," Adrian says. His fangs descend slowly. "But me first."

He traces my cheekbone, then slides his hand into my hair and tugs me forward, gentle enough that it feels like a question. I shut my eyes and go with the movement. He pauses with his mouth near my neck and inhales deeply. I twitch and clench my hands to keep from jerking away. Neckers do this all the time. It's no big deal. Maybe if I repeat that enough, it will feel true.

Adrian leans in even closer, his breath tickling my ear, then licks a stripe across my neck. He steps back with a shit-eating grin. I stumble forward at the abrupt loss of support.

"Delicious," he says, smacking his lips.

I look at him, incredulous.

"You just wanted to lick me?" I demand, wiping at the smear of saliva on my skin.

He shuts his eyes and shakes his head.

"Hardly. I want to drink until there isn't a drop of blood left inside of you," he opens his eyes, "but I learned to resist such urges hundreds of years ago."

I stare at him confused.

"I drink my blood from goblet now. I feed because I must, but I don't let the hunger control me. Do you understand?" He asks.

I drop my hand to my side. "Yes, but I can't get people to pour their magic into a goblet."

"No, but you can take a little from many people," Adrian says seriously. "Reilly found you one donor, and however unwilling you might think he was, you didn't really hurt him. Quit fighting him on it and start finding a solution."

"Why do you care?" I ask.

"Because I believe the prophecy," Adrian whispers, a sad smile crossing his face.

"What does that have to do with me?" I ask, even though the answer has been pressing in on me for weeks.

"Don't be willfully ignorant," Adrian says with an unimpressed look.

My mother has said I was born with a burden, but it can't be this. I don't want to be part of a prophecy. Hell, I don't even think I buy into the idea of it.

"Now," he says, holding out his hand. "I want to feel it. And don't stop until I tell you to."

I take his hand carefully. "I won't take enough to seriously weaken you."

"You'll take as much as I want you to take," Adrian says with a frown.

"You don't understand—"

"I understand enough. I want to *feel* and I want to *know*," Adrian interrupts. "Do what I ask or I really will feed from you."

I lift his wrist to my mouth and bite down angrily. I hate being threatened. His blood rushes into my mouth and I pull on his magic sharply. My eyes close involuntarily. This is power unlike any I have felt before. Adrian must be ancient. Strength flows into me like a river, but I wonder if I would even be capable of taking all of it.

"I thought it might hurt," Adrian gasps.

I look up. His eyes are wide, and his lips parted. He almost looks like he is enjoying it.

"But this is something else. It is indescribable."

I hum in agreement and continue feeding. I feel so warm. The hunger is both desperate and for the first time, completely satisfied. I want more because it is so good, not because I feel weak.

A slight tremor shakes down Adrian's arm. His brows are pinched together now, and the strange blissful look is gone. I slow the pull on his magic. Despite his insistence that I do not stop until he says to I don't want to hurt him.

He looks at me, and his eyes seem tired. I try to pull off his wrist, but he grabs the back of my neck and holds me still.

"No," he says firmly. "Not until I say."

I grind down with my teeth and growl around his wrist. Despite wondering if I could take all of his magic, I can already feel the strain from what I have taken. He hasn't been this weak in centuries.

He grits his teeth, breathing faster and faster until he's panting harshly. I reach inside of him, as deep as I can, and pull hard on the magic remaining, then jerk out of his grip.

Adrian falls to his knees but glares up at me.

"I said—"

"No," I snap. "I'm not killing you, and I'm not leaving you defenseless."

He huffs but lifts his hand toward me. "Help an old man up."

I roll my eyes and pull him to his feet. He stands in front of me, pale and shaking, and satisfied.

"You're insane," I say, shaking my head.

"I'm not the one that talks to ghosts," Adrian says.

I feel the blood drain from my face. No matter how much Adrian claims to know, he shouldn't know that.

"What...how?" I ask.

"You've been touched by the dead," he says. "I can see it on you."

"You're a vampire, you can't see something like that. No one can," I say, confused and frustrated.

"You of all people should know it's never that clear-cut," Adrian whispers. He tucks my hair behind my ear and for a moment my nose fills with the scent of familiar herbs. "She is still watching even though she can't be with you, she always will be."

I bite the inside of my cheek to keep from visibly reacting.

Adrian smiles and sweeps past me. "I'm sure Reilly is terribly worried I'm molesting you in here.

You should rejoin your friends before he tries to do something heroic."

I remain frozen in place. Despite all logic, I believe him. Perhaps just because I want to.

The curtain opens with a swish and Reilly soundlessly appears in front of me.

"Olivia," Reilly says quietly, concern etched on his face. "What did he do to you?"

"Nothing," I say, shaking myself and taking a deep breath. "Let's go."

He grabs my arm as I turn away. "I will kill him if—"

"Reilly, I'm fine," I say firmly. "He didn't hurt me, at all. Stop acting like you're some kind of knight in shining armor. You spent months threatening me and everyone I care about. You of all people should know I don't scare easy."

I turn and walk away, leaving Reilly to follow. Ever since the Summit, he has acted like I'm breakable. It's confusing, and I don't trust it.

## 11

"I don't trust this," Elise says, interrupting my thoughts as she parks the car. "There's something they aren't telling us."

I haven't been paying attention to the conversation going on around me. Everything Adrian said last night has been weighing on me. The prophecy. Memories of my mother.

Dealing with the NWR isn't a waste of time, but I'm itching to do something else. We have to get the spell book from Cesare soon. Reilly had told me earlier this evening that the clan members he can trust are meeting with us tomorrow night. Tonight can't go by fast enough.

"Stocke was suspicious as well," Reilly agrees.

"We know the NWR is planning something for the full moon," Zachary says. "Keeping the packs out of the forest should keep them safe."

"We'll see," I say, patting the pockets of my jacket. They clink, stuffed full of brews.

"How many did you bring?" Zachary asks, incredulous.

"As many as I could fit," I say with a grin.

He shakes his head and opens the door to the car.

We climb out and head up the front porch steps. Last time I only saw one small area in the back of the house, I'm curious what the rest will be like.

Elise knocks firmly and a few seconds later the door swings open. Colin welcomes us with a grin.

"Welcome to the Grzeski pack house," Colin says as he waves us inside. His eyes land on Reilly and his nose twitches.

The front of the house is even nicer and cozier than the back. The entryway is stately with dark wood floors and a high ceiling that extends up to the second floor. The staircase curves up to a balcony that overlooks the open space. I can see the back of a couch. It must be set up as another sitting area.

A small head pops up from the back of the couch, then two more. I wink at them and hear a squeal. The heads disappear. Colin looks up as well and smiles.

"Ian's daughter and my other nieces and nephews," he explains.

"I think I saw them last time I was here," I say as we walk farther into the house. Whatever they cooked for dinner smells delicious, and meaty.

"They are hard to contain, so that's not surprising," Colin laughs.

Reilly, Elise, and Zachary head into the dining room to greet everyone, but I tap on Colin's arm.

"Could you show me where the bathroom is?" I ask.

"Sure," he says. He leads me down the hall and around a turn. "Just down there. The door on your left."

"Thanks," I say over my shoulder as I head in the direction he pointed.

The bathroom is sleek and roomy, especially for a guest bathroom. I wash my hands and wipe away a smudge of mascara under my eye, then lean against the sink with a sigh. I've spent all my time recently working for JHAPI I can't stop thinking about what happened at the Summit. About what my mother said.

Every time I look in a mirror I hope to see her standing behind me again, but she never is. I rub my arm absently. Sometimes my skin still aches a little, but it's a phantom pain. The welts are gone and so is she.

I open the door and almost step on a little girl that was apparently trying to peek under the door. I freeze with one foot in the air as she scrambles backward. She sits back on her bottom and looks up at me with a determined expression.

"I wanna see your fangs," she exclaims before clamping her hands over her mouth like she's shocked she managed to say it out loud.

Impressed at her nerve, I grin and pop my fangs out. Her eyes go wide, and her jaw drops.

"Wicked," she says in an awed whisper.

"You should see Reilly's," I say. "They're even bigger."

"Whoa," she says, a new plan already forming on her face.

She turns her head down the hall, hearing something I can't, then scrambles to her feet and runs away. She slips around the corner just before Ian appears at the end of the hallway.

"I see you've met my youngest," he says, motioning in the direction the girl just disappeared.

"Apparently," I say, shoving my hands in my pockets. "What's her name?"

"Eliza," Ian says, coming to a stop in front of me and blocking the hallway.

"I'm sure she's a handful," I comment, not sure why Ian is striking up a conversation with me alone.

"She seems fearless. Those are always the kids getting into trouble."

"That is very true," Ian agrees with a laugh. He looks at me contemplatively, sliding his hands into his pockets.

"Did you have a question?" I prompt, trying not to sound rude. I'm not going to stand here all evening while he sorts out his thoughts.

"You said that you are half witch, and half vampire," Ian says finally. "However, that doesn't explain how you can use different types of magic."

I shrug. "I'm unique, I guess."

"Can you use every type of magic?" He presses.

"No," I tilt my head, considering how much to explain before deciding on blunt honesty. "Only the types of magic I've stolen from other paranormals."

His mouth thins as my words sink in. "You steal it?"

"Borrow might be a better word," I say thoughtfully. "Or copy? They don't lose their magic permanently. Depending on how much I take they can recover in a day or a couple of weeks. I keep what I take though."

He grinds his teeth together. "And how many people have you stolen magic from?"

I shake my head and sigh, then try to walk past him, but he grabs my arm. I look down at the fingers clamped around my arm, then slowly back up to his face.

"Let go of me," I say, letting some anger leak into my tone. "Or do you want to see how it works?"

He releases my arm, but his lips curl into a sneer. "Is that a threat?" he growls

"I haven't taken magic from anyone that didn't deserve it, or give the magic to me willingly," I bite out. "But I'm not here to be interrogated."

"I don't know if I trust you," he says, his voice low and dangerous.

"And I'm sure I don't trust you," I say. "Are you going to tell us the real reason you asked the entire team to come to dinner?"

His face closes off and his eyes go hard. "I don't know what you're talking about."

I tilt my head to the side and tap my ear. "Lie."

Ian steps to the side, out of my way. "Perhaps it's best if you rejoin your team."

"No kidding," I mutter as I brush past him and walk down the hall. I round the corner and almost walk into Reilly, who was walking in the opposite direction. Reilly stops and looks back over my shoulder at Ian, something passing between them.

"It's fine," I say, just above a whisper.

Reilly nods, then follows me toward the dining room.

The dining room table is actually two huge tables set end to end. It's set with plates and silverware, but the food is laid out buffet style in the adjoining room. The pack is still milling around and chatting.

Corinne has managed to include herself in a small circle of women and is talking animatedly about something. Ivy is hovering close by, but like most of the rest of the team, the pack just walks around her without a word. Stocke has also found someone to talk to, but they don't look happy about it.

"What a warm welcome," I murmur to Reilly.

"Everyone is on edge," he replies just as quietly. "They're not just suspicious of the team, there is something else going on."

Colin walks in holding a huge tray of freshly grilled burgers. He carries them through the crowd toward where the rest of the food is laid out. A couple of people try to grab a piece of meat as he passes them, but he dodges the attempts.

"Dinner is ready," Ian announces. "Please, let our guests get their food first."

I reluctantly grab a plate and while Reilly sits down at the table. The wolves look at him and whisper among themselves. I fall into step beside Elise. She is looking particularly bitchy.

"What was that all about?" Elise asks, nodding her head toward the hallway.

"No clue," I reply.

We near a small group of werewolves standing near the entrance to the kitchen.

"Traitor," one of them whispers as Elise walks past.

She doesn't flinch or acknowledge him in any way. I stop and glare at him.

"You want to try that again?" I hiss. First Ian, and now this. If these assholes are going to ask us here, without even telling us the truth about the situation, they can at least try to be polite.

The werewolf looks me up and down and turns away dismissively. My fingers twitch with the urge to zap him, but I feel a presence at my elbow.

"You aren't going to pass on one of my famous burgers are you, Olivia?" Colin asks, squeezing my elbow gently.

Colin is lucky I like him. I tear my eyes away from the asshole that insulted Elise and shake my head. "No way, I'm starving."

"Come on then," Colin says, guiding me away with a relieved sigh.

I rejoin Elise in the line. She's staring straight ahead with a blank expression, but I can tell she's furious. I pull on my vampire magic, and all the chatter grows in volume. I can pick out what she's hearing, and can't turn off. The word traitor is used a lot, along with other less flattering terms. I don't know how she isn't shifting and ripping them all apart.

We move through the line quickly and take our seats. Reilly frowns at my plate of food, but the burger smells amazing. I tap my fingers impatiently against the table as we wait for the rest of the pack to get their food. Elise had warned us that it was an unspoken rule to not eat until everyone was seated. Personally, I think it's a dumb rule. My burger is getting cold.

Colin sits down across from me and Reilly with his own plate of food.

"Where are you from originally, Agent Hawking?" Colin asks, drawing her attention.

"New York," Elise says, "but not the city. My pack is in the north-eastern part of the state."

A slender woman with dirty blonde hair sits down next to Colin and beams at me.

"Hi, I'm Keri," she says, extending her hand across the table. "We sort of met."

"Oh," I say, leaning over to shake her hand. "Nice to officially meet you."

"My memories of the whole thing are really fuzzy," she says, still smiling. "You seemed so menacing out in the woods, but I wasn't really thinking straight. All I remember is that you tackled Colin. I thought you were trying to kill us both."

Colin lays his arm over the back of her chair and looks at her fondly. That explains a lot. He hadn't mentioned she was his girlfriend, or at least that he wanted her to be.

"You were pretty drugged up," I say with a polite smile.

Ian stands at the end of the table, and the conversation quiets. "I want to thank the JHAPI agents for joining us today on such short notice," he says, nodding toward Agent Stocke. "I hope that they can one day be our trusted allies, and not—"

A sharp, urgent howl interrupts his speech. Several of the weres jump to their feet and Ian's face shifts into a growl.

"Secure the perimeter, go now!" Ian shouts.

"What is going on?" Stocke demands, jumping to her feet as well.

An explosion rattles the windows and shakes the entire house. Ian tilts his head back and howls.

Fucking werewolves and their stupid secrets. I leap to my feet and grab a brew from my pocket. The room is filled with the sounds of bones shifting and the angry growls of wolves. Stocke is shouting at Ian, but he is not listening.

Ian shifts from man to wolf in one fluid motion and bolts out of the room.

"Spread out, but stay with your partner," Stocke shouts over the chaos.

Staci draws a small gun from her waistband and follows Stocke out of the room.

"Ian," Reilly growls at me.

I nod, and we run out of the room, everything else fading into slow motion as we move. I can barely keep up with Reilly as I navigate the tight turns of the hallway.

Gunfire cuts across our path, shattering the windows at the front of the house. I drop down into a crouch a few feet from Reilly who is kneeling behind a sofa. He peeks up over the back and holds up five fingers. There's five of them.

A howl comes from directly outside.

"Shit," Reilly says, jumping to his feet and lunging toward the broken windows.

I follow him, but a child's scream from overhead brings me to a halt. Gunfire cracks in the back of the house, but all my senses are focused on the sounds of a fight upstairs. I turn and sprint up the stairs following the rabbit-fast heartbeat of Eliza.

The open area on the balcony is empty. Something heavy crashes into a wall at the end of the hallway. I run toward the furious growls and sounds of cursing.

A man, half-shifted, lies dead in the doorway. Past him, two men dressed in black with guns slung over their shoulders advance on the children. I don't know how they got in here so fast, but I can only imagine what they would do if they managed to kidnap the pack leader's kid.

The man on the left has a net that crackles with electricity when it brushes against the floor. The other has one of those poles with a loop on the end meant to catch dogs. Eliza dodges a throw of the net but takes a hit from the pole, protecting the two smaller children clinging to each other behind her.

Rage fills me. All the power I took from Adrian courses through my muscles and magic sparks on my fingertips. The man with the pole looks back and goes for his gun, but he doesn't have time to reach for it before I grab his head and twist. His neck cracks and he falls to the ground, limp.

The other man lifts his gun and shoots, but too slow. I lunge to the side, the bullets striking the wall, and dart behind him. I kick him square in the back, and he flies into the dresser with a thud, his head hitting a corner with a loud crack. Not taking any chances, I stomp down on the back of his neck, killing him as well.

Eliza is watching with wide, glowing eyes. Her tiny body is shaking with a power she can't control yet. Her hands are half shifted into claws and fur lines her face. Werewolves can't fully shift until puberty. I'm shocked she's even gotten this far. The other two children begin to cry as I approach. Eliza turns to try to reassure them.

"Eliza, on my back," I command as I scoop the other two children up, putting one on each hip. Terrified of me, they struggle, kicking and biting, but I don't care. I can't leave them here.

Eliza climbs up on my back and wraps her legs and arms around me.

"Hang on tight as you can. We're going to go fast," I say, adjusting my grip on the other two.

"Okay," she whispers in a scared voice. She tightens her grip more than a human child would be capable of.

I run. The sounds of fighting are still concentrated toward the front of the house. I leap from the balcony, not bothering with the stairs, and land in the entrance to the hallway. Eliza whimpers but maintains her grip on me.

The faint scent of Colin and Keri floods my nose. They're nearby.

"Colin!" I shout, running toward the scent.

Keri appears from around a corner and runs toward me, relief clear on her face.

"Colin is out back looking for kids. We couldn't find them," she says grabbing one of the kids that reaches for her with a sob. "They were supposed to be downstairs. This way."

We slip into one of the rooms and shut the door behind us. Keri pulls a rug back and opens a hidden trapdoor.

"There's a tunnel that leads to a safe house down

119

here," Keri explains as she drops the first kid in. I hand her the other kid, and then Eliza, who begins to cry at being separated from me.

"I have to stay with them," Keri says.

"Go," I nod. "I'll cover this back up."

She drops down after the kids. I lower the trap-door and press it shut. The sounds of crying abruptly stops. Soundproof. I put the rug back in position, then hurry back to the door and listen for any sounds of movement outside. I need to get back to Reilly. Stocke had wanted us to stay with our partners, and I don't want to leave him on his own, but I don't know where he is now.

Another explosion rocks the house, closer this time. I stop hesitating and rip the door open, running toward the last place I saw Reilly and Ian. Outside, light from the full moon illuminates the corpses that litter the front lawn. Both human and wolf, but thankfully mostly humans dressed in black. A fireball erupts behind me, billowing over the top of the house, but oddly it has a face. I grin, it must be Hu.

A body goes flying through the air from the corner of the house I'm facing; I run toward it. As I round the corner, I see where the fight is. Reilly is moving almost too fast to see leaving bodies in his wake. Ian clamps his jaws around a man's throat and drags him backward with vicious shakes. A dozen werewolves are spread out around him working in groups of three or four.

The NWR are advancing in small groups toward the side and back of the house. One person in front is holding a large black shield that stretches up above their heads and extends down to their feet. A small window allows them to see where they are going. The men behind him lean around, firing steadily as they walk.

Most of my team have taken up positions inside the house, leaning out to shoot then retreating to safety. The bullets dent the shield and slow their progress, but they can't penetrate the armor. The NWR is keeping up a constant barrage of gunfire; it's almost impossible for the team to retaliate.

I grab a brew out of my pocket and throw it at the closest group of terrorists. The vial breaks against one of them, and their hands fly to their throats as the oxygen is sucked out of the air. The man with the shield drops it. Bullets strike his chest, knocking him down. Two wolves jump into the midst of them, finishing what I started.

I flex my fingers and sprint into the battlefield. Electric magic flows down my arm and stretches out like a whip. Hu had shown me how to hold on to the magic and control it. Now, it's time to test it out.

I'm run at another group of three from the side where they're vulnerable. The closest terrorist is firing steadily as he follows the man holding the heavy shield. I flick my wrist toward him; the whip of electricity cracks against his side and the gun. His screams and curses as all the muscles in his body contract at once. I strike again, pumping electricity through him until he drops. A curl of smoke rises from his corpse.

The other shooter switches angles to face me, but I'm already swinging the magic toward him. It smacks him in the face, an arc of bright white lightning jumping from him to the man holding the shield. They both fall, spasming violently. I strike one last time, killing them both.

A gunshot cracks behind me. I duck and lunge to the side on instinct, hearing an enraged growl behind me. Elise has the shooter by the arm. She drags him to the ground and pounces on him.

"Dammit," I mutter, realizing I let an attacker sneak up on me just like in training. There are so many sounds and smells, it's impossible to keep track of everything even with heightened senses.

A loud pop and the smell of gasoline draws my attention back to the fighting. My eyes widen in horror. Near the back of the house, a terrorist wields a flamethrower, fire spewing out almost a hundred feet in front of him. Ian is in the path of a wide stream of fire, but he isn't moving fast enough. The flames swing toward Ian as he charges the group in front of him, completely unaware.

Reilly appears behind the man with the flamethrower, but he is not fast enough. Ian is engulfed in flames as Reilly tackles the man. Reilly rips his throat out with his teeth, blood spraying through the air like a fountain. Ian howls in pain, writhing on the ground in an attempt to put out the flames.

I run toward Ian, everything around me seeming to slow as I move faster than humanly possible. Reilly beats me to Ian, jumps on him, and rolls. The flames envelop them both, and the smell of burning flesh permeates the air. I don't know how Reilly can stand the pain, but he doesn't let go.

I get within reach of them and smash a deoxygenation potion down on Reilly's back. The flames go out as the air is stripped of oxygen. I hate the feeling, but grit my teeth against the discomfort and pull Reilly away from Ian's blackened body, pumping healing magic into him in the brief moment I'm touching him. Reilly's face and chest are burned, but it's already healing thanks to him being a vampire. Reilly doesn't even pause. Instead, he turns and leaps toward a terrorist that lifts his gun in our direction.

Ian jerks and whimpers, but can't get to his feet. The fur has been burned almost completely off on one side and his eyes are swollen shut. Vampire magic surges through me, giving me strength. I scoop Ian up and race inside the house away from the fighting. I jump through a broken window and search for a spot out of sight to set Ian down. Cook and Staci are on the other side of the room shooting out of a different window.

"Is he going to live?" Staci shouts over her shoulder.

"I hope so," I shout back.

"Take this," she yells as she tosses a bright green vial at me. I snatch it out of the air. "Healing brew."

I pour the brew over the wounds then wrap my hands around his head and push magic into him. There is so much damage. He is covered in burns on the outside, and his lungs are scorched.

I start with the worst of it, healing his lungs first as the brew seeps into his skin. His body heaves as he regains the ability to breathe and begins to struggle. I lay down on top of him to keep him from getting away. He growls and tries to bite me.

"Ian," I snap. "Let me heal you dammit."

He continues to growl but stops fighting me. I push more magic into him, and his accelerated ability to heal allows my magic to work better and faster. The burns change from black to red. They are still oozing, and disgusting to look at, but he's isn't in as much pain anymore.

I have used more magic in the last twenty minutes than I ever have before. If I hadn't fed from Adrian the night before, I'd be passed out on the floor right now. Even so, my healing magic is weak, and I'm running out of energy. I can't risk exhausting myself and becoming defenseless. My hands start to shake and I pull away from Ian.

He rolls up onto his feet, huffing in pain.

"That's all I can do," I pant as I stand. "Stay in here until you've healed more."

He lets out a noise that implies I must be stupid and runs toward the exit. I grit my teeth and follow. I guess I can't blame him for being unwilling to let his pack fight without him. Two wolves flank Ian, protecting their injured Alpha as he fights. Despite the still-healing burns he is still moving as fast as ever.

I grab a brew with each hand. It's time for me to go back to the basics. I lean out of the window and throw the first one. It shatters against a tall black shield. Green flame crawls over the top, dripping down like liquid. It will burn through that shield eventually no matter what it's made of. Based on the screaming, it's also burning through whoever is holding it.

I run over to where Staci and Cook are still crouched and stand just behind Staci's shoulder. As they lean out to fire, I step forward and throw another green fire brew. My aim is off and it hits the ground, but the liquid fire still splashes up someone's leg.

Stocke shouts something I can't quite understand over the noise. Ian howls and the wolves immediately cease attacking as they run for the house leaping through windows and open doors. I peek around the corner and realize why they retreated.

A spray of bullets takes out three of the five remaining groups of terrorists. The other two swivel to face the new threat, but the shields can't hold up against whatever is shooting at them now. An armored vehicle rounds the corner, a gun mounted on the roof that is firing in rapid succession.

From the other direction, I hear a roar. A wall of flame morphs into the snapping jaws of a dragon made entirely of fire. It surges toward the terrorists, blocking them in. The terrorists make no move to surrender, and likewise, they are shown no mercy. When the last man falls, the pounding gunfire finally ceases.

Stocke steps out of an open doorway, gun still held at her side, and waves at the armored vehicle. The door opens, and two SWAT team members jump down. They keep their guns at the ready and scan the area for threats as a third man hops down. He removes his helmet and looks around, then walks toward Stocke, trusting his men to cover him.

"We have the front of the house cleared," he shouts across the lawn. "Everyone needs to go through here," he points at the space between the truck and the house, "and stay on the front lawn. Anyone wandering around could trigger an explosive."

"Got it," Stocke shouts back. "Everyone move."

I follow Staci and Cook around to the front of the house. Ian, still in wolf form, limps along just ahead of us. He stumbles; the wolf next to him crouches down to catch him. The wolf lets Ian lean on him, and they continue walking slower than before.

The pack collapses on the front lawn; many of them are injured. My hands itch with the desire to heal them, but I can't help them all no matter how much I want to.

Staci runs to her car and opens the trunk. She pulls out a bag and shouts for Cook and Stocke to help her. They pull out vials of healing brews and hurry over to the injured. Relief floods through me. Staci came prepared.

Hu, Brunson, and Ivy walk over to Stocke. Hu glances at me, and I give him a thumbs up. That fire magic was impressive. He grins in acknowledgment then turns back to the conversation with Stocke.

A red truck appears at the end of the driveway, rumbling toward us with its big diesel engine. The SWAT team responds immediately, aiming their guns at the truck, but Stocke runs over and explains that it's a pack member. Jimmy parks on the grass and pops out of the truck. His usual, carefree expression is gone as he surveys the pack.

He goes to Ian first, but Ian snaps at him then begins to shift. It's slow and looks painful. The burns stretch and crack as fur gives way to skin. He is healing from the shift, but he's still in bad shape. The shift completes, but Ian remains on his knees.

"Heal the others first," he demands, looking at Jimmy.

Jimmy shakes his head but hurries over to the wolf that looks the worst off.

A pack member runs out of the front door, frantic. "Ian," he shouts. "Luke is dead, and the kids are gone."

Ian growls, the sound resonating through everyone. Ears perk up all around us as the pack goes back on alert.

"Everyone spread out. Find their trail—"

"They're with Keri," I say, interrupting before Ian sends the pack running all over the property. "In the tunnels under the trap door in that room."

"You saw them?" Ian bites out.

"The NWR got in the house and trapped them up-stairs where they killed Luke. They were trying to capture the kids, but I got there in time to stop them. Eliza had been fending them off," I explain. "She was very brave."

Ian nods and motions at the werewolf that ran out of the house. "With me," he says before sprinting back in the house.

"Are you hurt?" Reilly asks from behind me.

I turn around and flinch at his appearance. "I think I should be asking you that," I say, reaching up to touch the still reddened flesh visible through his shirt. It was burned almost entirely off when he saved Ian.

"It's healing on its own," Reilly says, grabbing my hand before I can touch it. "Don't waste your energy on me."

"At least get a brew from Staci," I say. "That's going to take a long time for you to heal completely."

"I will later," Reilly says. "Do you need to feed?"

"No, but I need a drink," I say, heading toward the house.

"You're going to steal their tequila?" Reilly asks with a smirk. "At a time like this?"

I roll my eyes. "Water, jackass."

Glass crunches under my feet as we walk inside. The once nice house now looks like a battlefield. A whimper draws my attention. Eliza is clinging to Ian in the hallway. He rubs her back soothingly, whispering something reassuring in her ear. If she had been taken, he would have been devastated.

Ian looks up and nods at me. I nod back, then continue on to the kitchen, not wanting to intrude in the private moment any longer.

The kitchen is almost untouched other than a tray of food that was knocked onto the ground. I step around the mess and dig through the cabinets until I find the cups.

"Stocke should not have agreed to this," Reilly comments. "And we shouldn't have come."

I fill the cup with water before responding. "Ian should have been honest."

Ian steps into the kitchen and crosses his arms.

"You knew I hadn't told you everything," Ian says. "Just like you knew I was listening right then; yet you all came tonight."

I shrug and take a long drink. "We suspected we were being used."

"Then why did you come?" Ian asks, tilting his head.

"JHAPI wants to stop the NWR. They want to do the right thing, so they had no problem being used. We all came prepared for a fight tonight." I hesitate, not sure how far I should push. "If we had known exactly what the threat was, we might have been able to stop them from getting in the house."

Ian clenches his jaw tightly, his eyes flashing with anger.

I spread my hands and shrug. "I'm just being honest. It would have been a fight and people would have died, no matter what. But the more JHAPI knows, the more they can help you."

Ian shoves his hands in his pockets. "I will take that into consideration in the future."

I bite my tongue to keep from calling him out on his bullshit. For someone as proud as Ian, even saying that must have been difficult.

"You saved my life," Ian says, looking at Reilly, then me. "Both of you."

"I was in the right place at the right time," Reilly says with a shrug.

"You still risked your own well-being to protect

me. That is something I would never expect from anyone other than a pack member," Ian insists. He pauses then approaches me. "You saved my daughter's life," he says gruffly.

I lower my eyes, not liking the lump that forms in my throat when I see the fear in his. "I'm glad I got there in time," I say quietly.

"I repay my debts," Ian says, looking at each of us in turn. "If either of you needs my assistance, I will come."

A pleased expression spreads across Reilly's face. "That debt may be called in sooner than you think."

## 14

I bounce my leg impatiently. Reilly said his clanmates would be here right after of sundown. It's been almost two hours and I'm still waiting. Reilly, however, is unconcerned and has been taking a ridiculously long shower.

Reilly exits the bathroom with damp hair. The scent of his shampoo drifts toward me. He's not wearing a suit like he normally does; instead, he has on...jeans. And a *t-shirt*. What the hell. It's black of course.

"They're late. Have they been kidnapped or murdered?" I ask, narrowing my eyes at him. "Also, I had no idea you even owned jeans."

"I prefer to wear a suit when I'm working," Reilly says, ignoring my question.

"You're always wearing a suit," I say.

"I'm always working," he replies with a grin. "And if they've been murdered, then it was either a ghost or their murderer that just texted me to say they are parking and will be up shortly."

"Ha. Ha," I say, not amused at his mockery.

He clears his throat and rubs his hand around his wrist like he misses the sleeves. "A few more people will be joining us this evening as well," he says. His heartbeat ticks up almost imperceptibly. He's hiding something.

"Other than Zachary and Elise?" I ask, suspicious.

"They'll definitely be here," Reilly says.

I sit up to press the issue, but a knock at the door interrupts. Reilly hurries over and opens the door wide. Ihaka steps inside first, grabbing Reilly's hand and pulling him in to press their foreheads together. Reilly claps him on the back and steps aside.

"Welcome to Los Angeles," Reilly says.

Ihaka walks inside with a bag slung over his shoulder. Viking follows. Rolf is his actual name, as I learned at Cesare's, but Viking suits him better.

Leslie walks in next, and she looks even better than the last time I saw her. She was always busty, but everything is particularly perky, and she has a new haircut that suits her well.

"Olivia!" She exclaims, opening her arms for a hug. I stand reluctantly and let her pull me into an embrace. She smells a little like Reilly's magic and a little like citrus from her shampoo.

"Has Reilly still been keeping you confined to his rooms?" I ask.

"Yes," Leslie groans. "However, it's kept Cesare from paying any attention to me, so it's all for the best."

Rolf settles on the far couch, resting his hands in his lap. Ihaka looks around the room, even pulling aside the thick curtains to check out the view.

Leslie glances at Reilly. "Have you been keeping him in line?" she asks me.

I laugh aloud. "As if that's possible."

Ihaka snorts from his position at the window and shakes his head in agreement.

Leslie grins. "I guess you have a point."

"Such disrespect for your sire," Reilly teases Leslie. He joins Ihaka at the window and they launch into a quiet discussion about something to do with the clan. Another knock at the door interrupts my eavesdropping. I walk over and open it, expecting Elise and Zachary. That is *not* who is standing in front of me.

"Surprise," Patrick says, boyish grin on his face as he leans around Javier's shoulder.

"What," I say as a statement instead than a question.

Patrick's smile fades slightly, the worry that I'll kick them both out showing on his face.

"I invited them," Reilly says from behind me. I turn to him, confused and surprised. Reilly winks at me and Javier and Patrick walk inside. Javier tugs the door out of my hand and closes it behind them.

"Has she gone mute?" Javier asks Reilly teasingly.

I try to glare at him, but my face isn't cooperating. Patrick stands in front of me and looks at me warily, then leans in and wraps me in a tight hug. I stiffen, but my arms go around him automatically. The familiar smell of his hair gel and the tight grip of his arms cuts through the resentment and shock. I melt into the hug and squeeze him back. I really did miss him.

Over Patrick's shoulder, I can see Reilly watching me. My heart twists. He did this for me. He may not have said *sorry* out loud, but this is better than that word could ever be. Reilly drops his gaze and turns away.

Javier is wrapped up in Leslie. She is clinging to him with tears running down her cheeks. When I first started working for Javier, I was convinced he was just another mercenary vampire, but it's obvious

135

he missed Leslie. Javier isn't an angel, but he's not all bad either.

I step back out of the hug and punch Patrick on the shoulder as hard as I can. Almost. I don't want to actually damage him. Patrick yelps and grabs his hurt arm.

"Dammit, you punch way harder now," he complains.

"Good, you deserved it," I say, brushing past him and plopping down on the couch. That's enough mushy stuff for now.

"Glad to see the two of you have made up," Javier says, pulling away from Leslie. "Patrick has been in a terrible mood since you left."

Patrick follows me to the couch and sits down on my left, wrapping his arm around my shoulders.

"No one else will come out with me to the bars and line dance," Patrick complains. "And it's terrible to line dance alone."

"Olivia? Line dancing?" Reilly asks with a grin. "That sounds fascinating."

I shoot him a glare. "I'm a fantastic dancer."

"I know," he agrees, his grin widening and his dimples growing more pronounced. I look away as I remember the heat of his body when we danced in that club in Vegas.

Leslie drops down on the couch and wraps Patrick in a hug. He hugs back, pulling her halfway into his lap.

"So you're a big, bad vampire now," Patrick says. "Is feeding on humans better than being fed from?"

"Mostly," Leslie says with a laugh. "I still miss it sometimes, but I think it's mostly nostalgic, you know?"

Patrick nods. "Yeah, I get it."

There is another knock at the door; I look back to

see Reilly ushering Elise and Zachary inside. Elise looks around, sniffing subtly as she scopes out the group.

Javier approaches first, extending his hand to Zachary.

"Agent Brunson," he says in greeting. "It's good to see you again."

"Mr. Moreno," Zachary says shaking his hand firmly. "Likewise."

"I didn't expect to see the two of you here," Elise says, shaking his hand as well.

Javier glances at Reilly. "The invitation was a surprise to me too. I'm curious what the purpose of this gathering is."

"You haven't even told them yet?" I ask Reilly.

"Told us what?" Patrick asks, leaning around me to look at Reilly too.

Reilly walks over and stands at the end of the couches. "Cesare Sangiovanni was recently appointed to the vampire council. This was just one of several moves he has made to himself in a position where he can force a change. He is a traditionalist, and he wants to go back to the days when vampires killed freely, and humans were seen as food."

"It's not exactly news that Cesare is a traditionalist," Javier says, walking around the other side of the couches to face Reilly.

"No," Reilly agrees. "However, Cesare thinks he has found a way to rise to power. There is something that has been trapped for centuries that, if released, would attempt to destroy every paranormal. Some call it a God, and I have been trying to confirm its existence for a while. I doubted that it could be real for years, but there are too many powerful people struggling to control it to doubt the existence of the Bound God any longer."

Javier taps his fingers against his leg. Patrick watches him, waiting to see what his reaction will be. If Javier walks out, I know Patrick will follow.

"There's also a prophecy," Zachary says from behind me. "We talked to one of Reilly's contacts night before last and discovered more about it. I'm still skeptical, but that doesn't make what Cesare is doing any less of a threat."

I shift in my seat at the mention of the prophecy and Reilly glances at me before returning his attention to Javier.

"You don't have to help us. I'm planning on killing Cesare, to put it simply," Reilly explains. "If I succeed, the clan will be mine, as will his seat on the council according to the old laws, which are still in effect."

I look up, surprised. I knew we were going to have to kill Cesare to succeed, but I had no idea it was going to catapult Reilly to such a powerful position. Maybe I should have suspected something like that was at play. Reilly is always thinking two or three steps ahead.

Javier tilts his head, considering. If he helps, the entire clan is in danger, but the reward if they succeed is huge. Part of me hopes he'll take Patrick and leave.

"Well, we can't let Cesare take us back to the Dark Ages," Javier says. "I will help however I can."

I shut my eyes and take a deep breath. Javier wants to do the right thing. I should be happy.

"Assuming we survive, I won't forget your loyalty," Reilly says seriously.

Ihaka approaches Javier and puts his hand on his shoulder. "Welcome to the family."

"What now?" Elise asks. "Defeating evil is great and all, but is there a plan?"

"Ihaka and Rolf have been watching and listening

to everything that has been going on at the clan-house," Reilly explains. "We need to know what exactly Cesare is doing, and when he is going to make his move. Rolf, please explain what you discovered."

Rolf leans forward, his bulky muscles flexing under his shirt. "There are rumors of someone being brought to the clanhouse unwillingly."

"Were you able to find out who?" Reilly asks.

Rolf shakes his head. "I was lucky to have overheard that. Everything that is happening is not part of the usual gossip."

"They might have been killed," Leslie says. "One of the neckers said he saw Cesare's bodyguard carrying something out to the trunk of his car. He thought it was a body, but it was wrapped up."

"It could have been a necker," Reilly says thoughtfully, crossing his arms. "Those deaths are always covered up to avoid issues with the council and public relations."

"He has been calling back vampires he sired that have more independence, and clans of their own," Ihaka says. "They don't often stay long, but it used to be rare for him to order one of them to return home once he allowed them to move away."

"If Cesare is planning on releasing this Bound God soon he may be preparing them to go into hiding," Reilly says, tapping his fingers against his arm restlessly. "We need to try to stay ahead of him. There is a coven that has been guarding this Bound God for centuries. We need to contact them. We need them as allies."

"Absolutely not," I bite out. How could Reilly even suggest that knowing what they've done?

"We can't take Cesare down with only the people in this room," Reilly argues. He barely glances at me before turning back to Javier like the issue is settled.

"Then we find someone else," I snap back. "The coven will betray us, and they will try to control me. You heard what Adrian said. Alexandra Hunt is a mean, crafty, power-hungry old witch. They're no better than Cesare."

"The enemy of my enemy is my friend," Reilly insists. "We have to be practical."

"I won't work with them," I say, standing up from the couch. So much for his apology. It was all calculated. He tried to soften me up so he could manipulate me. The t-shirt and jeans were probably all part of the act too. Fucking asshole vampire.

"The decision isn't up to you," Reilly bites out. "You will do as I say or—"

"Or what?" I demand, taking a step toward him. "Are you going to threaten to kill Javier and Patrick again? Or will it be someone else this time?"

Reilly clenches his jaw, and the muscles of his neck stand out. "No, but you will be dooming us all if you don't cooperate."

I scoff and shake my head. "We don't need them. If you tried, you could find another way."

I turn and walk away. Zachary is staring at his hands frustrated, but Elise nods her head at me. She has my back at least. My car keys and jacket are on the little table in the entryway. I grab them and yank the door open, slamming it into the wall.

"Go with her," Javier says to someone else.

"Reilly, they killed her mother, you can't expect her to work with them," Zachary argues. The door shuts behind me, and I tune out the rest of their conversation.

Patrick catches up to me in the hall and wraps his arm around my tight shoulders. "Fuck that guy, right?"

"I want to shove him off a bridge," I snap.

"How about we find someplace with tequila so you can cope with all this pent-up rage?" Patricks suggests with a grin.

"You're a bad influence. Shouldn't you be telling me to cope with my problems like an adult?" I ask with a raised brow.

Patrick pouts. "I would never."

I relax a little and let him guide down to the parking garage. He takes the keys; I climb into the passenger seat.

"I found this awesome country-western bar on-line," he says with a mischievous look. "We're gonna get our groove on."

I laugh, but my thoughts are still back in that hotel room where Reilly is continuing his plans without me. He's wrong about the coven. They're going to stab him in the back and fuck me over. I don't understand why he's refusing to see that.

## 15

I peek one dry eye open, and sure enough, the knocking is not part of my dream. With a grunt, I push up into a sitting position and swing my legs over the edge of the bed. My pants are laying on the floor in the middle of the room where I pulled them off and dropped them the night before.

I shuffle over and pull them on. The knocking increases in urgency and I smooth my hair down as I hurry toward the door. Through the peephole I see a young, slender guy wearing an actual cape. There's no doubt in my mind Adrian sent him. I pull the door open.

"What?" I demand, my head still aching from last night's drinking and the rude awakening.

The boy bows and holds out the rectangular, black velvet pillow in his hands toward me. Perched on the top of the pillow is a blood-red envelope, my full name written in calligraphy on the front, and a single white rose.

Adrian certainly has style. I pick up the envelope and the rose. The boy stands abruptly and walks away without uttering a single word.

"So weird," I mutter as I shut the door.

The envelope shimmers as I examine it. The back is sealed in black wax that is stamped with a rose. I dig my nail under the wax and open it. It's stuffed full with a thick letter. Adrian must be as talkative in letters as he is in real life.

I plop down on the sofa in the sitting area and pull out the thick parchment. As I unfold it another piece of paper falls out. I set it aside and read Adrian's letter first.

*Dearest Olivia,*

*You are the key...*

*I do love the drama of that statement.*

I can practically hear Adrian's voice, purring with excitement at his own flair. Still, my fingers dent the paper as the reminder of my place in all of this sinks in. Adrian had said he cared because he believed the prophecy. Somehow he already knew, or at least suspected, I was the key before we came to Fangers.

*The only way to kill a god is with another god. Of course, the Bound God is not really a god, and neither are you. I think you'll find the enclosed photocopy of Izul's diary particularly enlightening, as I did.*
*Also, you may find it interesting that your dear friend, Reilly Walsh, came back to visit me last night with some additional questions. I did not expect you to be willing to ally with the coven that caused your mother's death, and since I am rarely wrong, I must assume you know nothing*

*of this. I do love a good betrayal, but I like you more than Reilly. You have a day's head start. Use it wisely.*

*All my love,*
*Adrian Cormer, Master of Intrigue and Information*

*PS. The book won't be the only thing worth taking from Sangiovanni. Do be thorough when you next visit him.*

I drop the letter in my lap and grind my teeth together. Reilly. Fucking. Walsh. I should have known he'd go behind my back as soon as I didn't fall in line with what he wanted. Did he really think that if the coven showed up, I wouldn't try to kill that bitch, Alexandra? This is all going to be so much harder if I can't work with Reilly, but he's making it impossible.

I grab the photocopy Adrian enclosed with the letter. He might enjoy the drama of announcing that I am the key to the prophecy, but I need an explanation. On one side is a scan of some kind of book with messy handwriting. Only a few of the letters are recognizable, and none of the words look like any language I've seen before. Thankfully, on the opposite side is a translation.

*...a mistake. Aris lust for power has created a monster that cannot be controlled. I should have listened to the goblin prophet Allaghar, but I believed in Aris' vision. Cadriel was a normal child, but as he grew in age and power, he began to rival Aris in his need to control everything around him. Aris cannot share power, and neither can he. He killed the fire witch that came to offer him her talent. We covered it up. It was stupid to believe that it was an ac-*

*cident, or that it was the first witch he had killed by taking
too much of their magic.*

*They call him a God now. No witch was ever meant to
wield all the talents, so perhaps he is a God. He borders on
invincible, and this war has gone on for too long already. I
worry that witches may be wiped off the face of the earth.
We only have one hope left, the only magic Cadriel has not
been able to steal. I go tonight to beg the nocte viator for
their help.*

Nocte viator. Stealing magic. My hands begin to
shake. He's not a god, but he is like me. I can imagine
all the things I could do if I stole and mastered every
type of magic. A fire witch that was Impervious
would be strong enough to take on an entire coven. If
the witch could also heal? Find? Had the speed and
strength of a vampire? Their only limits would be
how often they could feed. I glance down at the
translation again. If Cadriel was killing openly, he
wouldn't have the same misgivings I do about
feeding off the unwilling.

I set aside the page and put my head in my hands.
Reilly thought he could test me and prepare me for
this fight, but he was wrong. Even Cesare was wrong.
If Cadriel is released from wherever he is, I won't be
able to kill him.

I pick up the next page. Izul stopped him somehow, I can only hope he wrote down some in-
structions.

*Cadriel is trapped for now in the shadow realm. However,
Allaghar warns us of the Day of Breaking. It was too much
to hope that Cadriel could be bound forever.*

*Aris is dead, so the task of killing Cadriel falls on me. Coven Praesidio has sworn to protect the secret of his location and search for the key to killing him no matter how many generations it takes. Cadriel was born from the ashes of a vampire, and to ash, he must return.*

Not helpful. Not helpful at all. A note in Adrian's handwriting is scribbled on the bottom of this page.

*The rest is in the book. Cesare has everything you need.*

My mother really didn't have any idea what she stole all those years ago. I refold the letter and the translations of Izul's writing, then rub my hands tiredly down my face. I have to get the book back like I promised my mother I would, but I will not betray her by working with the coven to do that.

Whatever that coven started out as they are just a bunch of fanatical psychos now. They hurt Leslie and Patrick, and they would have killed the entire clan just to get to me. People like that can't be trusted. Eventually, they would create someone else like me, and seek to control them just like Aris tried to do.

Reilly had kept me in line for a while with threats he hadn't intended to carry out. I have no doubt Alexandra Hunt would follow through on her threats, just like Cesare will if he finds out what I'm planning.

I can't do this alone, and I'm hoping I don't have to. I stand up and walk to my room. It's time to pack my bags and then see if there is anyone I can trust.

Zachary hands the letters back to Elise.

"You really buy this prophecy stuff?" He asks.

I take a deep breath, steadying myself to explain. "Those welts I had, they were from an accident when I tried to Find my mother, back when Reilly first showed up in Texas."

Zachary's face shifts to alarm. "You tried to Find someone that is dead?"

"I wasn't sure," I say. "Before your dad was killed, he found out that her death certificate was faked. All of it was. Reilly told me that he hid it from me."

Zachary scratches his chin and frowns. "I'm sure he meant well."

I smile at him sadly. "I know he did. I've never doubted that. Searching for her was an obsession for me back then. I would have done anything to track her down, and that wasn't healthy."

I sit down on the edge of the bed. "Anyhow, Reilly made me think there might be a chance she was still alive. I didn't know what I was doing, but when I searched for her, I didn't come up empty-handed. I somehow Found her ghost or soul, whatever you want to call it. I saw her everywhere for a while, and she spoke to me. She told me about the Bound God, and she said I had to stop him."

Elise drops the letters on the bed. "And you believed what this hallucination told you?"

"Yes," I insist. "It was her. Believe me or don't, but I'm sure of it."

"Ok," Elise says, shrugging. "Does the prophecy give any hints to how you're supposed to take down this god?"

"*The Key must be found, lest Chaos consume and*

*magic be lost, the Key must return to ash what was born of it,*" I recite with a sigh. "So, not really. But, I do know that I need to get the spell book my mother stole back from Cesare. Along with whatever Adrian was hinting at in that letter."

Elise snorts. "Cesare is not going to just hand it over."

"No, which is why I'm going to Find Maybelle and ask for her help," I say.

"What? Why?" Zachary asks.

"She helped my mother steal it last time. She stole it from the coven no less," I explain. "If anyone can help me, it's her."

"Will she help you though?" Zachary asks, his face showing his skepticism. "She did disappear when the coven was hunting you down."

"I think so," I say, twisting my hands together. "I have a feeling Gerard will help me convince her to."

"Reilly could probably get you into Cesare's without raising suspicion," Elise says.

"No," I say firmly.

Zachary sighs. "I know you're angry, but we might need him."

"I won't let him hand the spell book, or me, over to the coven," I say.

"Do you really think he would?" Elise asks.

"Yes," I nod. "If Reilly thinks it would help stop Cesare, he would do it without hesitation. He doesn't care that they would try to control me. He can't see that the coven is just as bad as Cesare."

"And they killed your mother," Zachary says, staring at the floor as he taps his hand restlessly against the desk.

"And that," I agree quietly.

"So, your plan is, run off and find Maybelle, then rob Cesare?" Elise asks.

"That's the short version," I confirm with a frustrated groan.

"You shouldn't go alone," Elise says, crossing her arms.

"I have to—"

"No, you don't. I'm going with you," Elise interrupts.

"You have your job here. Stocke will ask questions if you disappear," I insist.

"I'll handle it," Zachary says. "Stocke will accept my explanation. Elise is right, you shouldn't do this alone."

I bounce my leg, anxious about Elise coming with me even though I need her.

"What we'll be doing is technically illegal too," I warn even though I can see from her face that her mind is already made up.

"It's the right thing to do," Elise says. "Stop trying to talk me out of it. I'm not letting you do this alone. You're part of this team, and you need help."

"Ivy is going to kill me for dragging the team into my personal shit," I say, putting my head in my hands.

Elise laughs. "She'll understand. She might seem like a stickler for the rules, but she would break them in a second if she knew what was going on."

I drop my hands and up look up, squaring my shoulders. I can worry about what's going to happen after all this once I survive it.

"Do you have a map in here?" I ask Zachary. "I need to Find Maybelle before we leave."

"Yeah, I'll grab it," Zachary nods. He digs through the paper on the desk until he finds a map of the country. "Here you go."

"Thanks," I say taking it and unfolding it across the bed.

"When do we leave?" Elise asks.

"As soon as you have your bags packed. Mine are already in the car," I say, cracking my knuckles before spreading my hands over the surface of the map. I close my eyes and let the magic fall from my fingertips, searching for Maybelle.

## 16

I nudge Elise. She blinks up at me groggily from the passenger seat.

"Wake up, we're almost there," I say as I pull into the gas station.

She sits up and wipes a line of drool from her cheek. "I'm hungry."

"You're always hungry. This place says it sells hot dogs," I say, pointing to the sign in the window.

"I'm going to die of food poisoning," Elise grumbles as she climbs out of the car.

"You can't, you're a werewolf," I shout over my shoulder as she heads inside. She flips me off.

I pump the gas, leaning against the dusty car. Maybelle is somewhere deep in the goblin reservation. We're going to have to sneak in and find her without getting caught. Somehow.

I rub my fingers across my forehead. The goblins are very private, and they don't take well to trespassers. They also don't accept visitors or pass along messages.

Elise returns as I finish pumping the gas with a dried out looking hotdog. She scarfs it down in three bites, glaring at me the whole time. I shake my head and smile as I pull back out onto the road.

As we draw closer to the reservation, warning signs appear every mile suggesting we turn back now; the final one says *DEAD END*. The road ends less than a quarter mile later. I wrap both hands around the wheel as we bump over the uneven ground.

A large yellow sign marks the location of the entrance. It's impossible to miss, but not in the least bit inviting.

*NO TRESPASSERS*
*NO SOLICITATION*
*UNAUTHORIZED ENTRY MAY RESULT*
*IN DEATH OR SEVERE INJURY*

"Friendly bunch," Elise comments as she ties her hair back into a tight ponytail.

"No kidding," I say. "This should be an interesting trip."

We climb out of the car, and I look back over my shoulder at the setting sun. Reilly will be awake soon. And pissed.

The door to the underground tunnel isn't locked. It creaks loudly, rust falling from the hinges as we pry it open. It hasn't been used in ages.

There are no stairs or ladder. It's just a straight drop down; I can't see the bottom.

"How far do you think we're going to get before they find us?" Elise asks, hands on her hips as she stares down into the inky darkness.

"Hopefully we make it to Maybelle," I say. "I'm not sure I want to consider the alternative."

I crouch down by the hole and pull on the vampire magic. My eyes adjust to the lack of light, and I can just barely make out something at the bottom of the pit.

There is a handful of small rocks scattered around in the sand. I grab one and drop it down the hole. It hits the ground in a little puff of dust after about a second.

"Can't be that far down then, right?" I ask, glancing at Elise.

She shrugs. "I can't actually calculate the distance by the time it takes for a rock to fall to the bottom of a hole, but sure."

"I should have brought Staci. I bet she could," I say, looking down the hole with a sigh. There's no other option, one of us just has to go down there and see. I sit down and swing my legs over the side. "I'll go down first just in case there's no way out of this hole."

"I don't have anything to pull you out," Elise says.

"Let's hope you don't need it." I twist around and slowly lower myself down until I'm hanging on by just my fingertips. I kick my legs out and hit dirt. I really hope the drop isn't too far.

I let go. My stomach climbs into my throat as the wind rushes past me. My feet hit the ground. I try to roll with the impact but collide with something big and hard.

"Motherfucker," I mutter, stuck upside down with an aching foot.

"Are you dying?" Elise shouts down the hole.

"No, but whoever designed this entrance should be shot," I shout back. I untwist myself and get upright. The hole doesn't lead exactly straight down, it

155

curves at a bit of an angle. There is a small area to land in, but it's surrounded by an uneven wall of boulders, which is what I rolled into. This isn't a dead end, but the way forward isn't exactly clear.

"There are five tunnels leading out of this one," I yell up to Elise.

"Shit, which one do we take?" She asks.

I gnaw on the inside of my cheek. "Give me a minute."

I don't have a map, but the Finding magic is tugging me toward Maybelle. The problem is that just because I know which direction she's in doesn't mean that tunnel will lead me to her.

I shut my eyes and extend my hands. Finding magic is dynamic. It isn't just about maps and straight lines. When I trained with Corinne, I was able to see her. The magic courses through me and drips from my fingertips, searching through the empty space for what I need.

I send the magic toward each of the tunnels and almost fall over as I get a dizzying vision of five different things at once. My eyes twitch, but I keep them squeezed shut and push the magic farther. I have to Find her. We've come this far and have risked everything for this chance.

The magic searches, showing me glimpses of rock and dirt. One of the strands of magic snaps back into me, and I grit my teeth. That's one tunnel eliminated. Vague images flash through my mind. Goblins. Caverns. Darkness. Another strand of magic snaps back, then another, and I drop to one knee. The last two strands wind farther and farther down the tunnels.

My arms shake with the effort of pushing the Finding magic farther than I ever have before. My right arm is wrenched forward. I get a bright glimpse of Maybelle's face. She looks over her shoulder, brows knitting together. Her lips move, but I can't hear what she says.

"Olivia!" Elise shouts. Her hand connects with my cheek, and I jerk awake with a gasp.

"Shit," I say, rolling up into a sitting position and holding my aching head in my hands.

"What the hell did you do?" She demands.

"I found the right tunnel," I say. "Wait, you jumped down here?"

"You made a really disturbing noise then went silent," she says, holding out a hand to help me up. "You wouldn't respond to anything."

I take her hand and she hauls me to my feet. "That took more out of me than I expected, but I know which tunnel we need to take."

The urge to get to Maybelle burns in my gut. I want to take off at a run, but that would be a sure way to get caught and executed or whatever the goblins do to trespassers.

Elise adjusts her ponytail and nods. "Lead the way."

"Remind me to buy you a beer after this is all over," I say, climbing over the boulder to my left.

"You're going to buy me a whole dinner at the restaurant of my choice and give me a foot rub," Elise says.

I laugh. "You are not getting a foot rub."

She grins as we walk into the narrow tunnel. "Maybe I'll let Patrick give me the foot rub instead."

I look back and raise a brow. "Patrick?"

She nods unapologetically.

"He seems like fun," she says, her eyes going distant.

I shudder and make a gagging noise. "Gross."

The tunnel goes down at a steady pace. After fifteen minutes of walking, we come to another sharp drop, though this one isn't as far as the drop into the tunnels. The ceiling is lower here. Neither of us has to duck, but Reilly wouldn't be able to stand upright here.

I keep my vampire magic close to the surface. I can smell no one has come this way in ages, but we can't risk walking into some kind of goblin patrol. Elise sniffs behind me every minute or so.

"It smells like dirt and magic down here," she says finally.

"Yeah, it's a strange combination," I agree.

I come to a halt. The tunnel splits, heading off in two opposite directions.

"Please tell me you know which way to go," Elise says.

"I think so," I say hesitantly. I take a step toward the tunnel on my right, but the magic halts me. I turn to the left instead.

We walk down the narrow passage quietly. We must be hundreds of feet underground now. It's getting cooler the farther down we go. I stop walking, and Elise almost runs into my back.

"Did you hear that?" I whisper. Something is moving in the distance. The sound is hushed but steady.

"Yeah," Elise says, leaning her head back and inhaling deeply. "I think it might be water."

We walk closer, taking care to be as quiet as possible just in case it isn't water making the noise. The sound grows louder as we approach until the rush of rapids is unmistakable.

The tunnel curves to the right and ends abruptly, dumping us out onto a small ledge with a long drop into a roaring river. A light spray of water hits my feet and legs.

"How far across is this thing?" Elise says, having to raise her voice to be heard.

I squint my eyes and peer across. There's absolutely no light down here, so even my vampire side is struggling to see very far.

"Too far to jump," I say.

"We can't swim in that," Elise says, bracing her hand against the wall to look over the edge and downstream. The ledge we're on is narrow and barely wide enough for three people to stand shoulder to shoulder.

"We might have to," I say, scooting toward the edge as well. My foot slips as a piece of rock breaks free. Elise grabs my arm, dragging me backward.

"Be careful," she snaps.

"Wait, did you hear that?" I ask.

"Hear what?"

"Exactly," I say, crouching down. "The rocks didn't hit the water."

I get on my knees and look directly down. The edge of something is bobbing in the water. I slide my hand down and feel that the ledge we're standing on curves back underneath us. I touch something that tickles my wrist and jerk back with a yelp. Elise yanks me backward.

"Sorry, sorry!" I say, rubbing my hand and shaking off the goosebumps. "It surprised me, but I think it was just a rope."

Elise huffs at me. "You're trying to give me a heart attack between the passing out and the almost falling and now the screaming."

"Shut up, it's creepy when you can't see what you're touching," I say as I lean back over the edge. Elise keeps a hand on my shoulder. I pat around until I find the rope again and tug on it. I can feel some resistance, but whatever is attached to the end slowly moves toward me.

I look down over the edge and see a small boat attached to the end of the rope. I look back up at Elise.

"How do you feel about whitewater rafting?" I ask with a grin.

---

"I will say again, that this is a bad idea," Elise says.

"Just get in the boat," I repeat. The wood is digging into my knees, and the bouncing motion is becoming unsettling. I want to get this over with.

Elise sighs, but slides down and drops into the boat in front of me. The entire thing wobbles and I dig my fingers into the sides and grit my teeth. I hate boats.

"Give me the paddle," she says, reaching her hand back while the other is latched onto the front of the boat.

I shove the paddle up toward her. She grabs it, holding onto it like a lifeline.

"It's easier to see down here," I say, my voice shaking just a little.

"Yeah, but all I can see is rapids and boulders," she mutters.

"Fantastic. I'm going to untie the rope now," I say.

Elise nods, and I twist around to untie us from the ledge. The goblins helpfully used a quick-release carabiner to attach the rope to the boat. I push the latch in, and as soon as I release the carabiner, the fast-moving water rushes us away. I scramble for my paddle as the choppy river tips us forward and backward.

"Go left!" Elise shouts, paddling as hard as she can.

I plunge my paddle into the water on the right side of the boat and paddle with her. We move to left just in time to barrel around a huge boulder sticking up out of the water. The current swirls around it and the boat turns sideways as we pass it. Elise jabs the boulder with her paddle and pushes us back straight.

"This is not how I planned on dying," she shouts.

"We're not going to die!" I shout back.

"Shit," she says. "There's a drop!"

I widen my knees and crouch down, hoping that might keep me from falling out. The rushing of the water grows louder. The front end of the boat tilts down. Elise leans back so far she's practically laying in my lap, and I'm doing the same. There's no time to scream before water is splashing over us.

The boat rocks violently and we are thrown in a circle. I paddle as hard as possible, but I can barely tell which direction we're headed in. The boat smacks into a boulder. The wood cracks and water pours over the side as the water traps us against the rock.

I shove against it with my paddle like Elise had done earlier. The boat creaks as we slide, then the current grabs us again. We're slung sideways, bouncing over the rough waves.

We ride the rapids, using our paddles like poles to fend off rocks jutting out of the water. There isn't time to think, only act. We're both drenched, and the onslaught is endless. My hands are almost numb from gripping the paddle so tightly.

"Not again," Elise moans.

The roar of water is even louder than before. There is no way to stop from going over this drop though.

"I can't see over the edge," Elise shouts, scooting backward. My heart pounds in my chest as we hurtle forward.

The nose of the boat goes over the edge, and my heart leaps into my throat. This drop is twice as far as the one before. It's longer than the boat.

We're falling. My knees raise off the rough wood, and I grab the edge with my free hand, desperate not to be flung into the rapids. The boat smacks into the water as it lurches violently, and the spray blinds me. I'm thrown forward, and my hands hit the bow. There's no one in front of me.

"Elise!" I scream, searching the white froth for her. A head bobs up ahead of me. I drop my paddle and scramble forward, leaning over the side and grabbing her as she goes back under.

I drag her up to the side of the boat, but the pull of the current keeps me from pulling her all the way in. She scrabbles at my arms, but we're both wet, and she's slipping away. I push the vampire magic into my arms, giving myself a surge of strength, and drag her back into the boat. She lands on top of me, coughing up water.

The boat bangs against something and cracks loudly. Elise pushes upright and grabs the only remaining paddle. She has a scrape across her chin that is dripping blood.

She shoves us away from the next boulder and the next. I sit behind her, panting and shaky. I wish I hadn't dropped my paddle, but there hadn't been time to do anything else.

"The water is calming down," Elise says, collapsing back onto her butt.

I sigh in relief and slump backward. "Some people do this for fun. They're idiots."

Elise snorts in agreement.

The rocking of the boat ceases, but the speed of the current doesn't slow down.

"I really hope there isn't a massive, deadly waterfall at the end of this," Elise says, staring up at the ceiling of the tunnel that is at least thirty feet overhead.

I kick her leg. "Don't even say that."

Elise grabs the bottom of her shirt and uses it to wipe away the blood on her chin. The scrape is already healing. I could heal it faster, but I can't risk wasting magic like that. Elise doesn't seem concerned about it anyhow.

"Are we still headed in the right direction at least?" Elise asks.

"Yes, we're getting close." Light flickers in the distance and I sit up. "Shit."

"What?" Elise asks, jerking upright. She spots the lights as well and picks up the paddle. "I don't see anywhere to get out of the water."

"Me neither," I say, scanning the river in the distance. The walls of the tunnel grow smoother. The light gets closer and closer. I let out a sigh of relief. "Just torches."

They line the walls with one every five or so feet. They don't use fire. I peer at the odd contraptions curiously. I wonder how they keep them burning. It doesn't seem like this river is traveled very often.

"I guess we're approaching civilization," Elise comments.

The river curves and widens. I notice the water isn't moving quite as fast here. A small wooden dock sticks out of a large, square tunnel opening. Elise paddles toward it, but the river is still moving quickly enough that we're being swept past it faster than she can paddle sideways.

"We have to go down that tunnel," I say frantically. The tug in my gut demands it.

"Then we have to swim," Elise says, still paddling as hard as she can. She's right though, with only one paddle she can't move the boat there.

"Let's do it then," I say.

She drops the paddle, and we both leap into the water at the same time. It's icy cold, freezing my lungs in my chest. I have a sudden fear that there might be some kind of mythological sea creature lurking in the murky green depths.

I paddle hard against the current, kicking my legs as fast as I can. It's slow moving, but we make better progress than we did in the boat. A human would have no hope of making, lucky for us, neither of us is human.

Elise reaches the dock first and reaches back to drag me to it as well. We climb onto the rough wooden boards and flop over, panting and exhausted.

"You always get into the craziest shit," Elise pants.

"I blame the prophecy," I say, breathing just as hard.

Elise snorts and bursts into laughter. I laugh right along with her, it's infectious. Something about being alive after that insanity makes all the worries of the past few weeks seem surreal.

I roll onto my knees and look down the tunnel in front of us. It's different from the others. This one is more well-used and is goblin-made rather than natural like the ones we came through. It's also lit.

"We're going to start running into goblins soon," I say.

"We'll be able to smell them coming," Elise says, tapping the side of her nose.

"Doesn't mean we'll have anywhere to hide," I say.

She shrugs. "That is a problem for future us."

We stand, and I ring out my shirt. The weight of water is threatening to drag my jeans down my hips.

"I did not dress with swimming in mind," I mutter.

"No kidding," Elise says, shaking water off her pistol. "It's good Glocks don't mind a little dirty water."

My hands fly to my jacket pockets, and I'm relieved to find there are at least a few vials still there. I take the remaining ones out to see which I lost. I hadn't even thought about it when we first got in the boat.

"Ready?" Elise asks.

"Yeah," I say, slipping the vials back in my jacket. "Let's get this over with."

A rush of wind blows across my face. I stop in my tracks. I didn't think there could be wind in caves.

"Did you feel that?" I ask, looking back at Elise. She nods.

I hurry forward and hear an odd noise, like someone is blowing across the top of a bottle. There is an opening in the wall of the tunnel. It's barely a foot tall, but it's twice as wide. Elise and I have to lean over to look through it.

"Holy shit," I whisper reverently.

The sight that stretches out beneath us is breathtaking. The city is massive, lights twinkling in the twisting spires as far as I can see. Thick support pillars extend from the floor of the cavern all the way to the ceiling. They must be a thousand feet tall.

There are squat, sturdy buildings and narrow ones that twist upward so far I'm not sure how they don't snap off. A perfect grid of streets is laid out among the buildings. Small patches of color lit by warm light appear to be gardens.

An enormous lake that takes up a full third of the

cavern is fed by a waterfall from the river. Boats, much bigger than the canoe we were in, dot the still surface of the lake. Steam puffs out of a large industrial building near the edge of the lake.

This is more than a city. There's an entire self-contained civilization down there.

"No wonder they haven't been in a rush to join the rest of society," Elise whispers.

The steady tap of footsteps interrupts our admiration. We jump back from the window and look around for any way to hide, but the smooth tunnel walls don't provide any options.

I grab Elise and drag her back the way we came. We go around the turn and press our backs against the wall, trying to breathe quietly.

The footsteps get closer and closer. Then they stop. I keep my eyes on the curve of the tunnel, sure that a goblin is going to appear any second.

"All clear on Skywalk," a gravelly voice says. He smells like metal and stone.

The footsteps start again but heading in the opposite direction. My shoulders slump in relief.

Elise nods in the direction of the goblin, and I nod back. We creep after him silently. Far enough behind the guard that we can't see him, but close enough to hear him.

The tunnel becomes more complicated, splitting off multiple times. The torches shift into odd little lanterns that glow softly. I keep mistaking it for daylight even though it can't be. The floors are smooth and well-traveled.

Every so often an opening appears with stairs leading down. I pause near one of the doorways, the tug in my gut pulling my attention toward as I try to walk past.

I point down the stairway and Elise nods. I feel jittery leaving our guard behind. It's easier when you know where the person you are hiding from is located. It's terrifying when they might appear in front of you at any moment and there is nowhere to hide.

The stairwell ends in a somewhat open room. Pillars, delicately carved with alternating patterns, support the ceiling.

New footsteps echo behind us. Elise and I rush toward the opening on the opposite side of the room. It's not until we're three steps down that I realize guards are coming from this direction too.

I skid to a halt and Elise tumbles into my back, but it's too late. Two goblins wearing leather vests and red linen pants appear in front of us.

"Trespassers!" One shouts. The other lifts his hand toward us and the ground beneath our feet groans and moves.

Elise drags me back up the stairs, and we sprint across the open room. Another pair of guards run out of the other stairwell.

I fall flat on my face as something bites into my legs. The stone floor is sucking me down like it's quicksand.

"Olivia!" Elise shouts, scrambling back to my side. Her hands and knees sink into the stone.

"I'm here to see a friend!" I shout at the guards, no longer trying to struggle. I can't break the stone. "She's one of you. She's a goblin, her name is Maybelle. It's about the Day of Breaking!"

One of the guards flinches at the mention of the prophecy.

"I know what the key to the prophecy is," I press on. "I have to talk to her, please!"

The guards stand in a circle around us. One of

them, the only one wearing a cape, steps up in front of me.

"What would a human know of the prophecy?" He demands, looking down at me with cold violet eyes.

"I'm not human," I say, smiling at him with a mouth full of fangs.

He hisses and lifts his hand. The stone tightens around my legs.

"Wait, wait!" I shout. "I'm not a vampire either. Let me show you. I'm a witch."

"That is not possible," he growls, anger darkening his face.

"Don't freak out," I say. I lift my free hand and push the electric magic into a small sphere. It crackles brightly. The goblins all take a step back. I close my hand, and the magic is snuffed out.

The goblin in charge narrows his eyes.

"They have come to assassinate the king!" One of them exclaims, pointing a bony finger in my direction.

Elise rolls her eyes. "I'm a JHAPI agent, not an assassin. We are here because we need to speak with Olivia's friend. Cesare Sangiovanni intends on releasing the Bound God."

A quiet gasp travels through the group.

"The vampire council would allow this?" The goblin leader asks, crossing his arms.

"They don't know about it," I explain.

"Bind them," the goblin says.

The other guards move around us, clapping thick cuffs around our wrists. The stone flows away from my feet and smooths back into the ground like it never happened. I had no idea goblins had magic like that.

We are put in the middle of the guards and led down the stairwell. The tug in my gut says we're headed in the right direction. The nasty looks we're getting from the goblins don't exactly fill me with confidence though.

---

"This is a disaster," Elise says, leaning her head back against the stone wall. She's being held in a separate cell across from me.

"Could be worse," I say, stretching my legs out in front of me. "We could have drowned."

She snorts out a laugh. "Right."

"I hope this wasn't a huge mistake," I whisper.

"You had to try," Elise says with a shrug.

"I can practically feel Reilly raging at me right now."

"I bet they're all throwing a fit. Poor Zachary," Elise laughs. "He's an angel for volunteering to stay behind."

"Or just smart," I say, nudging at a loose pebble with my finger. "Maybe he knew we were doomed."

"They may not execute us," Elise says thoughtfully. "They may just keep us in these cells until we're old and frail."

"Yeah right," I scoff. "By the time the guards got us back here, they seemed convinced we were assassins. Shitty assassins, but definitely up to no good."

There's a crash from the direction of the guards. I scramble over to the iron bars attempt to peer down the hallway, but the cells are slightly recessed. I can't see anything.

Quick footsteps head toward us, and a squat goblin appears, panting. His face looks strangely familiar.

"Gerard?" I demand in shock.

"You're later than I expected," he says.

Another goblin with curly red hair held up by a lime green scarf and light scars on her green face appears behind him.

"You really got yourself in trouble this time," Maybelle says with a fond smile.

My eyes go wide, and a smile spreads across my face.

"Maybelle! How did you even know we were down here?" I ask as Gerard kneels in front of my cell and begins fiddling with the lock.

"I've been keeping an ear out," Gerard explains. The lock opens with a pop, and the door swings outward. "I knew you'd be here soon."

"Who is this?" Maybelle asks suspiciously as she points at Elise.

"Agent Elise Hawking, she's-"

"Agent?" Maybelle barks angrily. "You brought one of them into this?"

"She's my friend, and she's trustworthy. She understands what's at stake," I snap back. "Get her out too."

Maybelle groans in frustration but nods at Gerard, who seems to be waiting for her approval. He kneels down and works on the lock to Elise's cell.

"Hurry," Maybelle hisses.

"I am," Gerard growls at her. The lock clicks open, and Elise hurries out of her cell.

"What now?" I ask.

Maybelle lifts her hand and a wave of magic splashes against my skin. I stumble with an embarrassing squeak. My arms are green, and my fingers are long and delicate.

"What the actual fuck?" I exclaim, looking at Maybelle in horror.

"It's just an illusion. I disguised you as guards," she says. "Now, come on."

I look down and see that I am wearing the red pants and leather vest we saw on the other guards. The goblin version of Elise looks at me, her face reflecting exactly how I feel. This is creepy. I want my body back.

We walk down the hallway. Two guards lay unconscious on the floor. Maybelle was not gentle with them. A short stairway leads back up to what is basically the ground level of the city.

I look around, nervous that we'll be spotted.

"Just act normal," Maybelle says, elbowing me in the side.

I straighten my back and try to look like I belong. Ahead near the doorway are two guards, but they're lounging in wooden chairs sipping on something hot. They nod absently as we pass by and I can barely restrain my sigh of relief.

We climb several more stairways before finally being released out into the city. It's louder down here. The rumble of engines in the distance competes with the rush of the huge waterfall that pours into the lake. I can't stop myself from gawking.

Maybelle takes my elbow and drags me along at a quick pace. The neat grid of the roadways that we saw from the skywalk was deceiving. Only the main roads are aligned in orderly grids. The streets that connect them are winding and confusing.

We pass one of the towering spires. There is a constant stream of goblins going in and out of the arched doorway. The base of the structure is bigger than I expected. They looked so delicate from above.

Gerard stops at a small house set amidst a huddle of larger buildings and unlocks the front door. We're ushered into a small sitting room, and the door is locked behind us. Maybelle waves her hand; the illusions fall away.

Another goblin, younger than Maybelle and Gerard, is sitting at a small table in the middle of the room flipping a knife end over end.

"Welcome to Donheim," he says with a mischievous grin.

"This is Kabs, my nephew," Maybelle says, pointing at the goblin with the knife.

Kabs grins and nods at us, his short black mohawk bobbing with the motion.

The small room we're in has stone floors and a small fireplace built into the wall near the door. A fire is crackling merrily inside it, but there isn't the slightest hint of smoke in the room. To my right, a narrow staircase leads to an upper level.

There's a teal couch across from the table with bright red pillows. It's good to see Maybelle's love of color hasn't changed just because her appearance has.

"How did you know we were coming?" I ask, turning to Gerard.

Gerard smiles showing slightly sharp white teeth. "The same way I knew we'd find you in Pecan Grove. I have the gift of foretelling. It's minor and short-sighted, but it helps when it can."

"You're a prophet? Like the one that prophesied about the Day of Breaking?" I ask, trying to understand.

Gerard waves away my suggestion. "A distant ancestor. There are others that still have his power. I'm not one of those favored families."

"And you," I say pointing at Maybelle. "You turned us into goblins."

"A simple illusion," Maybelle says, shrugging.

"Is that how you made it seem like you were a human for so long?" I ask.

"I worked with an enchanter to create a more powerful version of my magic, but that isn't important right now. What the hell were you thinking trying to sneak in here? Donheim is well guarded, and there are constant patrols. Honestly, I don't know how you survived the trip down the river," she rants. The tone of her voice is so similar to the times she chastised me for trying to date men who weren't good enough for me that I can't help but smile.

"I missed you too," I say fondly, pulling her into another hug that muffles her complaints.

"You came here for a reason. What do you need?" Gerard asks, interrupting our reunion.

I turn to Maybelle. "Cesare Sangiovanni has the spell book you and my mother stole. I need it, and I can't steal it from him on my own."

"Why?" Maybelle asks, eyes widening in horror. "That thing has brought nothing but trouble."

"Cesare wants to release the Bound God. That book has something to do with it," I explain. "I don't know what, all I know is that I have to get it."

"The Bound God," Kabs asks with an incredulous laugh. "You actually believe in that crap?"

"Hush," Maybelle snaps at him.

Kabs stills and his face pinches together and looks at all of us. "You're serious."

"I'm the key to the prophecy, aren't I?" I ask Gerard.

He nods solemnly.

"How long have you known?" I ask, anger churning in my gut. He could have told me.

"I suspected," Gerard says unapologetically. "I've only known for sure since I dreamed that you were coming here for Maybelle's help."

"You don't have to do any of this," Maybelle says, crossing her arms. "Stay down here with us. You could sell your healing salves. I could make you look like a goblin when you need to go out."

"I can't Maybelle," I say, surprised at her. "I can't let everyone I care about get slaughtered. And if this god gets released, Donheim won't be any safer than anywhere else."

Maybelle turns away, pacing the room in agitation.

Elise looks at me with concern. I shrug. I knew convincing Maybelle wouldn't be easy, but I hoped she would come around once I mentioned the Bound God.

Gerard sighs and rubs his fingers over his eyes. "She's right, Maybelle. You can't hide from this any more than she can. You've known that for a long time."

"I don't believe in fate," Maybelle growls at him. "I make my own way, always have."

"This isn't about fate," Gerard growls back. "You set things in motion when you stole that book, and these are the consequences."

Maybelle continues to pace, her hands clenched into fists at her side.

"Come on, Auntie," Kabs pipes up. "It's not like you to back down from a challenge. Stealing from a vampire sounds like a good time."

Maybelle shoots Kabs a glare before turning back to face me and crossing her arms.

"You'll do as I say without question," Maybelle

says, finally agreeing to help us. "There will be no unnecessary heroics. No stealing anything else. And we are not going to try to kill Cesare."

I nod quickly. "I just want the book. None of us have a hope of killing Cesare on our own."

"I want to help," Kabs says, twirling the knife around and slipping it back into the sheath at his waist. "You'll need me anyhow."

Maybelle presses her lips together in disapproval. "I don't want you mixed up in this."

Kabs rolls his eyes dramatically. "Where have I heard that before?"

"Let Kabs go," Gerard says, his eyes distant. His words feel heavy like they mean something.

Maybelle looks at his expression and deflates. "Fine. Let's all rush headlong into danger and certain death."

"Do you really think we don't have a chance of doing this successfully?" I ask, sinking down into a chair by the table.

Maybelle sighs and shakes her head. "If we're careful, and if you all listen to me, we can do it. Probably."

"What's the plan then?" I ask, leaning forward.

"How well do you know the layout of the clanhouse?" Maybelle asks.

"Fairly well," I say, thinking back to the multi-storied mansion. "It's fairly straightforward. I saw the spellbook in Cesare's study."

"We'll go in during the day," Maybelle says.

Gerard shuffles around the furnace, swinging a pot over the fire. The smell of some kind of herby soup fills the lower level as Maybelle goes through the details of her plan. My stomach growls. I have no idea how long we were wandering in the tunnels before we made it here, or how long they had us in those cells.

With the planning complete, Gerard dishes up bowls of a thick, creamy soup. Elise sniffs it suspiciously before eating, but I shovel it in my mouth without question. I'm too hungry to be picky. It's weird, but not really bad.

"You work with JHAPI?" Kabs asks, looking at Elise and me.

Elise nods. "I've been with the agency for five years."

"Maybelle and Gerard won't talk about their time on the surface," Kabs says, leaning forward. "What are humans like? Scared of everything?"

"Have you never been out of Donheim?" I ask, stirring the hot soup to cool it down.

He shakes his head. "No one really leaves Donheim," Kabs explains. "And if they do, they never come back. Except for these two idiots."

Maybelle rolls her eyes. "It's no better or worse than Donheim."

I smile as the two continue to bicker. Maybelle seems fond of Kabs.

After dinner, Maybelle shows me and Elise the small room we'll be sharing tonight. Or today. I pause, realizing I can't quite feel if the sun is up or not.

Elise heads back to the living room to take Kabs up on his challenge to a game of chess. Maybelle gets two glasses of red juice that smells like strawberries and plums and leads me out to a small balcony, leaving the door open behind us. I sit down beside her and stare in awe at the view. It's dark on the lake, but the water is dotted by the lights of fishing boats. The bright points bob and move around the lake like slow-moving stars.

"It's beautiful," I say.

She nods. "I suppose it is. I haven't appreciated it in years."

"Why?" I ask.

"The closer you are to the lake, the less you matter here. Humans value waterside properties, but goblins don't view it the same. Fishermen are not necessarily poor, but the work they do isn't really respected. Being near the lake is either a necessity or all you can afford," she says with a sigh. "Let's just say I've lived by the lake for a long time."

"What have you been doing here since you got back?" I ask.

"Getting people what they need," Maybelle says with a wan smile. "Gerard and I have always been good at that."

The cafe back in Pecan Grove was the most popular restaurant in town. If the apothecary had opened, it would have been just as successful. Maybelle had been universally loved by the townspeople.

"I'm sure you're the toast of the town," I say taking a swig of my red juice.

She snorts. "Hardly. We came back here out of desperation. We're surviving, but no one was happy to see us."

"Except Kabs?" I ask, looking back over my shoulder. He's laughing at the table with Elise, apparently winning the game of chess.

Maybelle shakes her head. "He ended up in the same rough spot I did at his age. The family kicked him out; I was glad to take him in. He's bright and motivated, he just doesn't always use his head before he acts." She takes a drink then looks at me slyly. "Like someone else I know."

I huff out a laugh. "I've gotten better at that."

She raises her brows.

"I have!" I exclaim. "I've been handling my problems like an adult."

"Says the woman that snuck in here with no plan and now wants to rob a vampire," Maybelle says. "Again, with no plan."

"It worked out," I say, grinning. "And you came up with a plan."

Maybelle shakes her head, and we fall silent as we look out over the lake. The twinkling lights of the boats bobbing across the surface make it look like the night sky is at our feet.

"We can do this, right?" I ask quietly. "We can stop him?"

Maybelle is silent for a moment before responding. "Of course."

The sun has been up for an hour. I tap my fingers against my thigh impatiently. The mossy ground beneath my feet is slightly damp. Elise is much better at waiting than I am. She is relaxed and leaning against a tree.

We're on a hill overlooking the clanhouse. The house is huge, but the estate it sits on is even bigger.

"How much longer?" I ask.

Maybelle lowers her strange, silvery binoculars (though I was informed earlier that they are *not* binoculars, they are a feat of goblin artistry) and gives me a look. "I can't summon neckers out of the house with my mind. We wait until someone leaves, then we intercept them. You know the plan."

Elise stands up straight. "I heard a door."

Maybelle scans the house, then nods. "I see them. There are five, more than enough."

Our small group follows Maybelle down the hill. She moves like someone much younger, and unexpectedly fast considering she's barely four feet tall. Kabs takes up the rear.

The neckers are walking towards an SUV parked around the back of the house; laughing and joking around if looking a little tired. They don't see us coming.

Elise kicks the first person in the side of the face then grabs the next closest one by the shoulder and jerks him around to face her, cracking him across the jaw. They both fall to the ground in a heap. Maybelle has a stranglehold on one of them, her hand tight over their mouth. Kabs has managed to wrestle the fourth to the ground and is punching them enthusiastically.

I grab the third from behind, pouring a thin line of knockout brew onto their face. She slumps in my arms, and I lower her to the ground. I quickly dose the rest of them lightly. They're humans, and they've been fed on; it doesn't take much to knock them out. They'll be out for at least an hour. If that's not long enough, then something has gone terribly wrong.

We drag the unconscious neckers into the garden behind the house and stuff them in a hedge.

"Come here," Maybelle whispers to Kabs. She focuses on one necker and puts her hand on Kabs shoulder. He morphs into a perfect doppelgänger of the man Elise knocked out. Maybelle repeats the process, making each of us look like a different necker.

My body doesn't feel different, and if I stare at my hand hard enough, I can see my real body beneath the illusion. That takes away some of the creep-factor. Maybelle's magic hasn't actually changed me. It really is just an illusion.

"So, we just walk in?" Elise asks.

"Yep," I reply. "We look like we belong. It shouldn't raise any suspicion."

"Just don't talk to anyone," Maybelle says before brushing past us and starting toward the house.

I follow her, Kabs and Elise hurrying after us.

Maybelle walks up to the door the neckers exited and opens it. I hold my breath as we go inside. This is insane. We're walking into Cesare's clanhouse, where he is probably sleeping right now, to steal something from his personal study. My mother would be so proud. I smirk to myself. The best part is that she actually would be.

I move up beside Maybelle and lead the group through the somewhat familiar house. I didn't spend any time wandering around while I was here, but I learned the basic layout. The ground level is feeding rooms, a kitchen, and a small medical area with brews for emergencies. The second level has more feeding rooms and a lounge with televisions and games. The rooms are all off in the different wings that are set aside for the older vampires that Cesare sired. Cesare's study is on the top floor. Of course.

I lead us up the sloping staircase and past the stained glass. Maybelle has to drag Kabs away from some of the art. Based on the whispers I'm overhearing, I think he wants to steal it.

Laughter rings out ahead, and my heart pounds in my chest. I'm irrationally afraid the illusions are going to fail as the two women round the corner. They stop laughing when they see us and look coldly at Elise. Well, at whoever they think Elise is.

We don't see anyone on the next level which gives the house a creepy, deserted feel. I know they're all just sleeping, but it makes me antsy. We walk up the final flight of stairs and I hesitate. This place all looks the same after a while.

"This way," I whisper, turning to the left. The hallway grows darker as we approach the study. The door lacks the guards it had last time, but I know it's the right one.

I point out the door. Maybelle walks over and

looks around, then crouches in front of it, deftly pulling a small lock-picking kit from her pocket. She picks the lock before I can ask how long it's going to take and the door swings inward. It's dark in the study; the fireplace is not lit this time. I walk in first, barely daring to breathe as I scan the room. It's empty, but I feel watched being in Cesare's area of the house.

Maybelle and Elise follow me inside while Kabs stays by the door and watches the hall.

"Where is it?" Elise whispers.

"I don't know," I whisper back as I pull on the vampire magic to increase my sense of smell. There is a lingering scent of old leather and magic in the room. I walk to Cesare's desk and begin poking around.

Elise and Maybelle spread out in the room moving books around and looking behind picture frames. I run my hand on the bottom of his desk. My fingers hit a bump. I drop to my knees and inspect it. The wood is slightly worn just behind the knot; I push on it firmly, and it slides backward. A soft click emanates from the desk as a panel cracks open.

"There's a safe," Maybelle says, rushing to the side of the desk.

The entire side panel swings open. Inside is a small black safe, an old one with a bronze dial and handle.

"Can you get it open?" I ask. "Or do we need to break it?"

Maybelle gives me a look. "Can I get it open? Of course, I can." She leans down and presses her ear to black metal, then begins to turn the dial slowly.

Kabs looks back and waves at us urgently. I run over to his side and peer out of the crack in the door. A man in a black suit with a gun clearly visible is walking down the hall. I shut the door, keeping the handle turned until it's fully closed, then releasing it slowly to avoid a click.

I turn toward Elise and Maybelle and press my fingers to my lips, then lean against the door and listen. The guard walks closer and pauses in front of the door. I hold my breath. His shoes squeak on the hardwood floor, then his footsteps lead away again.

I slump in relief and wait until he's headed back down the stairs to crack the door open again. Kabs nods at me and takes up position to watch the hall once again.

"I've got it," Maybelle says.

I hurry over to her side as she opens the door to the safe. There are a couple of odd trinkets inside, but the only thing I care about it the creased, leather-bound book inside. It smells so strongly of magic that my nose twitches.

I reach my hand inside and pick it up, careful to not brush against anything else in the safe. It's heavier than I expected. A strange symbol is engraved on the outside.

"That's it," Maybelle confirms.

"Let's get out of here," I whisper. Adrian had hinted there was something else for me to find at Cesare's, but without any idea what it is, I can't risk wandering around looking for it.

"Wait," Maybelle says. She grabs a book off the shelf from the other side of the room and hurries back over to me. The book morphs into an exact copy of the spell book I'm holding.

"How long will it last?" I ask.

"Until he opens it and realizes it's a fake," Maybelle says, setting the copy back in the safe and closing it. "Knowing it's fake will shatter an illusion like this one."

Kabs looks back at us. "Still clear, we should go now."

We file out of the study, shutting the door behind us. My stomach twists with the urgency to get out of here. It's hard to walk when all my instincts are telling me to run.

A door opens ahead of us, and a bleary-eyed necker stumbles out. His hair is sticking up in every direction and dried blood is flaking off his neck. He scratches his stomach and glances at our group, then pads past us. Hopefully on his way to take a shower.

"Katie!" A man says sharply behind us. Shit. I was distracted by the necker in front of us and didn't hear him. We all come to a stop and I hesitantly turn around. The man is walking toward us with a puzzled expression on his face. He's looking right at me. Dammit. I deftly move the spell book behind my back as I turn to face the necker.

"Yes?" I ask with a tense smile, hoping he is actually talking to me.

"What are you doing here? I thought you were going into the city today," he says, suspicious.

"Change of plans," I say with a shrug.

He throws his hands up and rolls his eyes. "Then I need your help downstairs. I let you have the day off for your errands, not so you could wander the house."

"My bad," I say, wiggling the spell book behind me. If I'm going to have to go with this guy, I can't keep it with me. Elise takes it and I try to look appropriately apologetic. "What did you need help with again?"

His irritation shifts into anger. "Don't be stupid. Come on," he says, turning and heading away from the group.

I look back over my shoulder. Elise is watching

me tensely. I mouth *just go*. Elise tries to follow me anyhow, but Maybelle grabs her elbow. She pushes Kabs after me instead, her touch morphing him into a replica of the man I'm following.

I nod and hurry after the man. My heart is pounding out of my chest. Elise has the book. She can get it out. That's the most important thing.

The man leads me to a massive industrial style kitchen and shoves a tray into my hands. "Get the meal ready."

The meal. Right. There are three refrigerators and a pantry big enough to hold a party in.

"Is a sandwich okay?" I ask hesitantly.

The man looks at me like I'm crazy. "You can give him a plate full of mustard for all I care. We just have to keep him alive."

What the fuck.

"Yeah, of course," I say, opening the closest refrigerator. The amount of food is overwhelming. I grab an apple and string cheese and put it on the plate. The necker is busy working on something else, so I grab a single serve bag of baby carrots. It's a balanced meal for whoever they have. Sort of. It doesn't sound like they treat him all that well.

Kabs steps around the corner into the kitchen, hidden by the refrigerator door, but I shake my head and mouth, *wait*. I want to know who they are keeping prisoner, and why.

"You done?" He asks.

I nod and point at the tray. "Yep."

Kabs slinks back around the corner and I shut the refrigerator door.

He gives me another look. "You're acting really weird."

"Sorry," I say, drooping my shoulders so that I look a little tired. "Got a little carried away last night, then didn't sleep well." I really need him to buy this act and stop being suspicious.

"Right," he says slowly. "Whatever, let's get this over with."

He picks up a bucket of water from the sink and leads me out of the kitchen. We go down a staircase I hadn't seen last time I was here. It's narrow and dark. The stairs aren't museum quality like the rest of the house, they're rough-hewn wooden planks. Kabs creeps quietly behind us, something the human necker wouldn't be able to hear. At least I have backup.

The clean walls of the upper levels give way to cold stone. I look around curiously as we descend two more levels of stairs. We reach an open area and I stop in my tracks. This is a dungeon. There are six cells carved right into the stone with dull metal bars. It would be pitch black down here if it wasn't for the bright light coming from one of the cells.

The necker walks up to the cell and I hurry to catch up.

"Bucket," he says to whoever is in the cell.

The prisoner, a rough looking man with the beginnings of a beard and jet black hair, walks up to the cell door with an empty bucket. The necker pours the fresh water into the bucket then waves me forward. There is a small space at the bottom of the bars to slide the tray.

I meet the man's eyes and the strength of his magic almost overwhelms me. It's dark, almost smoky, and intoxicating. I want to drink it down. Understanding clicks in my brain. This is what Adrian meant in his letter. The other thing worth finding.

With a sharp, quick motion I smack the tray into the base of the necker's skull and he drops like a bag of rocks. The prisoner freezes, looking at me in surprise.

"What the hell are you doing, Olivia?" Kabs asks from behind me, still looking like a perfect copy of the necker I just knocked out.

The prisoner looks at the man on the floor, then back up at Kabs, clearly confused.

"We have to get him out," I say to Kabs.

"No," the prisoner says, speaking for the first time. "You're not taking me anywhere."

"Are you seriously refusing to be rescued?" I ask, incredulous.

The prisoner crosses his arms and plants his feet. "Yes."

"Why?" I demand, stepping up to the bars.

"None of your business," the man hisses. "Now get out!"

I narrow my eyes. "No. I don't know why, but I need you. You're coming with us."

"You don't even know who I am, why do you think you need me?" He asks, taking a few steps back.

"What do you know about the prophecy of the Day of Breaking?" I ask.

He laughs. "Plenty. Too much in fact."

"I'm the key to the prophecy," I say, trying not to sound pretentious.

The man's face shifts, then he shakes his head. "It doesn't matter."

"What are you talking about? Of course it matters. I can still stop Cesare," I insist, smacking my hand against the bars.

"It doesn't matter," he says, walking back up to the bars until he is inches from my faces, "because the Bound God has already been released."

"What? How? When?" I ask, all the color draining from my face.

"Which question do you want me to answer first?" He responds sarcastically.

"When?" I ask again, my voice edging into a growl.

"The night of the full moon," he says.

Four days ago? I pinch my brows together. Nothing has happened. The world hasn't ended, at least it hadn't before Elise and I got to the goblin city.

"Why hasn't he brought about the apocalypse yet?" I ask.

"I don't know, you'll have to ask him," the prisoner mocks, snorting in derision.

"How was he released?" I ask, gritting my teeth.

"I set him free," the prisoner says, turning away. He rolls his shoulders like he's trying to work out tension. "I did it."

I step back, stunned. "Why?"

"So many questions," the prisoner says. "None of this matters. It's done. Run far away from here and try to survive whatever comes next."

"No," I growl out. "I'm not running. If the god has been released, I'll just have to kill him."

"And how do you think you're going to do that?" The prisoner asks.

"I'll figure it out." I pull a knockout brew from my pocket and throw it at him. It breaks against his chest despite his attempt to dodge it. He falls flat on his face. "Get the cell open, Kabs. I'm bringing him with us."

"Maybelle is going to kill both of us," Kabs says as he runs up to the cell. He presses his hands against the stone wall. It moves under his hand, creating an opening.

I run into the cell and pick the prisoner up, throwing him over my shoulder with a grunt. "Let's get out of here."

We creep back upstairs and through the silent halls. This place is dead in the early mornings. Most neckers will sleep until two or three in the afternoon at least. That doesn't mean no one is awake though.

A shout from above us has me stopping in my tracks.

*"Wake Cesare up! Two neckers have the prisoner!"*

Shit. "Kabs, run," I hiss. They must have had security cameras down there.

We sprint, skidding around a corner in the kitchen. The backdoor is locked, a silent alarm flashing in red above the doorway. I take a half step back, then kick it firmly. The door cracks but doesn't open, so I kick it again. It breaks in half and I force my way out.

We run across the back lawn. I can smell that Maybelle and Elise passed this way recently. I risk a glance behind us; the men are just now exiting the house.

Kabs disappears into the trees ahead of me and I

run faster to catch up to him, letting the sluggish vampire magic give me more strength. Maybelle and Elise appear in front of us and I skid to a halt.

"I specifically said no heroics!" Maybelle hisses at me.

"I need him," I say firmly.

"Why is he unconscious?" Elise asks, pulling her gun.

"I had to knock him out," I say uncomfortably.

"He didn't want to be rescued," Kabs explains. "Refused our help and tried to make us leave."

"You…" Maybelle throws her hands up in exasperation. "You *kidnapped* some necker—"

"He's a witch," I interrupt. "I don't know what kind. I've never felt anything like him before, but he's powerful."

"Well, there's no going back now," Elise says. "Let's get out of here."

"Elise, you take Kabs," I say. "Maybelle, get on my back. Elise and I can run faster than either of you."

Maybelle looks skeptical, but she climbs on my back, wrapping her arms around the unconscious witch instead of my neck. It's awkward, but it'll have to work.

Elise runs ahead of me, Kabs gleefully clinging to her back. I'm glad someone is having fun. The sound of our human pursuers fades as we quickly outstrip them. Our car is parked over two miles away. I won't be able to keep this pace up the entire way.

"Elise, slow down," I gasp. She slows to a jog and I catch up to run beside her. "I can't hear them anymore, can you?"

"No," Elise says, not out of breath at all. "We'll make it back to the car."

We run the rest of the way in silence, both of us listening intently for any sign that they're catching up. Roots stick out of the uneven ground, threatening to trip me with every step I take.

The car is parked on a deserted, dead-end road that winds through the forest. Maybelle climbs down from my back and Kabs hops off Elise.

"Looks alright," Maybelle says uneasily.

"I don't smell anyone," Elise comments.

We hurry over to the car and pile inside. The witch is stuffed in the backseat between Elise and Kabs while Maybelle claims shotgun. I crank the engine and peel out.

---

The prisoner is tied to a chair, still unconscious. Elise and Kabs have gone to get us food and phone chargers since both of our phones are dead. Maybelle is pacing the motel room floor.

I have read and re-read the translation of the same passage in the spell book at least five times. It's wrong to call it a spell book. It's half spell book, half Izul's diary. He was a brilliant man, but he let Aris influence him to use that intelligence in terrible ways.

*We captured Cadriel, but to really kill him, he must be drained of his magic. The idea that we must create another abomination to kill the first one is unthinkable. I will keep the knowledge for now, just in case we must use this last resort.*

"We might have had a couple of days without Cesare looking for us if you hadn't taken him," Maybelle says, interrupting my thoughts.

I close the book with a sigh. "I know, but I couldn't leave him there."

Maybelle rubs her bony fingers down her face then looks at me. "What's done is done."

Guilt at dragging Maybelle into this mess settles in the pit of my stomach. I grab my wallet and pull out the shiny black credit card I never gave back to Reilly.

"Go back to Donheim," I say, holding out Reilly's credit card to her. "This will get a rental car and whatever else you and Kabs want to take back with you."

"No," Maybelle says pushing my hand away. "I'm seeing this through."

There is a quick rap on the door then Elise and Kabs walk in. The smell of delicious, fried food hits me. My stomach rumbles.

"He's still out?" Elise asks.

"Yep, but he should be waking up any minute now," I say as she hands me a bag of food.

Elise unpacks the chargers and plugs in our phones. "Find anything else in that book?"

"Nothing I haven't already shown you," I say, tapping my fingers against it.

A groan draws my attention to the prisoner. He twitches and I watch him impatiently. Waking up after being hit with a knock-out brew is a slow process. Your brain wants to stay asleep, but your body is hopped up on adrenaline as it tries to fight off the effects of the brew.

His eyes snap open and he tries to move, but we bound him tightly to the chair. He isn't going anywhere.

"Wha...th...fu..." He slurs.

"Finally," I mutter. I walk over to stand right in

front of him, grabbing his face to get him to focus. "Hey, what is your name?"

He jerks his face out of my grip and he looks around the dirty motel room. "None of your fucking business," he snaps in anger. "You have no idea what you've done."

"Fill me in then," I say, spreading my hands wide. "All I do know is that you, supposedly, released the Bound God even though you know about the prophecy. So far, you sound like an asshole."

He bares his teeth at me. "You sound like an idiot."

"Oh no, now my feelings are hurt," I say sarcastically. "Are you going to insult me or give me answers?"

Elise flicks her claws out behind me, shifting just enough for her hands and teeth to begin to change. "Answers would be good," she agrees with a threatening grin.

The prisoner snorts and rolls his eyes. "You don't scare me."

Elise sighs. "I told you this wasn't going to work."

"Maybe Staci will want to test her new truth potion on this guy," I say, gritting my teeth.

"If what he's saying it true, we don't have that kind of time," Elise says, shaking her head. "We have to contact JHAPI soon and we can't sit around in this motel room waiting for him to come to his senses."

"Fine, call Zachary if the phone is charged enough," I say. "We should warn them at least."

"Let me go," the prisoner growls.

"No," Elise and I say in unison.

"You have no reason to keep me," he insists.

"Explain to me why you let the god loose, and I'll consider letting you go," I say, leaning down to speak to him at eye level.

"Cesare would have killed me if I hadn't," he spits out.

"Lie," I say, crossing my arms.

"What are you?" he asks, narrowing his eyes. "You aren't a werewolf like that one," he says jerking his chin toward Elise. "You can't hear my heartbeat."

"Give me your name and I'll tell you," I say.

He stares at me, still furious. "Felix Rust."

I don't recognize that name. Maybe Zachary or Reilly will. "I'm half witch, half vampire," I tell him, holding up my end of the bargain.

His eyes go wide. "You're like him," he whispers.

I snort. "Yeah, an abomination according to Izul. Key to the prophecy has a better ring to it though."

"The prophecy is just meant to comfort foolish people that don't want to understand how the world works," Felix sneers. "I don't care about it. I only want to protect—" He trails off without finishing his sentence and shakes his head.

"How can you say you don't care about the prophecy? It came true. You caused the Day of Breaking," I say, throwing my hands in the air.

"Of course the prophecy came true," Felix sneers. "You trap someone powerful, eventually they are going to get loose. It was the inevitability of failure, not fate."

"What are you trying to protect if you don't care about stopping Cadriel?" I demand.

"My granddaughter," Felix bites out. "Justine. After Cesare captured me he told me I could either help, or he would kill her. If Cesare could get to me, then I have no doubt he could get to her too."

I rub my temples. "It still doesn't make sense. If Cadriel has been loose for days why didn't he immediately attack?"

Felix sighs. "He was weak. He couldn't even stand when he first re-entered this world."

"Why? And what do you mean he re-entered this world?"

"Ignorant children," Felix mutters before responding. "What do you know about the nocte viator? The shadow walkers."

"That they died out a long time ago and they could travel in shadows or something," I say, trying to remember exactly what Hu had said about them.

"Wrong and wrong," Felix says with a sigh. "The shadow walkers while in the cover of darkness manipulates space and time to travel to a realm that is outside of both. Time passes differently there; sometimes slower and sometimes faster. If you travel in that realm you could end up somewhere completely unintended in the physical realm if you don't know what you're doing."

That explains the bright light Cesare had on this guy in that prison cell. The blinds are all open and the late evening sunlight is still pouring into the room, but the sun will be setting soon. Felix has just been buying time and waiting for the sun to set. He knew we couldn't keep him here.

"And Cadriel was trapped there?" I ask.

Felix nods. "A shadow walker can bring anyone and anything into the realm if they are strong enough."

"But that person can't get out unless they can use that type of magic?" I ask. It's starting to make sense.

"Correct," Felix says.

"Let me guess, you and Justine are the last two shadow walkers left in the world?" I ask.

"Most likely," Felix says, his eyes distant. "Cadriel began hunting the shadow walkers hundreds of years ago trying to steal the magic. After he failed, and we trapped him in the shadow realm, Izul tried to finish the job. He thought that if the magic died out, then Cadriel would be as good as dead. Some of my ancestors hid in the shadow realm for years in order to avoid being slaughtered, and so, we survived. Unfortunately."

"You really think it would have been better for Izul to have succeeded?" I ask, horrified.

"This magic is a curse," Felix snaps. "Even to this day we are hunted, not to be slaughtered, but to be *used*. Cesare isn't the first, and he won't be the last."

"Look," I say, rubbing my hands down my face. "We can't keep you here. I know you're gone as soon as the sun sets, but if there is anything you know that might help me kill Cadriel, please tell me."

"There is no way you can win," Felix says. "Just run and hope for the best."

I grit my teeth and turn my back on him. "Let's call Zachary."

Elise turns her phone on and it immediately buzzes with missed calls and messages. "Zachary has called nine time," Elise says, looking worried.

She dials his number and puts the phone on speaker. It rings twice.

"Elise?" Zachary asks, sounding somewhat frantic.

"Yes, what's going on?" She asks.

"The witch council was attacked last night. It was a massacre, only one of the council members survived. No one knows who is responsible, and the witches are refusing to let JHAPI inside." he says. "Whatever is in there has them terrified."

"Shit," I say, sitting down heavily on the bed.

"Zach, the Bound God has already been released," Elise says, glaring at Felix. "It must have been him that attacked the council."

"You and Olivia need to get back here as soon as

you can," Zachary says, fear evident in his voice. "Reilly has been...angry since Olivia left. We talked him out of trying to work with the coven, but I don't know if that will last."

"If the coven shows up, I'm killing Alexandra Hunt," I spit out angrily. "If Reilly tries to stop me, I'll kill him too."

"We'll have your back, but I hope it doesn't come to that," Zachary says with a sigh.

Felix looks at me curiously. "What do you have against Alexandra Hunt?" he asks.

"She killed my mother," I say before turning back to the phone. "Zachary, as soon as the sun sets Cesare is going to know that he was robbed. Tell Reilly and make sure no one goes back the clanhouse."

"What do we do now that this thing is loose?" Zachary asks.

I look down at my hands and spread my palms wide. There is only one choice. "I'm going to Find him, and I'm going to kill him."

"Do you have any idea how to?" Elise asks.

I look up. "The spell book says he has to be drained of magic to have a chance of killing him. That's something I can do if I can get close enough. I have to try."

"You won't be able to just walk up to him," Felix scoffs.

I turn on him, furious. "No shit," I snap. "If you don't have anything helpful to add you can shut up or I'll knock you out again."

"If you want to have a chance of killing Cadriel, you'll have to trap him in the shadow realm again," Felix snaps back.

"And are you volunteering to do this?" I demand.

"No," he says, his face shifting as he decides something. "Can you take someone's magic without killing them?"

"Yes, it just depends on how much I take. If I take all of it, they will die," I explain. "Why?"

"I don't want Cadriel or Cesare to take over the world, but I'm not willing to fight. I'm done being used. Let me find my granddaughter and ensure her safety. After that you can take my magic and do what you want with it," Felix says. "Either way, I'm leaving as soon as the sun sets."

"Why are you offering to help now?" I ask, suspicious of this sudden change in heart.

"Hunt killed my son," Felix says gruffly. "I feel more inclined to help someone that hates her just as much as I do."

"It's a deal then," I say. "How long will it take you to find Justine?"

Felix shrugs. "There is a safe house she is supposed to go to if something every happened to me. If she's there, I'll be back soon."

"And if she isn't?" I ask, narrowing my eyes.

"Then I don't know how long it will take," he says, unconcerned with my desperation. "Wait here for no more than three hours. If I'm not back before then, assume I'm dead and all hope is lost."

"If you can't show me how to use the magic, it will be pointless though," I say, frustrated. "I don't automatically know how to use magic I take."

Felix snorts. "That shouldn't be a problem. I can teach you."

"Can you teach me in a couple of hours?" I ask.

"Were you not listening to the part where I can manipulate space and time?" Felix retorts sarcastically. "When we enter the shadow realm, I can make sure time is slowed for us."

I cross my arms. "Then it's a deal."

"I'll call you back, Zachary," Elise says.

"Fine, but as soon as Reilly wakes up Olivia's phone is going to be ringing off the hook. She should probably talk to him soon," Zachary says.

"Oh, so now he wants to hear what I have to say?" I mutter sarcastically.

Elise smirks and hangs up. I look out the window, the sun is half set already. I can feel it in my bones, and I suspect Felix can too. Grabbing the knife on the bed, I lean over and cut the ropes that bind him to the chair.

He nods gratefully and rubs his wrist. The sun sinks below the horizon, and the air Felix shakes. Smoky magic curls around his extremities. I meet his eyes as the deep purple magic wraps around him. His body fades into the smoke, then is gone.

I stare at the spot he once occupied and curl my hand into a fist.

"Do you think he's coming back?" Elise asks.

"I really hope so."

I stop pacing and scuff the weird stain on the carpet with the toe of my shoe.

"It's been three hours," Maybelle says. Again.

"I know," I admit. "I'm going to wait just a little longer." I can't give up yet. Felix hadn't been lying when he said he would return, and he did say time passed oddly in the shadow realm. He's not that late. Yet. My phone buzzes in my hand and I glare at the caller ID. It's Reilly again.

The temperature of the air drops almost imperceptibly and the smell of magic fills my nose. I step back as the air in front of me shimmers, then splits open. Dark, smoky magic pours out like fog and pools on the floor. Felix slowly comes into view along with a woman behind him. When he had said granddaughter I thought she must be a child, but Justine is my age. Judging by the sneer on her face she is not happy to be here.

"You're late," I say, tension making me sound angry.

"Yet, you're still here," Felix says with a shrug.

"I still don't think you should do this," Justine says to Felix, though her glare is fixed on me.

"My decision is made," Felix says calmly.

Justine takes a step forward, her long black pony-tail swinging behind her. "If you kill him, I will make you suffer."

"I don't need you to threaten me in order to avoid doing that," I say calmly before turning to Elise and asking, "Ready?"

"Yes, we'll go back to the team as planned," Elise agrees, her lips are pressed tightly together in disapproval. "Will I need to come back here to pick you up tomorrow at sunset?"

"No, if Olivia can't find you by the time we are done training her, then she might as well not show up for the fight," Felix answers for me. He thrusts his hand out. "Take everything you can without killing me. There's no point in giving this to you if you end up weak."

I nod and wrap my hand around his wrist. The first pull is always so satisfying. Hunger stirs in my gut, eager for more.

Felix's magic is strange. It's obvious he is powerful, but it doesn't feel anything like the cold, deep magic of a vampire. The magic has no weight to it. As I take it, I feel lighter. The smoky magic seeps into every corner of my body.

Felix shudders as he begins to feel the drain. Justine grabs his arm to support him and looks at me with undisguised hatred. I pull on his magic faster. I don't want to draw this out.

His hand twitches and his arm shakes as he struggles to remain standing. Just a little more, he's almost at his limits. Felix's knees give out and I drop his arm. Justine catches him and lowers him to the ground. The unfamiliar magic drifts inside of me.

Felix looks up at me. "That was unpleasant," he says in a rough voice.

"So I've heard," I agree.

"I can still feel the magic, you didn't take as much as you could have," Felix accuses.

"If I take the absolute most I can without killing you, you'll be unconscious for a long time," I say. "I need you to train me still."

Felix nods in understanding, but he doesn't look pleased. "Justine will take us into the shadow realm where we can begin teaching you."

Elise grabs the keys off the table. "How long will she be gone?"

"Until tomorrow after sunset," Felix says, struggling to his feet. "That will give us five times that long in the shadow realm. It will have to be long enough."

"Don't do anything stupid, Olivia," Elise says.

I grin. "I would never."

Justine rolls her eyes and stretches her hand out to her side, magic rolling out from her body. The purple magic creeps upward and the air itself splits open, revealing absolute darkness. Felix walks into it without hesitation and disappears into the inky black hole.

"Go," Justine says, "I'm not holding the portal open forever."

I walk up and tentatively reach my hand into the darkness. It vibrates along with the magic I just took from Felix, but it's cold. Taking a deep breath, I plunge through the opening.

The room doesn't fade from sight like I expected. I can still see and hear. A strange current tugs at my legs. My hair waves around my head, being pulled in one direction as though it's caught in a wind.

I turn in a circle and see Maybelle watching silently, arms crossed, face concerned. Kabs looks eager, about ready to follow me through the portal.

Elise's heart is pounding in her chest as she stares at me, but it's like she's looking straight through me.

"We're no longer in the physical realm," Felix says.

I jump and stumble backward with a scream. I thought I was alone.

Felix chuckles. "However, we're not completely in the shadow realm either. She will fade from sight soon."

Justine appears in the darkness. The cold seeps through my jacket as the motel room becomes blurry, like I'm looking at it through gauze.

For a brief second I feel like I'm falling, then a new world starts filtering into view. My feet slip slightly and I look down. There's sand under my feet. It's silver and glows faintly. A steady, cool breeze blows it across my feet. The sand is heaped into dunes all around us and scattered with silvery trees and shrubs bent from the constant wind.

Something wriggles under my foot and I jerk away. A strange, glowing worm pokes its head out of the sand, then sinks back in and disappears.

"What was that?"

Justine shrugs. "I call them glow worms, but no one has bothered to learn much about them. Look up," she says. "That's where it gets good."

I do as she says and stop breathing. The sky looks close enough to touch. I've never seen an aurora borealis in person but I don't think it could compare to this. Every color I can imagine is streaked across the sky in constant motion. Bright flashes of lightning cut through the colors every few seconds. It's like some kind of cosmic storm.

"It's beautiful," I say reverently.

A fist appears in my peripheral vision and I duck on instinct, stumbling backward to avoid the next strike. Felix sits off to the side watching, unconcerned, as Justine shifts her stance and prepares to attack me again.

"What the hell are you doing?" I demand.

Justine charges, pulling a thin stick off her back. I duck under the first swing and slam my fist into her stomach. Justine wheezes as she's thrown back half a step. She tosses the stick to her other hand and swings again, striking from a different direction this time. I catch the stick and kick, but she checks the kick and shoves me back.

"She's not completely hopeless," Justine comments, looking at me critically.

Electric magic sparks from my fingertips as I keep a safe distance between us. "You're supposed to be training me, not trying to kill me," I snap.

"If you use magic in this realm, you will attract some unwanted guests," Felix warns looking suspiciously at the sand dune to our left.

"Unwanted guests?" I ask, looking around. "People live here?"

"Not people," Justine says. "The shadow creatures. They feed on magic. If they smell it, they come running; and they are vicious. They might show up regardless, but using magic is like lighting a beacon."

"You can't fight them off with magic either," Felix explains. "Anything you throw at them they simply absorb and grow stronger from it."

"And bigger," Justine says with a shudder.

"How am I supposed to train here if I can't use magic?" I demand.

"You need to learn how to control the shadow walker magic. That is the one type of magic that you can use here. The shadow creatures hate it for some reason," Felix says. "It can't hurt them, so I've never been sure why. They run from it though."

"And is Justine going to keep randomly attacking me?" I ask, glancing at her.

"Perhaps," Justine replies with a grin.

"The best way to learn, is to do. Come sit down and I will explain the basics," he says, pointing to the ground in front of him, "then the real training will begin."

I walk toward him while keeping a close eye on Justine. Felix sits down cross-legged, and I drop to the sand in front of him.

"Now, in order to bring more than two or three people into this realm, a portal must be open. With enough focus and magic, you can create a portal that will stay open for minutes, or even hours. But when you fight Cadriel, what you want is speed; creating the portal is slow. Besides, you don't want to leave an exit he can just stroll out of if he kills you," Felix explains. "There is a faster way to move while you are in this realm."

Justine runs toward me and I jump to my feet, but a wave of the dark shadow magic swallows her up. I freeze, looking at the spot she was just standing. A kick sweeps my legs out from underneath me. My back hits the sand; Justine looks down at me with a grin.

"You can slip into the in-between to travel faster and avoid an attack," Felix says.

"Or catch someone by surprise with an attack of your own," Justine finishes with a sly grin.

She's way too happy about getting to knock me down. This training is going to be even tougher than Hu's.

"You can break into arguably the most well-protected clanhouse in the continental US, but you can't manage to avoid walking face first into a kick? Good to know," Felix snaps sarcastically.

Justine snorts, the first thing I've seen resembling a smile pulling at her lips.

I spit a glob of blood out onto the silvery sand and press my hand against my cheek. It's swelling and probably already showing a bruise. My legs shake as I push back up to my feet.

Justine is already moving again. I slip backward into the in-between, the place between realms. The magic carries me as I push through the current that tugs at my legs; Justine's hazy silhouette follows me. I push back into the shadow realm, putting on a burst of speed, and charge the place I think she is going to end up.

Training without being able to use the new offensive magic I have stolen is difficult, but necessary. I used to be able to take on anyone with nothing but a few brews in my pocket. The electric magic has become a crutch and my weakness at the same time. I can use it better now, thanks to Hu; but it still tends to exhaust me. I haven't wanted to risk using the vampire magic either. Justine is faster and stronger than I am without it.

Even though I want to quit, I could do this for hours if I had to. The shadow magic doesn't drain me as quickly as the others. It moves through me, in and out, like I'm breathing. It's almost inexhaustible.

Justine appears in front of me and I dart to the side but trip. Sands gets in my eye as I tumble down the short hill.

"Did I give you my magic so you could run around like a damn chicken with your head cut off?" He shouts, his face red. "Use your brain! Think ahead!"

I scramble to my feet and dodge Justine's strike. She advances, twirling that stupid stick like a baton. I want to rip it out of her hands and beat her with it, but I'm lucky if I can dodge a few blows. I'm completely on the defensive here. Even when I was training with Reilly, it wasn't this bad. That asshole must have been going easy on me.

Again and again, I slip out of the way just in the nick of time. As I duck under another swing I realize I've been missing something obvious. I keep using the shadow magic to move myself into the in-between, but that's not the only way I can use it. Gritting my teeth, I push the magic out underneath Justine's feet and open the ground beneath her.

She falls; the stick slips from her hand as the current sucks her down. I run forward, concerned for a split second, but a kick against the back of my legs stops that in its tracks. My legs fly out from under me. All the air is knocked from my lungs as my back hits the ground.

"Finally," Justine says, standing over me with her hands on her hips. "I thought you'd never think of it."

"You could have just told me," I say, exhausted.

Felix appears over me as well, still pale. "Then you would not be learning to think for yourself. Cadriel will be neither slow nor stupid. You have to be able to think outside the box, and faster, if you are going to survive a fight against him."

"Fair point." I take a deep breath, then push up into a sitting position. "Why am I not thirsty?" I ask, still trying to catch my breath. I should be dying of thirst after the time we've spent exerting ourselves.

"Because this isn't real," Justine says. "You don't need to eat or sleep here."

"This place is fucking weird," I say under my breath. "Why are you helping, by the way?"

She seems to hate me, but she's putting out a lot of effort to help.

Justine looks away. "Felix said Alexandra killed your mother."

I nod.

"She killed my parents as well," Justine explains. "My dad believed in all this prophecy shit. I don't, but he would have wanted me to help. So I am."

"How do either of you know about the prophecy?" I ask. "It isn't exactly common knowledge."

"We were part of Alexandra's coven. The Praesidio," Justine says.

I swallow uncomfortably. I suspected as much, but hearing it said out loud still makes me sick to my stomach. They seem to hate the coven as much as I do at least.

"Get up," Felix barks at me. "There's no time for this."

The hours blend together and I lose all sense of how long we've been here. My arms and legs have become a mass of bruises, but I can't risk using the healing magic. After a particularly brutal knock-down, Felix finally allows me a break since I can no longer stand.

"How much longer?" I ask. I won't quit, but I can't deny I'm hoping this is almost over.

"It's been about six hours, I suppose," he says, squinting at the horizon. "We still have what will feel like days before it will be night again in the physical realm."

I shut my eyes and shove down the urge to flee back to the real world.

"You can go after him now; you will fail, and he will continue. What use is that?" Felix asks calmly, sensing my frustration.

"I know," I bite out. "I'm not giving up."

"You are learning more quickly than I expected," Felix says, offering the first compliment I've heard him utter. "You'll keep getting faster."

Justine walks over and holds her hand out to help me up. I take it despite wanting to lay down for a while longer. She looks me over, pursing her lips.

"Do you have a healing brew in your jacket?" She asks.

"I think so," I say.

"That shouldn't attract the creatures," she says. "Use it and let's get back to work."

I down the healing brew and the aches fade.

Justine tosses me her staff. "You should learn to use this too."

I wrap both hands around the smooth wood and brace myself for her next attack.

---

A warm trail of blood slides from my nose over my lips. I wipe it away with the back of my hand and regret using that last healing brew hours ago. My left leg ache from a strike Justine got in. I think it might have split the skin. She holds the staff loosely and watches me, waiting for me to make the next move. She took the staff back a little while ago after she decided I had gotten the hang of it.

I step backwards into the in-between. My feet slip in the current and I fall. I can't breathe and I grasp at the air uselessly. Gritting my teeth, I force myself to stop panicking and let the shadow magic lift me back up. I fall out of the in-between and hit the sand. Justine is a few strides away, giving me time to jump back up to my feet and face her.

"Enough," Felix interrupts, "it's time to return." He points at the edge of the horizon where a red moon is beginning to rise in odd, jerky movements. Once second it's just peeking over the horizon, then I blink and it's halfway into the sky. It feels like I've been here for a week.

Justine puts her short staff on her back and nods at me. "Good luck," she says. It actually seems like she means it.

"Do you think I'm ready?" I ask Felix, staring out at the blood red moon that hovers dully against the backdrop of the brilliant sky.

"No, not at all," he crosses his arms and sighs. "Maybe if you had five or six years of focused training and few more types of offensive magic, but —" He trails off into silence, simply staring straight ahead.

The ever-present wind blows sand over my bare feet. I wiggle my toes, trying to remind myself this isn't just a nightmare. This is my new, and possibly brief, reality.

"Is he really as powerful as a god?" I ask. The question has been weighing on me. A god sounds invincible. Then again, so did the Witch Council, but they're all dead now.

"I don't know," Felix says, rubbing his hand over the scratchy stubble that has almost grown into a full beard since his imprisonment. "I hope not."

I turn my head just enough to see his reaction to my next question.

"You and Justine aren't coming with me, are you?"

He looks down, his face drawn and tired. "No, we aren't."

"Can't blame you, I'm not even sure why I'm going sometimes," I say with a sharp laugh.

He claps his hand on my shoulder, giving me a tight, unhappy smile. "Wouldn't want to waste all this training, now would you?" He asks.

"Definitely not," he agrees. "Use your Finding magic and let it guide you to your friends like we talked about. Just remember, it will draw the shadow creature to you, so move quickly."

Felix claps my shoulder one more time, as if he's trying to reassure himself, then steps away. His footsteps fade away, the swish of the sand blending into the rush of the wind in my ears. Justine's magic vibrates behind me as she carries them into the in-between.

I face the vast, rolling dunes, and for a moment I feel overwhelmingly lonely. This place is beautiful, but desolate. I turn away from the view. Whether I'm ready or not, and whether I succeed or not, it's time to go do everything I can to fulfill my mother's last request.

I'm doing the *right* thing, and, despite how much I wish Felix and Justine were coming with me, I won't have to do this alone.

## 23

S and falls over my feet as I climb up the steep sand dune. The Finding magic tugs me forward like a guide. Nothing looks familiar here, but I'm almost there. Reilly is close, well, as close as he can be when I'm in a place that isn't even real.

A weird, yipping noise breaks the silence. I turn around slowly. Dark shapes watch me from the bottom of the hill. I step back and the creatures break into a run, heading straight for me. Shit. I turn and run in the direction the magic is pulling me. I crest the hill and it immediately slopes downward. Half-slipping, half-running, I careen down the sharp incline.

The yips turn to pained-sounding howls. I slide to a stop and lift my hands. The shadow magic begins swallowing me. The creatures reach the top of the hill and sprint toward me. Justine was not kidding about their size. They're larger than wolves with teeth like lions.

If I can get Cadriel back into the shadow realm, he may not want to risk using magic, which would give me an advantage with my brews. If he does use magic...there has to be some way to turn that to my advantage too.

The creatures and the silvery sand fade into shadow, and the current of the in-between tugs at my feet. I manage to keep upright, but it's a struggle. The soft white of the hotel room shimmers in front of me. I'm shaking from fear and the exhaustion. My leg is killing me.

Shadow magic pushes me forward and I stumble into the midst of a crowd of people.

"Olivia!" Elise cries in relief. She catches me as I slump forward.

"How did she do that?" Someone asks in the background.

"Nocte viator," Hu answers, his voice reverent.

I nod. "Yes, Cesare had captured one of the last shadow walkers. That was how he released Cadriel."

"What the hell did Felix do to you?" Elise asks.

"Training," I say with a dry throat. It seems like all the thirst I hadn't felt in the shadow realm is making itself known now. I look up and realize the entire JHAPI team is here along with Reilly, his clanmates. The only people missing are Javier and Patrick.

Maybelle and Kabs are watching a few steps away from the rest of the group. Maybelle looks uneasy, but she gives me a small smile and nods in greeting.

"And I thought we were hard on you," Elise says, shaking her head. "Someone bring her a healing brew."

Reilly is standing behind everyone else, his arms crossed, glaring at me. He's furious. I expect him to come yell at me but he turns and walks into his room. Ihaka follows him.

"I couldn't use magic in the shadow realm," I explain to Elise. "And I ran out of healing brews."

Staci hurries over with a healing brew.

"Thanks," I say before swallowing it down. The relief is immediate.

"Where are Patrick and Javier?" I ask.

"They went back to Texas to get the rest of the clan that is going to join the fight," Elise says. "I guess you learned how to use the shadow walker magic?"

"Well enough," I confirm with a nod.

Stocke steps forward. "I understand that you and Reilly have disagreed on how to move forward. However, while you were gone, the team filled me in and, after the attack on the council, I have been able to persuade JHAPI to throw their full support behind this mission," Stocke says. "Did you learn how to kill this Bound God?"

"Maybe. I have an idea at least," I say, my mind still whirring with all the possibilities. "I need to get Cadriel back into the shadow realm where it's not safe to use magic. The creatures that live there feed on it, and if you use anything but shadow walker magic, they come running. That will either keep him from using magic at all, or make it harder on him the more he uses."

"And if it doesn't?" Zachary asks, always the skeptic.

"If he kills me, then he's trapped again," I say with a shrug. "It's a win-win."

"You can't go fight him alone," Elise says, shaking her head firmly. "That's just a suicide mission."

"It might be suicide for whoever joins me," I protest.

"No," Zachary says. "I agree with Elise. You have to take backup. I'm going with you."

"I'm going too," Elise says. "Partners stick together."

I look at her with wide eyes, but there isn't a trace

of hesitation on her face. I don't want to get either of them killed; this is my burden not theirs.

"I'm in as well," Hu says as he steps forward and puts a hand on my shoulder. "I want to see the shadow realm."

"If that's the only reason I can just take you there right now," I say, frowning at him.

"That's not even close to the only reason," Hu says, nudging me. "I'm going."

"And I came to finish this," Maybelle says, walking over to stand beside me. "I want to see this creature killed. My illusions will help you."

Kabs pops up beside her and crosses his arms. "Where she goes, I go."

Maybelle doesn't argue, so they must have talked about this already.

"Don't even think about arguing," Elise says.

"No one else," I say firmly.

Stocke nods in agreement. "The rest of the team can back you up from outside. What supplies do you need?" Stocke asks.

"Some basic brews, maybe," I say, thinking through the possibilities. "There isn't much that can help me fight Cadriel."

"Cesare has to know we're planning something," Stocke says, looking around the room at our small group. "JHAPI will do everything they can to stop him while you take on Cadriel, but we could use some more backup."

"There's someone I can call," I say. Ian said he owed me and Reilly a favor. This is a big one, but I'm calling it in. "Do you know where Cesare is?"

"Cesare has been seen near the witch council, and we think Cadriel is there as well. As far as we can tell, he never left after storming inside and killing half the council. Do you have the strength to Find Cadriel?"

Stocke asks, looking at me skeptically. "We need to be sure before we charge in there with no idea what we're up against."

"I think so. I'm not magically exhausted, just physically," I explain.

"I can help her Find him," Corinne says, stepping forward. "It'll be easier if we do it together. I have the experience, and Olivia is surprisingly powerful."

I look down at my clothes. "I'm just going to go change real quick," I say.

Corinne nods and I hurry to my room. I strip out of my sandy jeans and jacket. Justine managed to tear a hole in the arm. My door opens and I look up to yell at whoever just walked in, but shut my mouth when I see that it's Reilly. He closes the door behind him.

"What do you want?" I ask as I turn away and strip off my shirt. If he wants to barge in while I'm changing then he can deal with seeing me half-dressed. I don't care.

"You could have been killed," he says in a tense, quiet voice.

"I could be killed tomorrow, too." I grab a clean pair of jeans and step into them. "Hell, I could be killed in the next twenty minutes. I'm not exactly living a risk-free life right now." I snatch a wrinkled t-shirt out of a pile of clean clothes and turn around to face him. "And it's not like I failed. If I hadn't gone when I did, we'd all be fucked."

"You jeopardized everything without even warning me," Reilly snaps, the anger finally surfacing. He stalks toward me, his jaw clenched tightly.

"You wouldn't even consider not working with the coven," I argue as he stops right in front of me. "I know Adrian told you how to contact them. Did you go behind my back and talk to them yet?"

Reilly leans in close. "I will not fail at this. Cesare must be stopped."

"No shit," I snap. "That's what I'm trying to do."

"Don't get in my way again," he hisses.

"Take your own advice," I say, shoving him away from me. "Don't get in *my* way. I'm going to kill Cadriel with, or without, your help. And I will kill Alexandra Hunt if I have to."

There's a single knock and the door opens. Corinne pops her head in. "You done, Olivia?" She asks congenially, ignoring that we're in the middle of an argument.

"Yep," I say, brushing past Reilly. "Definitely done." His angry heartbeat thunders in my ears as I walk out of the room.

The rest of the team is standing around the edge of the room, and one of the couches has been shoved out of the way. A large map of Washington state is rolled out on the floor.

"I'm going to guide the magic," Corinne explains, hands on her hips as she checks to make sure the map is smooth. She looks up at me. "You'll have to trust me, and it will feel a little odd, but it's much less risky than even a normal Finding."

Reilly walks past us, nods at Ihaka, and the two leave the hotel room. I tear my eyes away from the door and focus on Corinne.

I nod. "Okay. Is there anything I need to do?"

Corinne holds out her hand. "Link your hand with mine and stretch the other out over the map."

I put my hand in hers and extend my arm over the map as instructed. Her magic flows out around us in a wave that tingles along my skin. I push my magic out. It rushes toward the map, eager to Find our target.

A gentle tug slows it down and the magic pulses.

Everything sways and I hear our heartbeats like an echo around us.

"That's it," Corinne whispers.

I look down. The map is covered in delicate, bright red tendrils of magic; more than either of us could have done on our own. The magic filters down until there is one strand remaining.

"Found him," we say in unison. Corinne releases my hand and with the final beat, my magic snaps back into me. I know where he is now. Nothing can stop us from killing him.

"He's definitely still at the witch council," Corinne says, turning to face Stocke. "We'll know if he leaves."

"Great work," Stocke says, nodding her head in approval. "I have the blueprints for the council building. Let's go over it and decide the best way to enter."

No one is paying attention to me for the first time since I made my dramatic entrance. I gladly slip into my room and close the door behind me, taking a deep breath. There hasn't been a moment to relax in days, and there isn't one now, but a few minutes alone is better than nothing.

I dial Ian's number. The phone rings, and I stare at the gleaming brewing equipment. It taunts me with a reminder of Reilly's manipulations. I pace the room, tempted to throw the cauldrons out the window, when a thought sparks at the edges of my mind.

Stopping in my tracks, I stare at the remnants of the last disastrous brew. I've been trying to find a way to cure my hunger. What if I've been going about it all wrong? What if...*oh*. This could change everything.

"Ian Grzeski," he says, answering the phone gruffly.

"Ian, it's Olivia," I say. "It's a lot sooner than I expected to have to make this call, but I need your help."

---

I step back and the smoky purple magic fades, taking the failed brew with it. It's clear what's missing from the brew now. Getting the final ingredient will be tricky though. My door opens and I jump, startled at nearly being caught.

"Ihaka?" I say, surprised he has come to talk to me.

He closes the door and sniffs the air. "It smells odd in here."

I point at the workbench. "Just trying something new," I say. It's not a lie, and my heartbeat stays fast, but steady. "Can I help you?"

"Did Reilly ever tell you about Ava?" Ihaka asks.

"No," I say questioningly. "Who is she?"

"The first vampire he sired. He turned her around two-hundred years ago," Ihaka says, walking farther into the room. "Perhaps you should ask him about her sometime."

"Why?" I ask.

Ihaka crosses his arms. "You do not understand him," he says. "And until you do, you will not be able to convince him when he is being stupid."

I snort. "Can anyone do that?"

Ihaka shrugs. "You might be able to, if you care to learn how. There is a reason that Reilly is so angry with you for leaving like you did."

"And? What is it?" I ask.

"That is his story to tell," Ihaka says cryptically.

"I really don't have time to dissect whatever trauma has caused him to be a manipulative asshole right now," I say, walking toward the door. I need to talk to Maybelle, but I don't want to leave Ihaka alone in my room either. "Do you mind?" I ask, opening the door.

He walks over. "It is important that you understand, and talk to him," Ihaka says. "But it's up to you."

"Thanks for the tip," I say, opening the door and waving him ahead of me.

He nods and leaves. I follow, but stop in the doorway. Maybelle is standing in a corner watching Kabs talk with Elise and Patrick.

I catch her eye and subtly motion for her to join me. She looks at Kabs one last time and shakes her head, then heads over. I shut the door behind us.

"I still don't like that vampire," Maybelle says quietly, glaring at the door like he might be standing right behind it.

"We agree on a guy for once," I say.

She narrows her eyes. "You haven't—"

"No," I say, cutting off her question. "Definitely not. I don't trust him."

"That hasn't stopped you in the past," she says slyly.

"I'm learning from my mistakes," I say, crossing my arms.

"What did you call me in here for?" Maybelle asks.

"I have a plan, but I need your help," I say.

She narrows her eyes. "Explain."

"Felix was right; Cadriel's escape from the shadow realm wasn't fate, it was just inevitable. We have to kill Cadriel. Trapping him again isn't enough, it will only ensure that eventually he will get out again, and the next time Cadriel might succeed," I say.

Maybelle nods. "I agree."

"I think I've found something in the shadow

realm that gives me a way to level the playing field between us, but I need your help to make it work," I say.

"My help?" Maybelle asks.

I nod. "I need to hide something from Cadriel until the last moment."

"What are you hiding? Some kind of trap?"

"Sort of," I say. "It's a brew. I haven't been able to make it work yet, but I've figured out the last ingredient I need."

## 24

"Please put your seats in the upright position as we prepare for landing," the pilot announces over the speaker.

The flight from Los Angeles to Seattle is shorter than I expected; we made it just three hours after sunset. My fingers dig into the armrest. Cadriel is close. I glance at Corinne and she grimaces; she can feel it too.

Patrick peers out of the window, then puts his hand on my knee. "Don't die, okay?" he says quietly.

"I'm not planning on it," I say, linking my fingers with his and squeezing his hand. He squeezes back. I'm grateful he's here, even though I'd prefer it if he wasn't going to be part of this fight.

The private jet Reilly hired for the team circles the city once before descending toward a small airstrip. The tires bump once as plane lands on the runway.

Everyone gathers their things, not that anyone brought much. I have a small satchel full of brews slung over my shoulder, but there was no point in bringing anything else.

Patrick joins Javier, Emilio, and the rest of their

clan. Leslie is with them as well. Emilio doesn't look pleased to be here, but I don't think I've ever seen him look pleased to be anywhere. He's wearing his usual suit with the lace cuffs despite the impending battle. I shake my head, amused.

Maybelle slips in front of me as the group hurries off the plane. "Stay close to me," she says quietly, glancing back to make sure I heard.

I nod. Reilly has been quiet for most of the flight. It makes me nervous.

We walk down the narrow staircase that unfolds from the jet. The airstrip is dark apart from the lights that mark the runway. Stocke and Corinne fall into step beside me.

"Do you have Cadriel's location pin-pointed?" Stocke asks, looking at the two of us.

"I can feel him," I say. "He's still at the witch council."

Corinne nods in agreement, confirming his position.

"Our backup is meeting us in a few minutes," Stocke says, nodding in approval. "And Ian's pack is almost ready. We're fortunate they agreed to work with us."

Maybelle stops abruptly in front of me. "Reilly," she growls.

People in black robes spread out from the dark hangar. My blood runs cold. I look at Reilly as he walks up behind us, disbelieving even though part of me expected this. I thought he would try to convince me one last time. I thought I'd have more warning.

"What did you do?" I demand.

"The coven will help us," Reilly says, his face set.

Maybelle steps up behind me and put her hand on my elbow. I curl my fingers into a fist and prepare to pull on the shadow walker magic. I can't risk being trapped here in some kind of fight while Cadriel is out there, free to kill.

"This isn't going to go how you think it is," I say coldly.

Stocke steps forward, angry. "This was not what the group agreed to," she says, sweeping her arm toward the coven.

Reilly clenches his jaw tightly as Ihaka and Viking step up on his other side. "You do not dictate who I choose to ally with, Agent Stocke."

"I can't believe you lied to her again," Patrick hisses from behind us.

I glance back. Patrick is furious, and Javier doesn't look much happier.

"You promised us honesty when we joined you, Reilly," Javier says coldly.

"I promised I would do everything I could to ensure we succeed," Reilly retorts.

"What a rag-tag little group you have put together, Reilly," a woman says, her deep voice booming across the empty space. She is wearing a fitted black robe and her gray hair is twisted up into a severe bun.

"Ms. Hunt, we discussed that you would come alone," Reilly says, gesturing to the ten witches behind her.

She steps slightly forward from the group and purses her lips. "I changed my mind," she says, settling with her hands on her hips. Her eyes find mine and she smiles. "Olivia Carter, we should have met long ago."

"I'm not sorry we didn't," I say, grinding my teeth together.

Alexandra turns her attention back to Reilly. "Reilly, be a good boy and bring Olivia to me. We need to go after Cadriel soon, but she will need time to adjust."

"You swore to me that you would fight alongside us." Reilly says, his posture changing subtly. "What are you doing?"

My fingers twitch. I want to pull her into the shadow realm right now and end this, but Reilly is hesitating. We need him on our side. If there's even the slightest chance he'll come to his senses, I need that to happen. I watch him from the corner of my eye, ready to disappear if he tries to grab me.

"She is a weapon. Someone needs to take control, aim, and fire. Otherwise, she is useless," Alexandra says, looking me up and down disdainfully. She pulls a glinting, silver collar from the pocket of her robe and presses her hand to the pendant hanging around her neck. "This is what will allow us to defeat Cadriel, and Cesare."

I stare at the collar, understanding and horror creeping over me simultaneously. "Those were supposed to all have been destroyed," I bite out.

The device is horrifying. It strips away the free will of whoever wears the collar, turning them into a zombie controlled by the witch that wears the matching pendant.

Stocke pulls her gun and aims it at Reilly. The rest of the team follows suit, half of them aiming at the coven as well.

"If that's what I think it is," Stocke begins. "Then you will have to go through us to get to Olivia."

"I thought I was going to have to hunt down my dear Felix, but using you will be much better," Alexandra continues, unconcerned by the guns pointed at her.

"You know Felix?" I ask, hesitating in my confusion. He never mentioned that he knew her personally. All Justine had said was that Alexandra killed her father.

She laughs and cocks her head. "He's my husband. Didn't he tell you?"

*Husband.* Not even ex-husband. He's still married to her. I look at the collar and Felix's words about being used come back to me. She probably put that *thing* on him, and she killed their son in her pursuit of power. She's a monster.

"Don't do this," I whisper, taking a half step back from Reilly. "You know it's wrong."

He clenches his jaw and looks at me, then looks back at Alexandra. His heart is racing almost as fast as mine. At least this isn't easy for him.

"This wasn't part of the deal," Reilly says, clenching his hands into fists.

"There is no deal," Alexandra shouts, anger contorting her face. "Hand her over, now."

"You're not taking her," Reilly insists, his voice shifting into a growl as his fangs extend.

"Do you really think you have a say in this?" Alexandra asks, sneering. "You made it easier for us to find Olivia, but I was always going to take her when the time came."

Reilly growls and shifts his stance. "You're exactly like Cesare."

"I'm nothing like that coward," she scoffs. "The vampires have proven they aren't fit to be in power. I am going to use Olivia to kill Cadriel, then the witches are going to govern paranormals once again."

Stocke shifts and points her gun at the coven instead. "You aren't taking anyone, and you sure as hell won't be ruling anything."

"Stupid human," Alexandra spits, rage shattering her haughty composure. "As if you could stop me."

Dark, smoky magic drifts from behind the

231

witches. I force myself to keep my eyes fixed on Alexandra, but I almost look down when the magic disappears. My nose tingles as the smell of Maybelle's illusion magic drifts toward me. She's hiding it.

Alexandra lifts her hand to the witches behind her and says, "Bring me Olivia."

The witches behind her fan out, preparing to attack. We outnumber them, but I still don't like our odds.

"Get out of here with whoever you can," Stocke whispers, looking back at me. "Get to Cadriel without us."

"Only if I have to," I whisper back. I won't leave my friends to face the coven alone, and I refuse to let Alexandra Hunt take anyone else that I care about from me.

The air splits open behind the line of witches and several fall into the dark fog that pours out. Justine appears out of the darkness and races toward Alexandra, a sword held in both hands.

Stocke opens fire, and the group splits apart. Reilly attempts to get in front of me, but I run to the side and lift my hands. Lightning erupts from my palms and collides with the stream of fire two witches are sending toward the team. I close my hands and crush their magic inside of mine, snuffing it out.

Hu runs forward and lifts a wall of flame between the group and the remaining witches. As the fire rushes by, I catch a glimpse of Justine advancing on Alexandra, who waits patiently for her next attack. Justine won't be able to kill her alone.

A rush of water breaks through the wall of fire and I sprint through the gap, moving vampire fast.

"Olivia, no!" Reilly shouts from behind me. I ignore him.

Justine swings her sword, but Alexandra waves her hand and a burst of water deflects the blow.

I catch Justine's gaze for a half-second and hope she knows what I'm thinking; we can do it just like training. Shadow magic envelops me as I step sideways into the shadow realm, just far enough to disappear from sight. I run toward Alexandra's shadowy silhouette.

"You idiot!" Alexandra shouts, her angry voice echoing through to me. "The coven's time is now, and you are working against us! You could have been my heir!"

"That's all you ever cared about!" Justine shouts back. "You let your own son die for this pointless shit!"

Justine dodges a wave of water and pours shadow magic into the ground right next to her feet, then drops the sword. It falls through the realms, but not in the direction it seems gravity would dictate.

I raise my hand and catch it by the hilt. The current tugs at my feet as I step back into the physical realm, already swinging the sword.

"This is for my father, you bitch," Justine growls.

Alexandra tries to turn toward me but the sword connects with her neck. The impact vibrates painfully up my arms as the blade cuts through bone. Alexandra falls, her head separating from her body.

Justine and I lock eyes, and for a moment, share a common sense of grief. Alexandra is dead, but that won't bring back either of our parents.

I look back at the others. A few witches are fleeing now that Alexandra is dead. The others are all dead, or unconscious. Viking is drenched in blood. He grabs a limp witch by the back of the neck and sniffs them carefully, then tosses their body aside.

Stocke is shouting at Reilly, he listens to her stoically. Ihaka is watching me. He shakes his head and turns away. I curl my hand into a fist. In the end, Reilly was on my side, but the betrayal stings. He was so easily blinded by his own ambition.

I toss the sword back to Justine. "How did you find us?"

"Felix told me you were concerned about the coven showing up to stop you. I followed you after I took Felix back to the safe-house and I overheard that vampire talking about Alexandra," Justine says, glaring at Reilly. "I knew I'd never have a better shot at killing her."

"Thank you for helping," I say.

"I didn't do it for you," she says dismissively, already stepping back into the shadows.

"I'm still grateful," I say.

"Don't waste my grandfather's gift," she says, her voice muffled as she disappears.

I take a deep breath and walk toward the group. And Reilly. Justine's fight may be over, but mine isn't.

"Can you give us a couple of minutes?" I ask, interrupting Stocke's rant.

She nods sharply. "I'm going to go make sure no one was hurt," Stocke says, turning away angrily.

I walk toward the hangar. This isn't a conversation I want to have in front of everyone else. Reilly follows me into the small waiting area attached to the office. I turn around abruptly.

"Don't *ever* do that again," I say, stepping in close and shoving my finger in his face. "I was starting to think I could trust you, and then you betrayed all of us."

"I couldn't risk failing," Reilly says, his eyes flashing with anger even as guilt bunches up his shoulders.

"Try again," I bite out.

Reilly turns away and drags a hand down his face. "I was trying to protect you. I thought that if we had more powerful people on our side that you would have a better chance of beating Cadriel. I didn't know she had that collar." He turns back, his face drawn, and looks me in the eye, "I'm sorry." He reaches out and drags the back of his hand down my arm, "Please, Olivia."

I grit my teeth. His heartbeat is steady, just like it was throughout his apology. He means it.

"If you pull something like this again, I won't wait to see if you come to your senses," I say firmly. People make mistakes. I know that better than most, but I also know that I won't keep someone in my life that lies to me. Ihaka's comments from the night before come back to me and I bite the inside of my cheek. "Who is Ava?"

Reilly looks up, his eyes wide. "Who told you that name?" He asks angrily.

"Just answer the question. Or are you going to try to insist on a question for a question like we used to do?" I sneer.

He looks away and sighs. He is silent long enough that I start to think he isn't going to answer me.

"The first person I turned was a woman; her name was Ava. She was a woman born before her time. Feisty, opinionated, brave," Reilly says, looking up at me with a pointed raise of his brow as if to say *just like you*. "She hated Cesare, and she convinced me to help her overthrow him. She said we could take over the clan and shape the future into something better. We could stop killing humans to feed. We could have peace with the other paranormal races."

Reilly shakes his head. "Cesare caught her. She managed to convince Cesare that I wasn't involved. He killed her and a few others. I escaped death, but not punishment," Reilly says, his hand reaching up to his shoulder. "Cesare expects betrayal I think. He rules by fear, not respect."

"The scars?" I ask quietly.

"Yes," he nods. "Whip a vampire long enough with

a silver-dipped cat-o'-nine-tails, pour holy water over the wounds, and even we will scar."

I stare at him, horrified. The agony he must have gone through is hard to imagine.

"How could you stand to stay with him after that?" I ask.

"Surviving has always been the most important thing," Reilly says, finally looking up and meeting my gaze. "I could have struck out in anger that day, but then I would be dead and no one would be trying to stop Cesare now. It was only a matter of time before he did something like this. I had to stay close and wait for the right time, and for the right people, to try again."

Ihaka was right. I could never have convinced Reilly not to work with the coven without knowing how desperate he is to kill Cesare. This is personal for him; it's not about ambition. I couldn't have done what Reilly did. I don't have that kind of patience. Then again, I probably would have just run away.

"Back when Cesare showed up at the hotel, you said I sounded like someone," I say quietly. "You meant her, didn't you?"

"Yes, you always have. Tough, determined, brash. You have more patience than she did though." He steps forward, watching me carefully.

My brain tells me to run far away, but as Reilly leans in close, our breath mingling, I find I don't want to. Just as I'm about to turn away, he shuts his eyes and pulls back.

"Elise is coming," he whispers.

I step away, relieved and disappointed.

Elise pushes the door open and approaches, eyeing Reilly warily. "Ian and his pack are ready for us."

"Took them long enough," I say.

"Are we going ahead with the original plan?" Elise asks as we walk back outside, the door swinging shut behind us.

"Yes, I'm sure Cesare is wondering where we are," I say, a smirk tugging at my lips. He has no idea what's coming.

The doors to the stately building lay broken in the midst of other rubble. Yellow police tape flutters in the gap left behind. Our footsteps echo through the ominously quiet atrium as we enter the former seat of the witch council.

The marble floors lead us straight ahead. On either side of the wide corridor are pictures of previous council members. Many of the portraits are burnt, some were ripped from the wall and lay shredded on the ground. Cadriel must have been angry when he came through here.

The corridor ends with a tall arch leading into an open room. Broken pews, once used for meetings, litter the floor between us and the raised stage the council would have given their announcements from. There is only one chair remaining. Cesare sits in it, his arm propped comfortably on the armrest as he waits.

"Reilly, I suspected you were not completely loyal, but this? Recruiting other clans to join your little mutiny?" Cesare gestures at Javier and the other vampires he brought with him, shaking his head in disapproval. "It reeks of desperation."

"You released something that has been bound for almost a thousand years, that you cannot control, just to kill the witches," Reilly says, his voice resonating through the room. He steps away from the group, putting himself between Cesare and everyone else. "Yet, you accuse me of desperation? That's weak, Cesare."

"Olivia will kill Cadriel for me, or return him to his shadowy prison," Cesare says, sitting up straight and waving his hand dismissively. "And after that, she will do whatever I tell her to do in order to spare the lives of everyone gathered here tonight. That is the difference between you and me, Reilly," Cesare continues. "I am willing to do what it takes. I knew you weren't the day you watched me kill Ava and didn't nothing to stop me."

Reilly growls at the mention of her name. "Today, you will be the one who dies."

Cesare laughs and snaps his fingers. Vampires stream into the room behind him. "You think you can kill me with a small JHAPI team and a weak clan?" Cesare asks, gesturing toward his clan. There are at least thirty of them.

Reilly smirks. "Did you really believe this was all of us?"

Cesare's smile fades and he narrows his eyes. "The coven didn't join you," he says, irritation slipping into this voice. "I have already been informed of how that fight went."

A long howl raises the hair on the back of my neck as it echoes through the entire building. It's impossible to tell what direction it's coming from as the rest of Ian's pack joins in. They got here almost an hour before us, just as planned. Cesare's fingers dig into the armrest. He wasn't expecting that at all.

A man with long blond hair slips out from one of

the doorways almost unnoticed. I make eye contact, confused to see Adrian here, and on Cesare's side of things. He winks at me.

"I've got this. Go take care of Cadriel," Reilly says, drawing my attention away from Adrian. He is looking back at me with determination burning in his eyes.

"Kill Cesare, for Ava," I whisper.

Reilly nods, flashing me a smile.

Cesare stands from his makeshift throne. "I will make you suffer," he growls.

Reilly turns back to face him. "Come down here and face me then," Reilly shouts.

Cesare moves in a blur, the vampires charging after him. Gunfire booms as fire flares up between the team and Cesare's clan. Werewolves stream into the room from every direction. Adrian kicks the throne into two vampires that make it past the fire, then leaps after it, a grin on his face.

Reilly and Cesare collide in the center of the room, exchanging blows too fast for me to see. They break apart and Reilly wipes a thin line of blood from the corner of his mouth.

I crouch down and press my hands to the floor. Streaks of lightning race toward two vampires. They jump away from the magic, but it arcs up and strikes their legs. They fall to the ground, convulsing.

Patrick and Leslie grab a vampire that leaps toward Corinne and Ivy. Corinne lifts her gun and shoots him in the face with a silver bullet, killing him instantly. Emilio has some kind of rapier. He moves gracefully through the fight, running the sword through a vampire's heart, then jerking it free. The vampire crumbles into dust.

"Olivia, we have to go!" Elise shouts.

I run back over to her, but a sickening crunch

jerks my attention back to the fight in the center of the room. Adrian is between Cesare and Reilly. The broken leg of the chair is jutting out of his stomach, blood flowing freely from the wound.

"You chose the wrong side," Cesare taunts, twisting the wood.

"I always did want to die gloriously," Adrian gasps, smiling despite the pain. He kicks Cesare, forcing him back and rips the piece of chair out of his gut.

"They'll be fine, Olivia," Elise says, jerking me forward. "Let's go."

Maybelle and Kabs are waiting for us in the shadow realm. I can't leave them there, vulnerable, for any longer than necessary. I force myself to turn away. We'll all die if Cadriel isn't killed. I have to believe that Reilly and Adrian can take care of themselves.

Elise, Zachary, Hu, and I sprint into the fray. Fire surges around us, forming a tunnel that protects the group. The Finding magic pulls me insistently forward. I know exactly which door will take us down to Cadriel.

---

The stairwell is steep and dark. My eyes water at the scent of decay which grows stronger as we descend. A scream rips through the air and I sprint ahead. Only Elise is able to keep up as I move vampire fast.

The door at the bottom of the stairwell is open, but a body blocks the path. I leap over the corpse and skid to a stop in a wide room. The ceiling is low and the lighting is dim, making the entire area feel claustrophobic.

A man with shaggy brown hair lifts his face from

where it's buried in a witch's neck. He drops her and turns to face us, blood smeared in the corner of his mouth.

Cadriel isn't tall, or muscled, but the sheer amount of magic held inside of him seems to have its own gravity. I can see why they called him a god. Fear curls in my gut as he looks directly at me.

"Did Cesare send me more food?" Cadriel asks, scanning the group curiously.

"Run!" A man screams from behind Cadriel, banging his hand against the iron bars he is trapped behind. "You will only make him stronger!"

I hadn't even noticed the cages behind Cadriel. At least a dozen witches are crammed inside the small space.

"Cesare didn't send us," I say, keeping an eye on Cadriel. "Your old friend Izul did."

The words have their desired effect. Cadriel's face goes red with anger and he hisses at me like a wild animal. I need him angry and unfocused for as long as possible. The group spreads out. We have to time this perfectly. I'll only get one shot to get Cadriel back in the shadow realm.

"Izul is dead!" Cadriel shrieks, his skin turning gray as he draws on imperv magic. "He is dead and I will kill the rest of the witches after I take their magic for myself!"

Zachary lifts his gun and fires at Cadriel several times in rapid succession. The bullets thud against Cadriel, but they can't penetrate his skin. Nothing can. Cadriel waves his hand absently and a gust of wind knocks Zachary to the ground.

The air around us shakes with his rage. Cadriel steps forward and lifts his hand. Fire erupts from his palms and rushes toward us, but Hu's fire magic collides with it, stopping it in its tracks. Hu falls to one knee. His arms shake as he desperately pushes back against the overwhelming power of Cadriel.

I run forward and send my electric magic racing over Hu's. The crackling, white light wraps around the fire like a net. Two against one, we slowly force Cadriel back.

Hu struggles to his feet and claps his hands together. His fire magic erupts, seeming to double in power. The three magics twist together, then collapse with a sharp crack.

Elise, already shifted, runs past Cadriel and nips at his heels, drawing his attention to give me a chance to create the portal. Magic pours from my hands, and the shadowy magic twists in the air. It is much more difficult to create a portal to the shadow realm that will last as long as I need, but Maybelle and Kabs have to have an escape route in case I'm killed.

I grind my teeth together. I'm almost done. Elise just needs to keep distracting Cadriel for a few more seconds. A faint step is all the warning I get before someone charges me from behind. Vampire magic rushes through my limbs giving me the speed to dodge their swing.

Zachary shoots the vampire attacking me, the bullet searing him all the way through with silver. I kick him, sending a surge of electricity down my foot and into his chest. The vampire drops, but there are five more running into the room.

"Hu!" I shout.

He turns and blocks them with a wave of fire. One of them runs toward the wall and kicks off of it, vaulting over the fire. Hu flings a fiery whip at him, but the vampire dodges that as well.

Zachary fires three rapid shots at the trapped vampires. The third hits its target.

"Just go!" Hu shouts. "We can hold them off!"

As much as I need Hu for this, I can't wait for him, and Zachary can't hold off the vampires alone. I grit my teeth and run straight at Cadriel.

Elise is darting back and forth, barely able to keep ahead of Cadriel. He isn't as fast as Reilly, but like me, he is almost as fast as a vampire. Elise spots me and leads Cadriel toward the hidden portal.

I charge him, pushing my speed to the limits. With one last push, shadow magic rushes out of me and the portal stabilizes.

A vampire swipes at Elise. She dodges the attack and darts to the side, away from the portal. Cadriel skids to a stop, unable to change directions as quickly as she can. I leap toward Cadriel. He turns halfway, his dark eyes locking with mine as we collide, and fall into the shadows.

We hit sand as Cadriel's fingers bite into my arm. Maybelle, who has been waiting for our arrival, waves her hand. The portal disappears behind an illusion, along with the cauldron I placed here the night before. Kabs presses his palms against the sand and pours his magic into it. I need the shadow creatures to come as soon as possible, and the best way to draw them in by using all the magic we can.

"I won't be trapped here again!" Cadriel roars as his magic plunges into me and yanks on the power inside of me. I fight back, reaching deep inside of him. Our magic slides together like nails on a chalkboard.

He shoves me away in shock. "What are you?" he demands.

"I'm just like you. A half-breed," I say, panting a few feet away from him. A strange, new magic prickles uncomfortably inside of me. My skin shifts to gray, becoming invulnerable. I didn't manage to get much, though, and the magic feels weak. It won't hold up against an attack for very long.

Kabs and Maybelle watch us uneasily as they wait

for the shadow creatures to appear, or Cadriel to attack.

Cadriel's face splits into a crazed grin. "Izul told me the knowledge to make another like me was lost," he says gleefully, reaching his hand out toward me. "No one could stop us if you join me. We are gods compared to them!"

I sneer at him. "Gods? Hardly. How many witches do you have to drain just to satisfy the hunger?" I demand. "I know the more you steal, the hungrier you get. And I just felt how much stolen magic you have inside of you."

Cadriel cackles. "Who cares?" he dismisses. "The power should be ours."

"You're nothing but a parasite," I snap angrily, then charge him.

Cadriel doesn't try to dodge my attack. We collide, rolling down the short hill we landed on, and the tug-of-war over the magic begins again. Cadriel's magic is harder to grab than a normal witch. My own magic spasms inside of me as he tries to steal it. I struggle to resist the pull while still trying to rip away every bit of magic I can from him.

The electric magic twitches inside of me, then begins to flow into him with a rush. I grab a brew from my pocket and flick the cork out with my thumb, but he smacks my hand away. The vial flies out of my hand, spilling the knock out brew onto the sand. I grit my teeth and reach deeper inside of Cadriel, ripping away a hot, powerful magic from him in return.

Magic and anger churns inside of me. I smack my hand to his chest and release a burst of fire. He jumps away, and wind rushes past me, blowing the flames to the side. He hits the sand a few feet away and slides further down the hill.

"You are going to kill us both using magic in this

place," Cadriel shouts, scrambling to his feet; looking at the hills in fear.

"As long as I take you with me!" I yell, lifting my hands again. Heat surges through my body, and fire erupts from my palms. Cadriel had stolen so much of it, and now the powerful fire magic is inside of me. Struggling to control the fire, it pours out of me and surges around Cadriel. I'm using too much, too fast, but it won't be reigned in. A wall of water splashes through the fire, dousing half of it. I drop to one knee as the magic snaps back into me.

"Look out!" Kabs shouts.

Hulking black shapes swarm over the crest of the hill and surge toward us like a river. The shadow creatures yip and howl, a bone-chilling noise that echoes around us.

"I warned you!" Cadriel yells.

The pack of shadow creatures race toward us, but Kabs sends his magic into the ground. A churning wave of sand shoots up, blocking their path. One of them falls from the crest and tumbles gracelessly down. Maybelle runs forward, spear held high and stabs down viciously on the back of its neck. It twitches once, then goes still. Others race down after it, only slowed by the obstacle Kabs put in their way.

Another small pack is charging in from the opposite direction. Kabs and Maybelle will barely be able to hold off the first pack, they can't stop this one as well. A shadow creature leaps at Cadriel and he kicks it, sending the thing flying. It hits the ground, claws scrambling for purchase as it slides a short way down the hill. Another charges him. He catches it by the neck and slams it onto the sand, but three more pounce on his back.

I run for the cauldron I left here the night before. Maybelle has it hidden, disguised as one of the many twisted shrubs that dot the sand. When I get close enough, I stretch my left hand out and channel pure magic into the cauldron, starting the brew.

I may be a vampire, and I may be able to steal magic, but I'll always be a hedgewitch first. Brewing was the first thing I learned. It's the one thing I have left from my mother, and it's a part of me now. Herbs and crystals are my usual ingredients, but they can't do what I need today.

My hair whips around my face and the ground vibrates under my feet. Grains of sand float up, hovering around my legs like stardust. Deafening thunder cracks through the sky overhead. The magic draws the attention of the shadow creatures. A few break away from the group, heading straight for me and the magic I'm wielding.

I pull the short staff off my back and race toward the next creature before it can attack me. It lunges, massive jaws opening wide. I swing low, catching it in the throat, then bring the staff down on its back. The creature stumbles. I kick back and catch another in the face, noticing it just barely in time. Lifting my hand, I send shadow magic toward the two standing close together, opening the ground under their feet. They are swallowed up by darkness and disappear.

Cadriel shouts in the distance, enraged, and lightning cracks through the air in a bright flash. The magic strikes one of the creatures, but it doesn't falter. It grows. Electricity crackles through its thick black fur as it doubles in size. The monster jumps at Cadriel, but he meets it head on, striking it as the imperv magic rolls over his skin.

Another creature creeps toward me, growling menacingly. Its muscles bunch as it prepares to leap. I take a step back and let the magic flow into the brew once more. Watching the creature closely, I grab the small knife from my waistband, switching to hold the staff one-handed. It leaps toward me, its teeth gleaming in the silvery light of the shadow realm. I deflect the attack with the staff and slash the knife across its stomach. Mottled black blood drips out of the creature, coating the knife.

I step back into the in-between. I have to do this while Cadriel is distracted, and I may not get another chance. Slipping back into the shadow realm, I duck down behind the shrub that hides the cauldron. This part is going to suck, but I can't risk using too little. Before I can over think it, I dig the point of the knife into my wrist. Blood streams out, but it doesn't drip on the sand, it flows into the cauldron in front of me. I scrape the bloody knife on the edge of the cauldron and the black blood of the shadow creature sinks into the brew as well. It churns, the color changing from green to black.

I don't know what the shadow creatures are, exactly, but I know they devour magic. I'll never be able to kill Cadriel while he has all of his. My blood mixed with the blood of the shadow creatures will be able to drain every last drop of magic from him and destroy it. I stir the brew with the knife. The contents of the cauldron twist and swirl together, changing into something powerful and terrifying.

I dart away from the cauldron. Cadriel is still distracted but he won't be for much longer. The shadow creature I cut attempts to charge me again. I bring the staff down on its head, then kick it under the jaw. It flies backward, unconscious and bleeding out.

A bolt of electricity flies toward me. I drop the staff and the knife, barely getting my hands up in time to counter Cadriel's attack. Lightning smashes into fire. The opposing magics twist together, electricity striking the sand in blinding flashes. The fire magic is almost uncontrollable, but the sheer power of it allows me to hold Cadriel off.

"Kabs!" Maybelle screams.

My focus wavers for a split second. Two creatures are running at him from behind. Kabs turns, and sand rushes up to block them just in time. Cadriel pushes forward, overwhelming my magic. I'm thrown back and tumble down the hill.

I jump to my feet but Cadriel doesn't run after me. He's staring at Maybelle, and at the spot where the portal is hidden. She kicks a shadow creature's head as it snaps at Kabs, then runs it through with her spear. The illusion flickers, barely enough to show the portal we came through, but he *knows*.

Cadriel looks down at me. "You shouldn't have tried to trap me here again," he spits out. He lifts his hand toward Maybelle, a dark and angry expression on his face.

"No!" I scream as I sprint toward her, slipping through the shadows to get there faster.

I move as fast as I can, the vampire magic pumping through my shaking limbs. The lightning is faster. It streaks past me, and straight into Maybelle.

The magic hits her as I leap from the shadows less than a foot away. She turns toward me; her eyes wide and fearful. The electricity jaggedly sears her skin, and she screams. White light pours out of the wounds as the magic rips through her.

She seems to fall in slow motion. My heart stutters as I reach for her, thinking that if I can just catch her, maybe I can save her. She hits the sand, and the bright electricity fades into nothing.

"Maybelle!" Kabs cries. The sand rises up around him, swallowing the last of the shadow creatures. He runs toward her.

I drop to the sand beside Maybelle and drag her

into my lap. Every ounce of healing magic I have rushes into her. Her scarred face is locked in a silent scream of pain, and her eyes are still wide with terror. The magic flutters through her, useless. It's too late. She takes one last shuddering breath, then goes still. She's gone.

I look up at Cadriel, rage unlike any I have felt before filling me. She was the closest thing to a mother I had left, and he killed her. He took her from me. The illusions Maybelle created shatter, the magic falling away like ash.

Cadriel runs toward the now visible portal. I roll into the shadows, letting Maybelle's body slip from my arms. As he reaches the portal, I step out of the shadows and lunge toward him.

"You're dead, you piece of shit," I scream as I wrap my arm around his neck, keeping him from taking the final step.

"I will not die here," he hisses, desperation giving him strength. He drags me forward, stepping halfway into the portal. Our feet slip from sand to the rushing current of the in-between.

In front of us, the air twists, revealing the underground room we came from. Behind us, is the dim light of the shadow realm. If he gets back to the physical realm, then all of this was for nothing. I bite Cadriel's neck, my teeth digging into the taut flesh. His blood fills my mouth, making my stomach twist in revulsion. I wrench magic and strength away from him. His steps falter as he is forced to fight back against the pull on his magic.

I drag him away from the physical realm. We fall and the current sweeps us downstream toward the cauldron. Cadriel elbows me in the cheek, catching my eye and knocking me aside. The skin splits; blood drips down my face. He pulls away, scrambling to his feet. I leap onto his back, clawing at his face and neck. Anything I can grab. He stumbles and I force us back into the shadow realm. I wrench his head to the side and drop my feet down to the sand for leverage. I just need to reach the brew. I only need a drop.

Kabs runs toward us with a battle yell, his hands outstretched. The sand under our feet rolls upward and we both fall. My back hits the iron cauldron. The brew erupts around us as it shatters. The black liquid falls on us like rain, seeping into our skin.

Magic drains out of both of us like a sieve. It feels like my soul is being ripped from my body. I never understood how much this hurt.

Cadriel shrieks in pain and anger. The warmth of the fire magic bleeds out of me, followed quickly by the shadow magic. The vampire magic is ripped away and my body grows weak. Cadriel pulls out of my grip and rolls away from me. Bright trails of magic flow out of him and into the brew. It hovers where the cauldron used to be; now a twisted mass of pure magical energy.

The last bits of magic I stole from Novak drain away, sparking at the tips of my fingers as it disappears. My body shakes as I struggle against it instinctively. Cadriel convulses, spit foaming at the corners of his mouth. Every muscle in his body strains against the brew.

The warm healing magic fades quickly. There was so little; it's easy for the brew to consume it. Tears gather in my eyes as the hedgewitch magic begins to drain out of me. Pain cuts through every cell in my body. It's the only thing I had left from my mother. I didn't think I would have to lose this too. I didn't think I would have to sacrifice everything to kill Cadriel.

. . .

The last bit of my magic seeps away. I'm empty. There's nothing left but loss and rage.

"What have you done?" Cadriel demands, baring his teeth at me like a wild animal. The portal is shaking unsteadily. It won't hold for much longer. He tries to stand, but his legs collapse underneath him. He crawls forward on hands and knees.

Howls erupt behind us and I hear the rush of sand as Kabs shouts a warning. I force myself to move. I have to end this. Every limb shakes as I lunge for Cadriel. My nails claw into his back, slowing his retreat. He grabs my hair and jerks me off his back.

He killed Maybelle. I won't let him get away with it. I grab his leg, clinging to it as he kicks back trying to hit me in the face. I push my feet into the sand and jump toward him. He twists unexpectedly, gets a hand around my throat, and forces me onto my back.

I grab a handful of his hair with one hand and yank him closer, then force my thumb into his eye. He screams as I crush it into his skull. Blood drips down my hand. I get a knee between us and push him off of me.

"No," he moans. "I won't stay here!" He turns away and drags himself toward the portal on his stomach, fingers digging into the sand.

A spear lands next to me. "Take it!" Kabs yells.

I grab the weapon and drive it into his leg. Cadriel howls in pain. I jerk it free then plunge it into his back. The spear hits bone, jarring my arm painfully. He wheezes as I stab him again and again. Maybelle's face as she fell is all I can see. I hate him.

"Just die!" I scream, my face contorted in rage as I plunge the spear into him again.

He claws at the ground, still trying to drag himself away. I grab his hair, wrenching his head back, and drag the blade across his throat. Blood sprays over the silvery sand, coating it with red.

Cadriel gasps for breath, coughing as his lungs fill with blood. Slowly, his body goes limp, then cracks. He collapses into dust.

I scoot away and fall back onto the sand; tears streaming down my face. My fingers tighten around the spear. He's dead, but Maybelle is gone and nothing will bring her back.

"Olivia!" Kabs shouts.

I force myself upright. Kabs swallows up the last two of the creatures in a wave of sand, but there are more cresting over the top of the hill. We're about to be overrun.

"Run!" I scream. The portal behind me is shaky. I don't know how much longer it will last, and I can't remake it.

"Kabs we have to go!" I shout.

"I won't leave her!" Kabs yells back, sobbing. He tries to pick her up, but she's as tall as he is, and he can't seem to get back to his feet.

I grit my teeth and jog toward him. Her body is cold and limp. My muscles strains as I lift her. She isn't very heavy, but I'm exhausted.

"Let's go," I beg.

Kabs nods and we run toward the portal. It's shrinking.

"Faster!" I yell. I pick up the pace, my legs and arms burning with the exertion. The portal shrinks even further, but we duck down and leap through together. The magic shudders as we pass through, then collapses and spits us out onto concrete.

"Stay down!" Zachary shouts.

Fire rushes overhead. Sweat drips down my forehead from the suffocating heat. The magic dissipates; I push up to my knees and hand Maybelle to Kabs.

"Stay with her," I say hoarsely. He nods and crawls closer to her.

Hu is still facing off with the same vampires. It's like we were only gone for a minute, instead of what felt like an hour. A wall of fire swirls around him, lashing out when one of them gets close.

Zachary fires twice and his gun locks back on empty. He scrambles for another magazine, but the vampire he shot is still running at him. Elise jumps, colliding mid-air with the vampire. She latches onto his throat and bites down hard, dragging him to the floor.

The ground beneath the other vampires churns and they sink into the stone like its quicksand. I look back at Kabs. The tears are gone, replaced with determination.

Hu shoves both hands forward and the wall of fire flares out. I choke down bile as the smell of burning flesh fills the room. Zachary shoots the trapped vampires, putting them out of their misery. When all that's left is dust, Hu lowers his hands and steps back.

"Is Cadriel dead?" Hu shouts across the room.

I nod once and Hu slumps in relief.

"Are they still fighting Cesare?" I ask as I glance back at Kabs. He is kneeling by Maybelle again, head bowed.

Elise woofs once, then sprints toward the stairs. That must mean yes. Hu runs after her. I try to follow, but I'm slow. I might as well be human now. There isn't a drop of magic left in me.

"Are you hurt?" Zachary asks, looking me over.

"Not badly enough to care," I say. "But my magic is gone." I look down at my hands. They're shaking. It feels like someone carved out all my guts. I can't fight like this.

"Gone?" He asks, his brows pulling together in concern.

"Yes, but there's no time to explain right now," I say, shaking my head.

"We'll get you a gun then," he says. "Come on."

I shake off the fear and jog after him. As we near the top of the stairs, the sounds of fighting grow louder and louder. There is a steady rap of gunfire in the background.

Zachary peers around the corner, then waves me forward. Stocke is behind a short wall with an AR-15 against her shoulder. She pulls the trigger every couple of seconds, her aim steady. Ian's pack has forced the vampires back, allowing JHAPI to pick them off from a distance.

Staci is crouched next to her reloading her weapon. She sees us and waves us over, kicking a backpack in our direction.

"There's more ammo in there, Zachary," she shouts over the racket.

"Olivia needs a gun," Zachary shouts back, digging through the backpack.

"Olivia, try the purple one," Staci says.

Zachary pulls out two magazines that fit his pistol then tosses me a purple gun with a large cylinder set on top.

"Is this a paintball gun?" I ask, confused.

Staci grins and nods. "Yeah, sorry it's all I have. I got some empty paintballs and figured out a way to inject them with brews."

"That's fucking genius," I say, lifting the gun and firing over the wall. The paintball splats against a vampire and she drops like a stone. At least I can still do this.

"Knock-out brews," Staci says, answering my unasked question. "I brought a non-lethal option just in case."

It's better than nothing. I fire steadily, dropping vampires when I don't miss. I'm more consistent when I'm throwing a vial but I have to be much closer for that, and vampires are fast.

Viking flies through the air and lands on his back, sliding toward us. A vampire that I recognize from Cesare's friendly little visit runs toward him.

"Shit." I leap over the wall and fire twice, but miss. I run toward Viking. The bodyguard reaches him first and rears back for a strike. I fire again and the paintball hits the bodyguard in the neck. He falls forward.

I shove the unconscious vampire off of Viking. He's dazed and his stomach is bleeding sluggishly, but he doesn't look like he's going to die.

A chuckle makes me look up. Cesare stands in front of me. His suit jacket is torn and there is blood on his teeth.

"I am going to enjoy killing you," Cesare taunts.

I don't see him move before I'm shoved back. Viking drags me away from Cesare. Reilly is standing between us, having blocked the attack.

The two vampires strike and dodge, each of them moving so fast my eyes can't follow. Viking keeps a firm grip on me, half shielding me from what's happening.

"Let go of me!" I yell. "Go help him instead!"

"If you are vulnerable Cesare will attack you again," Viking says, holding me a little tighter just in case I try to flee. "That will distract Reilly."

Ihaka and Ian, in wolf form, charge in from opposite sides. Ihaka is holding a short wooden spear.

"Cadriel is dead," I shout, still straining against Viking's grip. "You hear me Cesare? He's dead! Your plan failed!"

Reilly takes a kick to the chest and flies a few feet backward. He skids to a stop, one knee and one hand on the ground.

"You will join Cadriel in death," Cesare hisses at me.

"You first," Reilly shouts.

He charges and Ihaka throws the spear. Ian jumps forward and lands on Cesare's back, grabbing the back of his neck with his jaws. Cesare growls and stumbles backward, trying to reach for Ian, who leaps away.

Reilly catches the spear in mid-air and plunges it into Cesare's chest. It pierces him through the heart, the bloody end jutting out of his back. Cesare falls to his knees, a sneer still on his face, and disintegrates into dust.

## 29

I t's over.

I'm sitting in a van with a shock blanket wrapped around my shoulders. I'm not sure what the purpose of it is, but it's warm and I'm shivering from exhaustion. Most of the team is milling around aimlessly. A few people dressed in uniforms are walking with purpose carrying stretchers.

Zachary and Elise walk up. Zachary steps in front of me, his expression full of concern.

"Olivia, are you all right?" he asks.

"Yes," I whisper. "Is everyone okay?"

"Ivy is pretty banged up, but she'll live," Elise says, her lips pressed into a thin line.

I shut my eyes and bury my face in my hands, relieved. I couldn't have taken another death. "That's good."

"I'm sorry about Maybelle," Zachary says. "I know she meant a lot to you."

I nod, not wanting to speak about her death so soon.

"How did you do it?" he asks. "It seemed like you were only gone for a few minutes."

"A brew," I say, dragging my hands down my face. "I realized how to make it work after failing to find a way to cure the hunger I've been struggling with. I found the last thing I needed in the shadow realm. A way to destroy magic."

"I guess that was the key the prophecy mentioned," Zachary says. "I didn't believe it until now, but it was true."

"Yeah," I agree. "Adrian thought I was the key. He was both right and wrong."

"Is your magic really gone?" Zachary asks.

"Yes," I say, looking down. Pain from the reminder of the loss twists in my chest. "I can't even brew now."

He puts his hand on my shoulder and squeezes it sympathetically. "You're going to be okay without it," he says quietly.

"Eventually," I agree, trying to smile, and failing. I can feel a distant echo of the hunger inside of me that I lived with for so long. I could steal magic again, but I don't want to be like Cadriel. I won't be a monster.

"You always manage to survive the craziest shit," Elise says. "You'll get through this too."

Adrian walks up, looking angelic despite leather pants. There is a bloody hole in his previously white shirt. He stops in front of me and smiles, his teeth stained with blood. "How does it feel to fulfill a prophecy?"

"Terrible," I say with a harsh laugh. "How'd you manage to survive getting skewered?"

He scoffs. "I'm not that easy to kill."

I shake my head and smile. "I'm glad you aren't."

"It appears you aren't either," he says, tilting his head.

"Just dumb luck," I say.

"Be proud of what you have accomplished," he says, putting a cold hand under my chin and lifting my face up to his. He leans in and kisses me soundly on the cheek.

I cringe and wipe the side of my face, smearing the lip-shaped imprint of blood.

"I'll see you again," he says. "Hopefully." Adrian turns and walks away.

Zachary shakes his head. "He is so odd."

"You are not wrong," I agree. I spot Reilly walking toward us. "Can you give us a minute?" I ask.

"Sure," Zachary says, shoving off the side of the van. He and Elise head in the same direction Adrian went.

Reilly's shirt is torn and stained red. His suit jacket is gone. Even his hair is mussed. He stops in front of me, his hand brushing lightly against mine.

"Fancy meeting you here," I say lightly. After everything that's happened today, I'm just glad Reilly is alive. I'm glad I'm alive. Any worry about tomorrow can wait until then.

Reilly wipes away the blood Adrian left on my cheek. "You killed a god," he whispers.

"And you killed Cesare," I say looking up into his eyes. I don't need to be able to hear his heartbeat to know he wants me right now, not when he is looking at me like that.

In some ways, I'm still not sure if I can completely trust Reilly. But there hasn't been a single person in my life, not even my mother or Brunson, that hadn't lied to me at some point. Reilly is beginning to feel worth the risk.

I lift my hand slowly, watching for his reaction, and wrap it around the back of his neck. His eyes drop to my lips and I pull him forward, taking the kiss I've been wanting for so long. It's better than my dreams.

One of his hands tangles in my hair and the other slips down to my lower back as he pulls me closer. I memorize the feel of his lips against mine. The warmth of his fingertips through my shirt. The hard press of his chest against mine. It all reminds me that I am *alive.*

## 30

The newly formed witch council sits at the table with the Director of JHAPI, the two official vampire council members, and the werewolf council. The team is briefing the councils on everything we just went through and reassuring them that the Bound God is dead.

Giving my testimony to the hearing was miserable, but it's over at least. JHAPI and the werewolves thanked me for my sacrifices. The witches were less appreciative, one of them even hinting that I must be part of some kind of conspiracy to cripple them. I'll never really be accepted by the witches. It shouldn't bother me, but it does. Especially since I've lost all my magic.

Most of the world will never know exactly what happened with Cadriel. The official press release says there was an explosion. Maybelle is receiving a medal for bravery posthumously. It's not enough, but there isn't really a way to thank someone who gave up everything like that.

The only good to come out of this is that the werewolf council is finally convinced JHAPI is not out to get them. Ian had a lot to do with that. It isn't perfect, but at least things are changing for the better.

The vampires have been shamed for almost letting one of their own get away with a crazed plot to take over the world. Reilly is hopeful that he can improve things for the vampires though. He certainly has his work cut out for him.

Agent Stocke finally finishes her testimony and the Director of JHAPI leans forward, clasping his hands together. "Agent Stocke, I commend you and your team for the personal risk you undertook in order to stop a madman," he says, glancing back at me and nodding in thanks. "I am appointing you as the lead liaison between JHAPI and the councils. Is there an agent that you would like take over your position as team lead?"

Stocke only hesitates for a moment before replying, "Yes sir. Agent Ivy Andreas has a healthy respect for the rules and a natural instinct for leadership. She will lead the team well if you give her the chance."

The director nods. "Thank you all for your efforts. This briefing is adjourned," he says.

I sigh in relief. It took several hours, but at least it's over. I'm the first one out of my seat, and I hurry toward the exit. The rest of the team is taking this opportunity to shake hands with the director and speak with the councils; I'm not interested in any of that.

The halls are packed with people today. I weave through the crowds until I reach the break room. There's a vending machine inside and I'm dying of thirst.

I cover a yawn and feed the dollar bill into the slot. It doesn't have tequila, unfortunately, but I'll take water over nothing. The bottle tumbles down and I grab it from the take out port.

"Olivia, I'm glad you're still here," Staci says, walking up from behind me. "I want to talk to you about something."

I jump, easily startled now that I can't hear people coming. I hadn't appreciated how much the vampire magic enhanced my senses until I lost it. "Sure, what did you need?" I ask.

"Stocke just approved my vacation request. Two weeks off," Staci says, crossing her arms like she's getting ready to argue.

"That's nice," I say, confused. "Are you going to visit family or something?"

"You lost all your magic, even the hedgewitch magic. I want you to take mine to replace it," she insists. "As much as you can without killing me."

I step back. "You don't know what you're asking—"

"Yes, I do," Staci says, closing the gap between us. "You love brewing. It's your life. I want to do this for you, it's not like I'm giving up my magic forever, it'll just be a couple of weeks before I can brew again. You killed Cadriel for us, it's the least I can do."

I stare at Staci with my heart in my throat. She has her jaw set stubbornly; she won't let this go until I agree. It's not like this is an offer I am going to turn down anyhow. She's offering me my life back.

"Okay," I say, my hand tightening around the cold bottle.

She lifts her chin and nods once, satisfied. "Let's go, Stocke is waiting for us."

"Right now?" I ask.

"Of course," Staci says, turning and heading down the hallway.

I follow, my heart pounding in anticipation. Staci walks into the same room we used for our team meetings and sits down in the closest chair. Zachary, Elise, and Stocke are the only people there.

Zachary nods and smiles at me.

"Take it," Staci says, holding out her arm.

"Are you sure?" I ask her again, trying to give her every chance to back out.

"Yes," she says, shaking her hand at me insistently.

There is no doubt in her eyes. No fear. I walk forward and take her hand. Her magic is warm and familiar. I ache to have that again.

"Thank you," I whisper.

She nods, squeezing my hand gently. I reach into her, and the magic I love the most begins to fill all the empty space inside of me.

## 31

Two weeks later...

"Are you nervous?" I ask.

"No," Reilly says, shaking his head slightly. "The ceremony is going to be boring. Besides, the council is lucky to have me."

I raise my brow at him. "You think very highly of yourself."

He grins, showing off his dimples. "I defeated a god and the most powerful vampire on this side of the world."

"Excuse you," I say, crossing my arms. "I'm the one that killed a god."

"I helped," he insists.

"You weren't even there!" I protest.

He grins mischievously. A knock at the door interrupts our argument and Javier walks in, followed by Lydia.

"Javier," Reilly says with a welcoming smile. "I'm glad you could make it. There are quite a few clans I want to introduce you to."

Lydia walks over to me. "Olivia, it's been a while," she says politely. Her greeting isn't exactly cold, but she seems uneasy.

"It has," I agree. "A lot has happened since the last time I saw you." An uncomfortable silence stretches between us. "Javier is finally getting everything he wanted. Recognition from the council," I say finally.

Lydia nods. "Yes, it's good to see him rising through the ranks. We've worked toward that for years."

"I'm glad it's Javier," I say, trying to reassure her a little. "He's a decent vampire."

She smiles proudly. "Yes, he is."

Ihaka opens the door and sticks his head into the room. "I hate to interrupt, but you are needed, sire," he says.

"Thank you, Ihaka," Reilly says before turning back to Javier. "We'll finish up this discussion soon, Javier. I promise."

I follow the group outside. Reilly waits for me by the door.

"Ava would have loved this," he says quietly.

"The boring ceremony? Or knowing that Cesare is completely defeated?" I ask, looking up at him.

"The latter," he says with a smile.

"Go make her proud," I say as we separate. Reilly continues on toward the stage and I slip out into the hallway to find my way to my seat in the audience. Stocke is waiting for me near the back.

"Agent Stocke, I thought you might be here today," I say, greeting her with a smile.

"Of course, I can't miss the appointment of the newest council member. I did need to talk to you though," she says.

"What's up?" I ask.

"You aren't obligated to work with Reilly Walsh anymore," Stocke comments.

"No, I'm not," I reply. No one else has mentioned it, but I have been thinking about it. It's strange to have my future so open again. It feels foreign.

"I'd like to formally offer you a position with the agency. You'd have to go through the second phase of training, and then you'd be assigned—"

"Sorry to interrupt, but the answer is no," I say, cutting her off.

Stocke looks surprised. "Can I ask why? I thought you'd at least consider it," she says.

"I have considered it. I thought the offer might come after everything, and since I'm special," I say with a rueful smile. "But I know what I want to do."

"You aren't going to be joining Reilly's clan are you?" She asks, looking toward the raised stage the council is walking out onto skeptically.

I laugh. "God no. I'm going to do what I wanted to do in the first place; open an apothecary." The laughter dies in my throat and I stare down at my hands, white-knuckled where they are clasped in front of me. I had wanted to do it with Maybelle. Hopefully, I can make her proud.

"We can help with that then. As a thank-you," Stocke says. "It was already put in motion in order to offer you the job; your record is being wiped clean."

Shock colors my face. "What?"

"Your felony," she explains. "It's being wiped from your record. You'll be able to apply for all the certifications you need to join that healer's guild or whatever it's called."

A weight I've been carrying since I was eighteen is lifted from my shoulders. I made mistakes, and paid the consequences, but having that follow me around for life was depressing.

Stocke claps her hand on my shoulder. "If you ever miss the excitement, let me know. The position is yours if you want it."

I nod, still unable to speak around the lump in my throat. Stocke smiles and walks away to find a seat. I look at Reilly standing with the vampire council. He's so young compared to the rest of them, but he's right where he belongs. We all are, finally.

Leslie is going back to live with Patrick and Javier for a while, despite Reilly being her sire. Kabs is back in Donheim though I suspect he won't stay there long. He is volunteering to be one of the first goblins to live openly in a human city.

And I'm going home. I don't know when Pecan Grove became home, but it has.

## 32

The old house has a new coat of paint. My mother had painted it bright yellow when we first moved in. It was a total eyesore, but she loved it. The new owners apparently did not. I can't really blame them.

The door opens and squat, middle-aged woman walks out with a sunhat shielding her face. She pulls on some worn out gloves and starts pulling weeds. I smile, glad someone is taking care of the place. The commercial on the radio ends and an upbeat song starts playing. I put the car in drive and pull away from the curb.

Every street I pass has its own memories. Walking to school. Playing with friends, not that I had many. I take a left and pass the hospital. It's huge now; updated with gleaming windows and a parking garage. When I used to go with my mother, it was dingy. At the time it was one of the smaller hospitals in the area. Everyone that couldn't really afford to go to the hospital ended up there. My mother brought healing brews every Sunday and helped everyone she could.

I tried to help too, in my own way, when I stole that healing magic. I hadn't realized it meant we'd have to stop going there completely. The old twinge of regret twists in my stomach. There were so many people that we missed out on helping. I can fix that now though. I don't have to hide anymore, and if my apothecary takes off, I'm going to start the volunteer work again.

After the hospital, the houses get farther apart. It's not quite out of the city, but it's not really in the suburbs either. The parking lot is just past the simple, iron gate that leads into the cemetery. There's no one here but me.

Thunder rumbles overhead as I climb out of the car and walk around to the passenger side to get the flowers. Looking down at my hoodie and wrinkled t-shirt, I have an overwhelming feeling of being under-dressed. I take a deep breath. It doesn't matter. They can't see me...most likely.

The gate creaks as I push it open and step into the cemetery. It swings shut behind me and I wind my way through the grave plots until I find what I came here for. The Brunson's are buried in a single grave, one on top of the other.

I stand at the foot of the gravesite and stare at the headstone. I'll always regret not seeing Debra again before she passed. Some selfish choices you don't get a chance to make up for and running away like I did is one of them.

I nervously adjust the flowers in the vase, then set them by the headstone. They're sunflowers. Her favorite.

"Zachary is doing good," I say quietly. "And I found my mom. I don't think I would have if the two of you hadn't taken me in when you did. So thanks." I shove my hands in my pocket. I'm not good at this, but I hope that wherever they are they can hear me, and they know I mean it.

The wind picks up and the first drops of rain hit my face. I pull my hood up and turn away from the grave. This was my last goodbye. The rain beats down harder, but I turn my face to the sky. The sun is breaking through the clouds illuminating everything. I smile despite the tears slipping out of my eyes.

## 33

The glass window gleams in the light of the street lamps. My feet are sore, and while my body is tired, my mind is still whirring from the excitement of opening day. Customers actually came, and better yet, they bought things.

Patricks holds out his hand for a high five and I slap my hand against it with a satisfying smack.

"I make a great salesperson," he says, leaning back against the counter with a pleased grin.

"You make a great flirt," I retort, smiling at him. He was actually helpful this evening. He strolled in a little after sunset and managed to sell as much as I had during the entire day. He kept winking at old ladies every time they picked up a salve.

Mr. Muffins winds between my legs and meows loudly.

"You were not helpful at all," I tell her, hands on my hips. "But if you're nicer to the customers tomorrow, I'll give you extra tuna."

She flops down onto her back and purrs loudly, acting like she's innocent.

"You're not fooling anyone," I mutter.

"Well, I'm going to head out," Patrick says, something off in his tone.

I narrow my eyes at him. "Why?"

The bell rings and I look up.

"Reilly?" I ask. He's wearing a black button down shirt over jeans. It's almost casual. My eyes wander past him to the three bodyguards right standing outside. "What are you doing here?"

"I couldn't miss opening day," he says with a grin.

Patrick hurries to the door, nodding politely at Reilly. He looks back over his shoulder and winks at me before hurrying out of the store.

I shake my head, but I can't hide the pleased smile. "What are you really in the area for? I know you didn't fly all the way from Seattle just to see me."

Reilly ignores my question and wanders down an aisle, pausing to pick up whatever catches his eye. I step over Mr. Muffins and follow him.

"You've been busy," he comments, gesturing at the shelves lined with brews and salves. He crouches down and inspects a little jar of cosmetic cream on the bottom shelf.

"Between brewing and still taking care of Javier's neckers, yeah, busy is one way to put it," I agree with a shrug.

"I was surprised to hear you were still doing that," he says, glancing up at me.

"They still need healing, and the brews can take care of that well enough. Javier asked for a few of the neckers to volunteer as part-time workers here, at his expense, in addition to my normal pay. He said to consider it a raise," I snort. "I think he just doesn't want to lose me."

"I can't blame him," Reilly says, standing up slowly.

I look down at my feet. He's not here for me. Thinking he is, is only going to get me hurt.

"You know it's strange," Reilly comments as he prods a vial of shimmery liquid. "We haven't actually been on a date yet."

I look up sharply, my stomach doing flip-flops. I open my mouth, but no words come out.

"I have reservations at a restaurant in Dallas. Supposedly, they have the best steak you'll ever eat." He holds out his hand. "Will you come with me?"

"Dallas is two hours away," I protest.

"I have a helicopter," he says with a grin.

I slip my hand into his. He twines our fingers and pulls me in close, wrapping his arms around me. Standing in my own store, with everything I thought I'd never get, is surreal. There are no more secrets, and no more prophecies. I close my eyes and bury my face in his chest. This is it. This is what it means to be free.

## A BIG THANK YOU

Thank you for choosing to read this series. I can't express how much it means to me to know that readers are sharing in the stories I have created.

Forbidden Magic is a special book for me since it marks the completion of my first series. Two years ago I didn't think I would ever finish a book. One year ago writing an entire series felt equally impossible. But here we are :) With a little elbow grease and a lot of sleep deprivation, I did it.

It's not over though! Olivia's story is complete, but I have more stories to tell, and I hope that you'll enjoy the next series just as much.

I received an email last night as I was putting the finishing touches on this story. Thank you, Corrie. It had been a long day (a long month really), and I was exhausted. Hearing from a reader reminded me why I love writing. It was exactly what I needed :)

Never hesitate to contact me! You can always email

me or shoot me a message on Facebook. I check the
Facebook group regularly as well. If you post there,
I'll see it!

# FOLLOW ME

If you loved this book, the best way to find out about new releases and updates is to join my Facebook group, The Foxehole. Amazon does a very poor job about notifying readers of new book releases. Joining the group can be an alternative to newsletters if you feel your inbox is getting a little crowded. Both options are linked below :)

Facebook Group:
https://www.facebook.com/groups/Thefoxehole
Newsletter: Get a prequel to Witch's Bite
https://stephaniefoxe.com/newsletter-wb/
Goodreads:
http://goodreads.com/Stephanie_Foxe
BookBub:
https://www.bookbub.com/authors/stephanie-foxe

Reviews are very important to indie authors, and help other readers that would be interested in a series like this find it. I also love reading your thoughts on the book.

To review any of my books simply go to the website below and pick one book or all of them.

FOLLOW ME

https://readerlinks.com/mybooks/764/1/1237

ALSO BY STEPHANIE FOXE

**Misfit's Series**
Misfit Pack
Misfit Angel
Misfit Fortune
**A new world of magic awaits!**

**Misfit Pack** is the first book in a new series by Stephanie
Foxe –

**Everything changed in a flash of pain and blood.**

All because she had to play hero.

Amber finds herself tied to two strangers, her humanity
stripped from her, and a heavy responsibility laid on her
shoulders.

Haunted by guilt and loss, she struggles to understand what
it means to be a werewolf – and an alpha.

Magic is commonplace, but there is a divide between
humans and supernaturals. There are rules. Expectations.

The title of alpha isn't given lightly, it's earned through a
Trial that will test her in ways she never expected.

Left with no choice but to fight for her new status as alpha,
Amber must pull together her fledgling pack of werewolves
that never wanted to be more than human. Time is ticking
as they prepare for the night that could tear them apart. If
Amber fails the Alpha Trials, they'll lose a lot more than
their humanity.

They'll lose their freedom.

**Start reading the first few chapters here:** https://
stephaniefoxe.com/misfit-pack-teaser/

www.stephaniefoxe.com

Printed in April 2023
by Rotomail Italia S.p.A., Vignate (MI) - Italy